Producer & International Distributor
eBookPro Publishing
www.ebook-pro.com

One Day I'll Meet You
Tamar Ashkenazi

Copyright © 2022 Tamar Ashkenazi

All rights reserved; No parts of this book may be reproduced or transmitted in any form or by any means, electronic or mechanical, including photocopying, recording, taping, or by any information retrieval system, without the permission, in writing, of the author.

Translation: Noël Canin

Contact: tamar.ashkenazi@moh.gov.il

ISBN 9798843223359

One Day I'll Meet You

A Novel

TAMAR ASHKENAZI

For Yuli and Yonatan,
If it weren't for you, this book wouldn't have been written. At all.

1

Sveta

Eight babies were born at the hospital during the night shift but only seven mothers were happy. For the eighth mother, joy in the pregnancy had faded during the fifth month when her husband was injured in an accident. Not even the birth evoked a need to touch or hug. Even when the baby cried upon leaving the womb, she couldn't find the words to soothe her. At that very moment, the baby's first missing experience was stamped in the memory book of her mind.

No-one waited impatiently to see her through the glass window. No-one said she looked like Mama or Papa, Grandma, or her brothers. No-one commented on who or what exactly she'd look like when she grew up.

Four days later, seven babies left the hospital, each one dressed in special, festive clothes, after being photographed held tightly in the arms of their adoring mothers and family members. At the same time, the mother of the eighth baby signed a waiver-of-rights document in the presence of the ward director, not before giving her daughter the name Svetlana, or Sveta for short, as if to bless her life with light. Another profound missing line added to the memory book in Sveta's mind – the waiver.

When she was two weeks old, dressed in a faded garment and wrapped in a hospital blanket, Sveta was transferred to Orphanage

No. 10 in St. Petersburg. A concrete wall surrounded the compound; accompanied by a nurse, she was taken through the green gate directly to the director's office. She examined Sveta, smiled at her, called her by name, adding "malinka" – she was indeed very tiny. She then gave the cook feeding instructions, not before she'd checked the medical file for sensitivity to milk. Asking the nurse to put Sveta in her designated crib on the second floor, she took the documents that came with her to the female doctor's office, "And not the male doctor's office," she emphasized.

Nobody approached her before feeding time.

Sveta had already heard the crying of babies in the hospital, and its intensity didn't alarm her, but accompanied her fifteenth night's sleep.

∼

Meals at Orphanage No. 10 were given at regular hours but this didn't suit Sveta. A storm of hunger would appear about half an hour before the institution's meal time, a late response, not adapting to her needs with small, more frequent meals. Time and again, when her mouth filled with milk, a little spilled from the sides of her mouth into her neck, and she'd cough. She'd almost choke when she tried to stop feeding. These were other lines engraved in the memory book of her mind.

When she saw faces, they were the faces of Katya, Zoya, Vera, Zina, Lena, or Margarita. But no face was engraved in her memory. Nor was the touch of the hands taking care of her whenever she needed a bath, a change of diaper, or feeding. She heard talking and even if the words weren't clear to her, the intonation certainly was; they were not soothing, caressing voices, but voices not intended for her.

The connection between hunger and food, a soothing voice and enveloping touch – the foundation for building trust, security, and love – didn't form, and nor did the longing subside. No-one talked to her, explained her day to her, soothed her when she cried, or related to her emotional experience. Even if she didn't yet understand, the sense of abandonment already smoldered, its roots deepening by the day. When distressed she still cried and, to soothe herself, she'd suck on her bent forefinger and pinky.

Despite all this, Sveta had something. Her alertness and direct gaze into the eyes of the person in front of her aroused affection for her. In time, she began to recognize Doctor Ira, who was a pleasant figure, coming to see her almost every day to caress, hug, and leave. Within a month, she began to recognize another figure, Klara the physiotherapist who took care of her twice a week. The experience of touch, massage, being rolled on a plastic ball, or a bubble bath – all evoked an abundance of sounds and gurgling, which, in time, turned to laughter.

Little Sveta wasn't able to satisfy her yearning for the doctor or the physiotherapy; the affecting experiences with them were only brief and blended with the figures of Katya, Zoya, Vera, Zina, Lena, and Margarita. On Sundays, the caregivers allowed themselves longer breaks and, in the absence of the director, took smoking breaks with Sveta in their arms, looking at them and smiling.

Her love of water was discernible when enjoying a bubble bath in the safety of a special inflated ring to prevent slipping and drowning. In contrast to the water, the material of the diaper and the clothes, hard from washing, always aroused discomfort, until they were softened by rolling from right to left and moving her arms and legs.

During the long hours between meals and sleep, when no-one approached her, she'd gaze at the ceiling. When a streak of sunlight appeared on the wall, she immediately examined it, passing on to the first bar of her bed, then the second, and the third…

Then, one day, without warning, when she was ten and a half months old, she was dressed in presentable clothing that was soft and pleasant and taken away by a woman she didn't know, who spoke to her in a language she'd never heard.

2

Ira

"Father is dead," I told my Yuri painfully. "He went with friends from work to the lake and drowned." I always worried when Slava went out with his friends after working at the garage. He'd say that they'd first open the bag of fishing rods and then they'd drink vodka, tell jokes, and chat while they waited for the fish to bite.

A few days previously they'd gone to the lake and my Slava fell into the water and drowned after drinking a lot of vodka. His friends were drunk and didn't notice. He was already dead when they found him. They helped me to arrange the cremation of the body and then we held a small funeral and buried the urn with the ashes. There weren't many people, just friends from his work, two aunts, and me. I had just started a new job as a neurologist and didn't yet have any friends. My family couldn't come; they lived far away, in a village in the Stavropol district.

I held Yuri tightly and then he lay on the sofa and fell asleep, his head on my knees, my hand stroking his head with monotonous movements. After helping him to get into bed behind the curtain, I felt I also needed a little vodka. Pouring myself a full glass from the open bottle, I sat down on the sofa, reminiscing about the period we'd met.

After high school, at the age of seventeen, I trained as a *feldsher*, a doctor's aide with considerable responsibility. I loved studying then and had good grades. I was also awarded a certificate of excellence and the teachers recommended my parents send me to Stavropol to study medicine. Because I loved children, I wanted to study at the pediatrics faculty at the Stavropol State Medical University. Studies were free and there was no problem. At first I was alone and new in town, but gradually I connected with girls in the class and learned to love the fast pace of life in contrast to the village. I enjoyed wandering through the beautiful town, each time discovering another corner of it: large squares, statues, and broad streets paved with large, light brown stone, on both sides of which stood high-rise buildings. In the village there were single-story houses with a large yard, animals, and vegetable gardens, and everything was surrounded by mountains and green fields.

We met in the Fall, in my second year of medical school. I was making a living then as a *feldsher* in the emergency room at the hospital for adults. I was doing the evening shift when soldiers from the Red Army brought in a soldier who'd been injured in an accident and the blood dripping from his head covered his face.

On instruction from the doctor, I immediately took pads and gently began to clean his forehead and cheeks. I didn't know where the source of the bleeding was, if it was only from the injury on the left side of his head or from another place. The soldier was vaguely conscious and we received information from his friends. As part of the medical team, I had to examine the wound myself. After his face was clean and the bleeding seemed to have stopped due to the pressure bandage, a surgeon arrived to stitch the wound. The soldier had bruises on his legs and arms, but the orthopedist who examined the X-ray determined that there were no fractures.

At the end of my shift I went to visit him. He had recovered a little, apparently due to the infusion of fluids he'd been given. I asked how he was, he nodded and I left. It wasn't acceptable for staff to interact with patients. The next day he was fully recovered and we chatted a bit. He said his name was Slava and asked for my name.

We married even before he was released from the army; a small wedding arranged by his friends. Mother sewed me a white dress and brought a veil from my cousin who had married the year before. The dress was a little big because with all the excitement I'd lost weight before the event. A few guests came from each side, everyone drank a lot of vodka; his friends from the army danced and sang, and it was a very happy affair.

After his release, Slava found work in a tool store, until I completed my training, and then we moved to St. Petersburg, where he was born. We found a communal apartment in the center, a beautiful place on Liteyny Prospekt, near the junction with Nevsky Prospekt. It was a huge apartment, maybe two hundred and fifty square meters. There were five rooms along the corridor, one for each family.

Our room was the first one after the entrance hall. In the corridor stood a refrigerator and shelves for shoes. On the left side was the shower and on the wall was a list with the day and hour each family could shower. We were listed on a Wednesday. There were only the two of us then, until Yuri was born, but we always had enough time to shower. Next to the shower, on a small shelf, was a communal telephone. At the end of the corridor, on the other side, was the toilet and next to that a communal kitchen, with three ovens for the five families and hot plates with four burners. It wasn't always enough and there were occasional arguments with the neighbors over the burners and the oven. We did the laundry in the kitchen in special pots.

However, I arranged the little apartment the way I wanted it. With his good hands, Slava hung up a curtain that divided the room into a living area and sleeping area and, after Yuri was born and grew up a little, Slava divided the sleeping area in two with another curtain, so we'd have a little privacy. Once we'd saved, we bought a wooden closet with a glass door where I kept crystal glasses and a pretty dinner service. After a few years, we brought in a chest of drawers and a mirror, which became my favorite corner of the home and was my very own.

The money we earned was enough for rent, telephone calls, food, and clothing and I got on with Slava's parents who were nice and received me kindly. At a certain point, Slava found work in a garage and once I'd completed my residency, I did another course and became a specialist pediatric neurologist. By then, Yuri was two and a half years old and went to daycare.

As part of my work, I was sent to Orphanage No. 10.

I heard Yuri whimpering in his sleep. I could still smell Slava in the home and it hurt me, so I poured another glass. I wondered how we'd manage now with only one salary. Not having an answer, I poured another glass and got into bed.

3

Ira

I got to work early. I knew that three new babies were supposed to arrive. Before their arrival, I finished examining the section of older children, aged three or more, and the intermediate section of children aged one to three years. There was a virus there and all the children had colds and blocked noses.

I asked the caregiver to boil a pot of water with chamomile leaves on a hot plate so there'd be steam in the room. It didn't always work, because the infants often touched one another, infecting each other, mainly when they snatched toys or bit one another. Sometimes they'd play together, but not much.

Afterwards, I hurried to do my morning rounds and examine the children who were sick. Six had already been reported. I examined each one in his bed. I listened to their lungs, looked into their ears, and made funny faces so they'd open their mouths wide. It didn't always work. I understood that Vitya was also sick and asked that they bring him to my office. Such a sweet child. Everyone knew he was "my child." On each floor, I had "my child." In the office I taught him to build a tower of blocks and clapped every time he succeeded. I loved his victorious laugh when he toppled the tower he'd built with one blow. He held out his arms to be picked up.

I fell in love with him from the first day. His mother, herself an orphan, gave birth to him at the age of sixteen when she left the boarding school she'd been living in and was on the street. She didn't know where she'd live, where she was headed, or what future awaited her. She didn't have minimal living conditions, and it wasn't difficult for the hospital to persuade her to give up her baby. I was distressed for her and for him. I knew that his chances for a good life depended on parents who would adopt him soon, and if he wasn't adopted by the age of three, he'd be transferred to a boarding school until he was fifteen and then turned out into the street, the same fate as his mother.

I didn't dare ask about it, I knew some things were "determined upstairs." Only the director decided which child should be adopted, and she didn't share her considerations with anyone. Although I wanted him to be adopted quickly, I also wanted him to remain a while longer with me.

When it was time for the ten o'clock meal, I had to return him to the group. I was leaving my office with him when, suddenly, I heard a shout from the second floor, "Ira, Ira, come quickly, she's convulsing!"

I immediately handed Vitya to one of the caregivers, went upstairs and into the office where I saw Yana, "my child" from the second floor, convulsing on the bed. She was only a year and two months old. Her left leg became rigid, and then the arm on the same side of her body; like a machine she rose up above the mattress and three seconds later fell back and again rose up. Even when her arm rose and fell, she remained hard as a stone.

I tried but failed to soften her arm and was afraid I'd break it. I noticed a triangular mark on Yana's face that began to turn gray and then blue. I saw that her chest wasn't moving, that, in fact, she wasn't breathing, and realized that if the convulsions didn't stop, I'd have to give her an injection.

The caregivers were ready beside me with a sterile syringe; all I had to do was connect the needle and draw the substance from the vial. With alcohol and cotton, I cleaned the area where I'd drawn out the substance. I removed any air from the needle, approached and injected her.

"Snap out of it! Snap out of it!" I cried to her. "Yana! Yana!"

She didn't respond. She might not have heard me.

Within four minutes the convulsions diminished and gradually began to disappear. I waited for a response, but she barely responded. I didn't know if she was awake or asleep, but finally, after eighteen minutes of nerve-wracking waiting, she fell asleep.

This wasn't the first time it had happened. When we received her, aged three months, in her medical file was a letter detailing the mother's situation and the sign "+" in the square opposite the diagnosis "epilepsy." She was also born premature, in the twenty-eighth week.

I was afraid that the convulsions had caused a further delay in her development and even, perhaps, a permanent vulnerability. During my residency in neurology, I'd learned that epilepsy in infancy might significantly affect development, so I always kept a close eye on Yana's weight and made sure she wasn't malnourished, but it was clear to me that she wouldn't develop like the other children.

To be prepared, I pinned a sheet of paper on the board with a table I made for the caregivers. On it they were to note down the date and time of convulsions as well as the number. I thought it right to do an EEG test for her as well, to examine the electrical activity in the brain and to consult with a colleague from my neurological studies regarding a change in dosage or even to change the medication. To be on the safe side, I asked that her bed be moved nearest to the door, near the large changing table so that the carer could maintain constant eye contact. I wanted the caregiver to be able to see Yana from the first convulsion.

Before leaving, I asked them not to wake her for a meal, but allow her to wake naturally, by herself. I reminded the carer that when she woke, Yana would probably be very tired and not able to eat with a teaspoon. I asked them to prepare a bottle of porridge for her.

At noon I returned to my treatment room to examine the new babies who had just arrived from the hospital. I wiped down the washable cover on the wooden table with a cloth and covered it with a new sheet. I also wiped the tray with its thermometers in alcohol, as well as the instruments for examining ears. The neurological instruments were the last to be cleaned and then I washed my hands, changed my apron and tied it around my hips.

The caregiver brought in the first baby. After I'd laid him down I started to examine his body. Movement, reflexes, and the fontanelle were all found to be normal. I took out my stethoscope and made sure the lungs were clean and the heart beat regular. I opened a new file and completed the data in the list on the form, such as weight, height, and everything else I examined. As I was measuring his head, the baby urinated on me, which usually happens if you don't diaper the baby before continuing the examination. The urine is sterile so I wasn't worried, merely wiped my face and finished the examination. I then called the caregiver to dress him and take him to his room. Only then did I sit down to read the letter from the hospital, in which they gave details about the mother – nineteen years old, healthy, blood tests normal.

Before the next baby came in, I changed my uniform. Two babies were then brought in. One apparently suffered from Fetal Alcohol Syndrome. Poor little thing, what kind of a future was waiting for her. Many young mothers either didn't know or didn't want to know the effect alcohol has on the fetus, or drinking was an emotional pause for them, as it was for me after Slava died. But when I was pregnant, it didn't occur to me to drink.

I finished examining the babies who were then taken to the baby room, each one to an iron bed with high bars. The beds were the only colorful items to decorate the room. Girls were given pink beds and the boys had the blue or green ones. I liked these colors because there were no pictures on the walls. We took great care to maintain the babies' hygiene and didn't want to hang any item or object that would gather dust. So the walls themselves were painted in a special, washable paint that could be washed with soap and water.

I finished the paperwork and wrote down instructions for the care of each baby. I gave the kitchen instructions regarding milk and porridge and returned to the second floor to see how Yana was doing. I was glad she'd begun to wake up and before I left, I repeated the instructions and asked them to offer her food every three hours, without taking into account the usual meal time for everybody.

My shift had ended. I left the orphanage with a heavy, worried heart. I knew that if Yana did not receive the medication the minute convulsions started, she might die, and I couldn't bear the thought of not being beside her. I was afraid the caregiver wouldn't notice in time, or too much time would pass before the doctor on the entrance floor was woken and he could go upstairs to prepare the injection. More than four minutes might pass and Yana would suffocate and die.

Before going into our building, I thought I saw Yuri approaching, his face looking down at the pavement. As he came closer, I noticed his hunched shoulders. He was carrying a loaf of bread he'd bought for our supper.

"How are you doing, Yurinka?" I asked.

"Everything's fine, Mama," he gave his usual answer.

We went inside and I immediately went to the kitchen to heat up meatballs and mashed potatoes.

He suddenly came in behind me and asked, "What do you think about someone who doesn't have enough food and pinches something without paying?"

What kind of a question is that out of the blue? I wondered, responding without thinking, "As I see it, food is first of all something basic and our body requires it. Whoever doesn't eat and doesn't have any food starves his body, which is unpleasant and also harms our health. Why do you ask, my boy?"

"Uh… I saw someone in the bread store steal a roll. There was a long queue and people stood and waited, apparently deep in thought and didn't notice. I didn't think it was such a bad thing, but I felt sorry for him because if he'd been caught it would have been very shameful."

"Food's ready," I said, looking at him with pride. I was glad he was compassionate and simultaneously sad that Slava didn't get to see him grow up. He'd have been so proud of him.

When we finished our meal, I turned on the television and we both watched ice dance with the couple Ludmila Pachumova and Alexander Gorshkov. After the children, my greatest love was ice dance. I went to every dance performance in St. Petersburg. Slava always bought tickets. He'd stand in queue for hours. Occasionally, he'd pay someone to give us good seats. After he died, the neighbors and Yuri sometimes bought tickets for me, but the pleasure of going out had diminished, replaced by dance on television. I loved the music, the soft and graceful movements, the spins and leaps. I almost stopped breathing until the dancers landed safely back on the shining surface of the ice.

That evening there was a performance that included classical ballet as well as artistic ice dance. The dancers were beautiful and flexible. I poured myself a glass of vodka, waving my arms as if in a dance, imitating the dancers' legs, until my thoughts, too, were dancing in an imagined circle, around sweet Yana, who came to mind. I hoped with all my heart that the night would pass peacefully and I poured myself a little more vodka.

In the morning I woke late and was stuck in a queue for the toilet. This held me back at least a quarter of an hour. Then I waited in queue for the sink. There were two sinks on our floor, one in the kitchen and one in the bathroom behind the curtain so as not to disturb anyone showering.

When I was finished, I returned to our little apartment to dress and comb my hair. The velvet curtain separating my sleeping corner from Yuri's moved slightly and I thought I saw under the blanket the slender arm of a girl. I wasn't sure. I stopped breathing for a moment, my chest constricted, and I felt my heart beat faster. I decided to ignore it and hurried out because I was already late. Worst case scenario, I could ask him that night.

As soon as I arrived, I went up to the second floor. Valentina, the director, didn't reprimand me for being late. The staff reported that Yana had slept well but not eaten much. I decided that I myself would feed her today. Unashamedly, I took her for a walk in my arms. Such a pretty little girl with light brown hair and the loveliest blue eyes I'd ever seen. I'd give anything to know what she'd felt and thought after waking from the seizure. She hadn't spoken a word, communicating only with head movements – up and down meant "yes" and from right to left meant "no." She also spoke a lot with her eyes. Before parting from her I sang her a song and, for the first time, she clapped her hands and opened her eyes wide.

I was on top of the world, because she really did look happy and mostly because I perceived it as developing communication with her. I hugged and kissed her and then went away, leaving her to be looked after by the caregivers.

I went down to my office to write to the hospital and make an appointment for Yana to do an EEG test and examine the level of medication in her blood, in order to find out if the dosage should be changed. I summed up her medical history since she'd come to us. When she first arrived, she had at least thirty episodes of convulsions a month. Later, with the help of medication, the number decreased to between fifteen and twenty. In the letter, I reported that on days she didn't feel well, or had a virus, the convulsions increased. Any loss of equilibrium brought about convulsions.

On days like these, I was so afraid I'd stay beside her until late at night, to make sure she didn't suffer respiratory arrest. It had happened the year before, when a baby died in my arms. I will carry him in my heart forever. For weeks afterwards I couldn't sleep. I blamed myself. I didn't speak to anyone. I'd come to work heartbroken, unable to look the staff in the eye, although medically speaking there was nothing I could have done. The district came to investigate. I was deep in sorrow and unconcerned by the investigation because I knew I'd done all I could. The investigators came to the same conclusion. But there was no comfort in this, and I couldn't bear the thought of it happening again, and to Yana of all children.

4

Ira

When I got home, Yuri was studying for a history test. This was his final year in high school and he knew he had to get good grades. I gazed at his face and suddenly remembered the day he was born, a blond, blue-eyed baby. When he was small, I always dressed him like a man when we left the house. Even when there wasn't very much money, I made sure he always had at least one pair of good pants, a festive shirt, nice shoes, and blue knee-socks. A good boy. He always did as I asked – went to daycare, to school, did his homework. But I'd noticed that lately, since he'd turned seventeen, he didn't always listen to me. He suddenly looked up and down in a way that wasn't like him.

"What's worrying you, my boy? The test?"

"Mama, do you remember my telling you about the boy who stole a roll from the bread store?

"Of course I remember. Talk." I sensed a sharp change of subject that had nothing to do with the test.

"Well, it was a girl, not a man. And it happened about two weeks ago. I followed her out of the store, she realized that I'd seen what she'd done and was alarmed. I approached her and promised I wouldn't tell anyone. I swore not to. After she calmed down, she almost swallowed the roll whole and thanked me. She was so hungry. I was sorry for her. I wanted to accompany her home, but she refused. And then we parted. I pretended to go in another direction and hid behind a building until she was far enough away and couldn't hear my steps. I followed her to a building in an adjacent road. She went inside a building but I couldn't see which apartment she entered."

I was astonished. He'd never spoken so much or so fluently. "Well, go on," I murmured.

Without eagerness or drama, Yuri quietly continued, "I waited about half an hour and approached the building, as if I lived there and wanted to go up to one of the apartments on a higher floor. I walked slowly and quietly and at the entrance, I checked all the corners. I saw the stairs and another iron door, probably to the basement. I climbed up to the last floor and didn't see anything, so I left the building and continued to look for her. She had the face of someone who was afraid, I couldn't stop thinking of her brown eyes. I felt like I wanted to know more. Hear more about what had happened to her. About her parents, her siblings, and why she was so hungry.

I waited at the corner of the street until it was dark, made sure there were no people around and then I returned, quietly, on the tips of my toes and tried to turn the lock in the door to the basement. It wasn't complicated, it only looked as if it was locked. I went inside. It was dark there, but fortunately there was some light from the moon and I managed to take a few steps. I couldn't see anything but smelled the unpleasant odor of damp and it was very cold, so I hurried away."

I sighed, as long as my boy doesn't get into trouble. Who wanders the night apart from drunks and addicts? "Just as well you got out of there," I said with relief.

He went on, "I walked away from there to go home and then, as I was walking, I heard running toward the neighborhood basketball court. It was rather strange at that hour, in the dark. I wasn't sure, but I thought I saw a figure in a dress, a girl. I decided I had to see from close up. I changed direction and walked quickly from the other side, and then I hid behind a bush. The figure approached quite fast and then I saw her – it was her, the girl with the roll.

"I came out from my hiding place and walked slowly onto the court so she wouldn't be alarmed. As I came closer, she stopped running. I heard her panting. She must have been running for some time. She looked back to see no-one was looking for her. Suddenly I found courage, approached and grabbed her hand, not too strongly but firmly, and asked what had happened. Who was she running from."

"Well, and what happened then?" I was becoming quite tense.

"We sat down on a wooden bench in the park, which seemed safe and relatively far away. She told me she was running away from her father. He beat her for no reason. Every day she had new bruises on her body. She said that nobody asked questions and that she wasn't the only one with marks like that, and that she managed to hide some of the marks under her clothing.

"She also told me that every evening her father drank a bottle and a half of vodka, beat and threatened her, while her mother said nothing. She also drank and he hit her too. Before she ran away, she'd received a terrible beating with a strap and felt as if her vertebrae was disintegrating and in the end she fell to the floor. When she saw her father so drunk and lying on the sofa and her mother unconscious on the floor, from alcohol or blows or both – she waited for the pain to pass a little and then she managed to crawl out of the house. She said she had no choice. There was no-one left in the world who cared about her. After three streets she had no more strength to move, and she went into one of the buildings where the basement was unlocked. She went inside and she'd been sleeping there ever since. It was two weeks now. In the same clothes."

I was astounded, but realized very quickly where this story was leading. "Yurinka, you have a good heart, and I realize she slept here last night. Do you think it's all right for her to stay with us? Her parents will be looking for her, and the police will come here."

He looked at me, disappointed, but then something mature appeared in his face and he said, "Mama, please. If you had seen how she wept and how lost she looked, you would have also taken her in. And I've promised her that you're a doctor and will take care of her, she has bruises all over her body. And she's been away from home for two weeks and nobody is looking for her."

I was so proud of him for his compassion and sensitivity but I was still concerned. "Yurinka, first, go and get her, and after I examine her I'll decide. And tell me her name."

His smile was worth everything.

"Lena. Her name is Lena. Thank you, Mama, I love you."

5

Tali

The Nursing School graduation ceremony was in full swing. In the audience sat my parents who came from the kibbutz and Benny, my partner of two years. Our relationship wasn't what it had been in the beginning, as far as I was concerned, anyway, but I thought it right to invite him. I was one of the outstanding students in my year, on the level of management and organization, as befits the daughter of the kibbutz cultural coordinator and newsletter editor.

While making my speech as student representative, I stood alone on the stage in the hospital lobby, wearing a white coat and a nurse's white cap edged on top with a narrow black line. Suddenly, in the audience, my eyes noticed Udi.

We'd only met two weeks previously, after Ruthi, a dialysis nurse, had spent two months begging me to meet him. I wasn't interested, after all I had Benny, and why should I meet a dialysis patient who was interested in me? But Ruthi said he'd noticed me crossing the corridor of the surgical ward and passing the treatment room where he and his mother were being instructed on how to carry out home hemodialysis.

Two weeks previously, when I had a growing sense that my relationship with Benny was coming to an end, I gave in. "In any case, in two weeks' time I'm returning to the north, to the kibbutz, and then going into the army, so all right, I'll meet him," I told Ruthi.

We met, one evening, after I'd finished my shift. I got into his car and proceeded to ask him a nurse's professional questions concerning his illness, and he went along with me. He was good-looking and very nice, but I continued to behave like a nurse the entire evening. When he took me back to the student dorms adjacent to the hospital, I realized that it was silly of me and perhaps arrogant to relate to him like that.

He didn't give up and we'd met twice more since then and now, seeing him at the end of the hall, while I stood on the stage, I felt butterflies in my belly. These shifted to feelings of guilt toward Benny, who was sitting opposite me in the third row and, fortunately, hadn't noticed anything out of the ordinary.

At the end of the ceremony, my parents returned to the kibbutz with three years of possessions that I'd packed up from my room, and I went with Benny to his home. It was a long and boring weekend, which I spent mainly missing Udi.

I secretly called my friend Ronni, who advised me with characteristic forthrightness, "If you don't feel anything for Benny, there is no reason to stay in the relationship, just part from him."

Since I was already in his home, I thought it really was the right time to part in a nice and respectful way and so, without preparation, but also without drama, I explained to him that it was over.

I couldn't make out if he expected it or if he was prepared because of the distance I'd shown him during recent weeks. In any case, he tried to dissuade me. I felt bad seeing him try to persuade me to continue, but apart from that, I didn't feel anything else for him. To my surprise, he even came to the hospital two days later to persuade me to return. I only felt compassion for him.

"It's over, Benny, go on with your life," I told him and, by the expression in his eyes, I saw he'd finally realized I meant it.

The following week, I spent time with Udi at his family home in Petach Tikvah.

The first few times I agreed to come to his home only after dark to avoid an encounter with his parents and grandmother. In the morning, I slipped out to the street to take the bus to the hospital. The family home included a villa for his parents, a house for his grandmother, and one for him. His older brothers were already married and only his younger brother was still living with his parents. Dialysis treatments took place in a designated room in his parents' villa during hours free of daily activities.

At dawn, Udi and his father would go out to work in their fields and his older brother joined them. They returned at eight for breakfast, a finely cut salad with onion, a fried egg, bread, and tahini. Just like kibbutz. Afterwards, they returned to the fields. Udi had dialysis three evenings a week.

I was in transition between the end of my studies and active service in the army. I had gone into the army before my nursing course as part of my army training in order to serve as a nurse in the military. Since I no longer had a place to live in Petach Tikvah and Udi had to get up early for work, I mostly stayed over at his place, and couldn't avoid an encounter with his parents and grandmother. I was very embarrassed and barely said a word in their presence beyond what was necessary.

Udi was a complete contrast to the young men I'd previously dated. Firstly, he wasn't from Kibbutz, but I forgave him for that because he was a farmer and he also dressed in accordance with the fashion codes that were familiar to me: jeans, checked shirts, and Palladium shoes. Something else that I had difficulty digesting was the American car he drove. It had leather seats that were too luxurious for a Kibbutz girl and, apart from that, he'd grown up in a house of people who supported the Maccabi football team, whereas on Kibbutz we, of course, belonged to Hapoel team. At first I didn't realize just how central a part this played in the life of his family.

Udi wasn't perturbed by the strangeness I felt and went along with what I wanted. I gradually dragged him to plays and exhibitions and he began to read the books I finished. All in all, he left cultural events solely in my hands. His friends were essential to his life. When I once said something silly to one of his friends, he didn't correct me in front of everyone but backed me up. Afterwards, on the way home, he explained it to me. I so appreciated it because I really did say things I shouldn't have said.

His illness played no part in our relationship beyond the treatments. Despite his health, which allowed him some indulgence, he didn't give up transporting goods to the docks at night or to the wholesale market. His modest but stubborn way of not seeing any block or flaw in the difficulties I presented in my views or desires – to give in to me but not to give me up – increased my confidence in him. I loved his speech, his voice, his smile, and most of all his hand holding mine as we strolled near the Antipatris Fortress when we wanted some privacy.

After enlisting and completing basic training, I did an officer's course after which I was assigned a position as a nurse in a government hospital near Petach Tikvah for a period of two years, when I moved in with Udi.

Debby, his mother, taught me all the secrets of the menu permitted for a dialysis patient. She soaked chips in water for a whole night before frying them, avoiding potassium-rich vegetables and fruits as well as proteins. He could only eat sugar and fat freely. The hardest was the limitation on drinking and I was amazed at how Udi didn't complain and managed by sucking ice cubes to cool down the body and soothe his thirst. The lengthy dialysis treatments were specifically set when games were broadcast, as befits a "football family." Udi's father, Moolie, had been a member of the Israeli national football team, his younger brother played for the youth team, and the entire family were avid fans of Maccabi Petach Tikvah.

The treatment itself made us all nervous, primarily connecting the dialysis tube to Udi's arm and the blood flow into the machine because of the danger of clots or bleeding. Udi would calmly insert the thick needles into his arm and thus, for four hours, we watched television with his friends who came especially to enjoy the food of the house prepared by his mother and grandmother. At the end of the treatment, he removed the needles himself and then began the ritual of cleaning the machine.

On the family farm there were no secrets and Udi talked about a wedding and children. I had no such plans. I wanted to finish the army first and then do a university degree. His mother already said that his aunt would sew my wedding dress and the event would take place on the farm lawn, like his older brothers. Joy and enthusiasm took hold of the entire family and each one in turn tossed out ideas for a buffet and lighting, and why not use the guest list from the previous weddings and when would we have a wedding tasting evening. I was very tense. It was far too soon for me but I felt reluctant to slow down the happiness.

When we were alone, Udi described how our firstborn would look and we amused ourselves with ideas about his qualities. Most of all I wanted him to inherit Udi's phenomenal memory for telephone numbers. At breakfast the next day, he again raised the issue of the child and my studies. He knew I intended on going to university immediately after the army, and I think it wasn't by chance he raised the subject in the presence of his parents because his mother immediately said, "Don't worry, I'll help you raise him while you study." I knew she'd keep her word.

My parents for their part were confused about my relationship with a "sick" man. They loved Udi very much but were concerned for me.

Roni was also uneasy. "Aren't you afraid?" she asked.

"No!" I responded. "I know Udi won't live to be seventy, but he will probably live until he's at least fifty."

I knew Roni had my interests at heart and only wanted to make sure I was aware of the situation. She didn't try and persuade me to leave him. She knew she didn't stand a chance.

Two months later we had a date for the wedding.

6

Ira

The sores on Lena's arms appeared to be infected. It looked as if she'd been burned with cigarettes. I began to clean them gently with a cloth and water and when I'd finished, I suggested she go and shower after which I'd bandage them. Fortunately, all this happened on a Wednesday, which was our family's day to use the shower.

I went with her to the shower to explain the taps to her because in our building hot and cold were back to front. I handed her soap and a towel, a pair of my underwear and a nightgown. I glanced at her through the curtain when she went in naked with her back to me. I barely repressed a cry of alarm; her back was full of scars and purple-yellow bruises. My whole body went cold. At that moment it was clear to me – she would remain with us.

The next evening, after she'd rested and eaten and was a little calmer, I managed to get her to talk.

She began to tell me her story, "Papa shouted at me, gave me orders and beat me every day, me and Mama. He decided everything at home. What I'd wear, who to talk to on the street and who not, what I had to do at home and at school."

Lena continued, "He spoke to Mama and to me as if we were his servants. He insulted us, said we were stupid. He always demanded and never said please or thank you. Only complaints. He shouted at me if I didn't do things exactly as he wanted. Once, when I answered back, he grabbed my head in his large hand and banged it hard against the wall. Everything in my head seemed to move and change places. I was so dizzy that I fell. Then, despite the trembling in my head I manage to cry out, 'Papa, why? I was a good girl,' and then he slapped my face to shut me up."

I felt as if I couldn't breathe. I couldn't hear such terrible things all at once. Even in horror movies they let you catch your breath. "Lena," I said. "What you've gone through is terrible. Come to me, I want to hold you. I'll be gentle, I saw the sores and bruises."

Trembling, defensive, she came closer to me. Only after she felt my light touch did she calm down and cautiously allow me to hold her.

After a few moments of silence, her eyes on the floor, Lena let out a deep breath. "Once, Papa threw the china bear my grandma gave me. It shattered in pieces. He knew I loved it. I cried a lot about that. Sometimes, he'd slap Mama twice for no reason, and then he'd order her into their bedroom. Mama would go in and I'd hear her scream with pain. After about a quarter of an hour she'd come out, bent over and weeping like a whipped dog

"And after Papa left the house, Mama would go to the cupboard, sometimes crawling because of the pain, and take out her bottle of vodka that she kept hidden in a paper bag. It was the only thing that calmed her down. She would cry and drink until she fell asleep."

I felt as if her words were tearing my arteries and veins and that everything was bleeding inside. And if that's how I felt, what had it done to her spirit? I was ashamed that I'd dared think she should go home. I called Yuri into the kitchen for a moment. "Lena will not ever return to her parents or to that basement!" I said.

He heard my voice tremble and maybe saw my moist eyes. I'd never let him see me cry. I'd always shown him he had a strong mother.

"Mama… so, she'll stay with us?"

"Yes, my boy. Lena is staying with us."

His eyes filled with joy and he hugged me.

I wasn't sure I'd made the right decision. I'd heard about good people who had taken people in trouble into their homes and regretted it, but I couldn't think of sending Lena back to that hell. Only someone heartless would do that. I didn't say so to Yuri, but I thought I'd at least give her a chance. Without promising anything. I didn't admit this even to myself, but I suppose the secret longing for a daughter crept into my heart, one that could never be realized because Slava had died so young.

Lena moved in with us and her parents seemed indifferent to her disappearance. Since the police didn't call the school, I assumed that they hadn't approached the police or looked for her. Neither did she look for them. She didn't seem to miss them. I wondered if I should occasionally suggest she reconsider going home. In the meantime, I got used to being a sort of surrogate mother to her. After a month, I had the courage to ask, "Lena, would you like to visit your parents?"

She didn't say a word but started to tremble and walk up and down the living room, murmuring inaudibly. Her body language expressed unequivocally that there was nothing to discuss. My question raised anxiety in her and I so regretted this. I immediately said, "Lena, you're family and you're staying here with us, all right?"

Many moments passed before she calmed down.

That night I suddenly woke up in alarm. It took me a few seconds to realize that Lena was crying out behind the curtain. Two or three cries, probably a nightmare, and then silence. I went back to sleep.

Lena continued to go to school in the mornings without fearing that her parents would look for her. I believed her when she said there was no chance they'd come looking for her. In the afternoon, she'd help me tidy and clean the apartment without my asking her. After about two months, she found work in a clothing store, where she cleaned, folded, and arranged the clothes on shelves. They paid her a pittance and would sometimes give her a garment that was slightly damaged. Lena knew how to sew and whenever we needed to fix a garment or tablecloth, I'd ask the neighbor if Lena could sew on their machine for half an hour. It was a Singer, an old but excellent machine, and our good neighbors always agreed. I liked them and, every season, always gave them a jar of the strawberry jam my mother picked and cooked.

7

Ira

I went to the treatment room on the first floor just as Klara the physiotherapist was giving Olga a hydrotherapy session. "Oy, our Olga, you are two years old already, how much longer will you wait for a family?" she said to her.

We all knew that her adoption would not be a simple one. Not everyone was willing to take a child with Down's Syndrome and Olga's face betrayed the syndrome: her eyes were almond shaped and slanted upward, her tongue stuck out slightly, and her neck was short and thick. Most people also knew that the syndrome was accompanied by health problems and intellectual and communication limitations, but her smiles and chuckles made up for everything. Maybe, I hoped, someone would fall in love with her.

"Klara," I said. "Do you remember Yashka, who stayed with us until he was transferred to a boarding school?"

"I don't think anyone adopted him," she answered. "Wait. I think someone called you."

"Who? From the second floor?"

"I think so."

I didn't hear anyone calling, but started to run in the direction from where she said she heard the call.

I knew where my legs were taking me – to Yana's room. When I arrived, panting, she was convulsing again. Only a week had gone by since we'd received the answers to the levels of medication in her blood and I'd raised the dosage. Since then she'd had no convulsions and I'd hoped we were on the right track.

"What happened?" I asked worriedly.

"She took a long noisy breath, as if she didn't have any air left, like a child with stridor," reported one of the caregivers.

"Since then we haven't seen her chest rise and fall," added the second caregiver.

They were already practiced and had prepared the syringe for me. I drew in the liquid medication from the vial, expelled the air from the needle and injected her. I looked at Yana. She didn't look good. I thought I shouldn't wait. I felt I was about to lose her and injected her again. I counted together with the caregivers: four seconds, five, six, seven, and then the first breath appeared, but apart from that no response at all.

I was worried. In the meantime, Valentina arrived. I immediately asked her permission to use the telephone in her office and ran to call Dr. Petrov at the children's hospital. I reported Yana's condition to him.

"Do you have oxygen?" he asked.

"We only have an inhalation machine."

"Give her an infusion."

"I'm not sure I'll find a vein in her condition, I'll try."

"Actually," he said. "Bring her to me now, at the hospital, in an ambulance!"

I quickly returned to Yana's room. Four minutes had passed since the injection, but there was no improvement, not even the slightest movement of the chest. I asked the caregivers to prepare me another syringe and was ready to administer another injection. In all my years in this job, I hadn't had a situation like this one.

I asked Valentina to call an ambulance and she immediately left to do so. In the meantime, I injected Yana for the third time. Four seconds, five... I waited for one more minute. Finally, she was breathing again. The rigidity of her limbs softened and passed. Finally, in a sense, I, too, breathed again.

The ambulance arrived. Yana lay lifelessly on gurney, she looked exhausted and didn't communicate at all. I hoped there was no brain damage. I got in with her and we went to the hospital. I held her little hand all the way.

When we arrived, the nurse in reception immediately placed a mask on her face and opened the tap on the oxygen balloon. A doctor gave her an infusion and took blood samples. I knew they'd also check the oxygen levels in her blood. I admired the doctor's hands of gold and the speed at which he found a vein for the infusion, but his face was grave.

Yana was then transferred directly to the children's ward, where I met Dr. Petrov, who received me warmly, apologized and rushed off for an emergency treatment. I remained beside Yana and waited for signs of waking. These usually occurred ten minutes after an injection, after which she'd sleep for long hours. I wondered why her responses were slower today. Was it because she'd received more than one injection? Was it because there'd been more convulsions than usual?

About thirty minutes later, Petrov arrived with a nurse. They stopped at Yana's bed and he said, "The large number of convulsions in a relatively short space of time must have affected her more."

He then gave the nurse instructions, "Continue with the infusion at the current pace, and you can stop the oxygen in accordance with the information regarding its levels in her blood. If she is alert, you can start to feed her. Tomorrow, we must do more blood tests, and if she's no worse, you can take her back to the orphanage." He said goodbye to me and left the ward with the nurse.

Suddenly all was quiet, apart from the sound of the linen and clothing wagon, the bottles' wagon, and occasionally a baby crying. I still hadn't released Yana's tiny hand. Slowly, she began to respond. A wan smile spread over her face, and I could feel her touch in my fingers.

Since long hours had passed since she'd eaten, and after I'd informed the nurses, who knew I was a doctor, I took a bottle of warmed porridge and checked its temperature on the back of my hand. I began to feed Yana, who sucked vigorously and after a few minutes, fell asleep. I covered her with a blanket and left the ward and the hospital, going straight to the bus station. When I got home I was so exhausted I barely managed to change into a nightgown, I fell into bed and slept.

I woke late and got ready as fast as I could. I was still worried about Yana but my first obligation was to my work. When I arrived at the orphanage, I immediately went in to Klara, who was just preparing the bath and work surface, changing sheets, and washing the physio balls. Apart from a diaper, the children were naked during treatments, so everything had to be very clean. While she finished the cleaning and preparations, I boiled water in a kettle.

Once a month, we'd go over her work-file, to update the development of each child and then we'd update the medical files. This time I didn't wait for the water to boil and started nibbling on the jam cookies. I had a need for sugar and caffeine.

Klara read out several diagnoses from her list, "Head tilting, problems with crawling, hypotension, meaning low muscle tension, increased muscle tone, asymmetrical functioning, and I don't think we'll have time for much more."

"We have three children who suffer from head tilt," I noted. "And asymmetry in all of them tends to be the left side."

Klara reported that Alex had greatly improved with the water therapy and that his short muscle was beginning to lengthen. It was too early to tell with Luda and Lilya, only a month had gone by since they started treatment.

"Can you add an additional weekly treatment for them?" I asked. Despite the heavy load she carried, it was important we do everything to avoid harming their stable development.

Klara correctly suggested we should decide this at the end of the daily treatment of all the children because we might reduce hours for someone and manage to add for someone else.

We then went on to the group of children who had trouble crawling. There were eight of them, and none of them managed to push themselves equally with two legs, the asymmetry was clear. Klara said that two of them dragged one leg and so she worked with them on strengthening muscle and joint flexibility. About Pavel, she said that it was enough she showed him the movement once or twice and he continued by himself in the cylinder in the play room.

"Jenia also does what he is supposed to but he tires quickly and then resorts to his original movement," she said, adding that with both of them she'd tried exercises climbing up a step, and in time she discovered that this was very effective, but only during the advanced stages of the treatment. Regarding the others, she noted that she worked mainly on flexibility of hip joints and massage and that they needed a lot of treatments.

In this way, without realizing it, time flew, and I still hadn't examined the sick babies. So I suggested we end with the low muscle tension group. The most prominent there was Olga, to whom Klara devoted many hours of hydrotherapy to strengthen her shoulders and pelvis. She didn't appear to be so weak and hunched, and when we touched her there was no sense of floppy contact. Out of the water, Klara worked with her on leg activity and had her walk on the floor after scattering toys along the way so that she had to pass them or change direction in order to advance. "She's been here for two years already. Who will take her? All the parents who come here ask for healthy children," said Klara sadly.

That's true, I mused, and although I could understand parents' preference for healthy children, on the other hand, I always have a sense of injustice, because the children who need love and treatments more than anything are those who ultimately receive the least. "I'm sure that anyone who takes her will gain a warm and loving child," I said.

"Come to her next treatment and see her response to music, how happy she is and how she moves. She doesn't stop smiling."

There was a sudden knock at the door. The caregiver from the first floor arrived to report that Olga had a fever – thirty-nine degrees already. I hugged Klara, thanked her for her wonderful work and hurried off to Olga. I found her flushed and hot.

I listened to her lungs; her breathing was fast and it was difficult for her to exhale, in addition to the cough and high fever. I had no doubt that she was suffering from pneumonia. I immediately went down to my office to dilute a bottle of antibiotic powder and asked the caregivers to give her water or tea to drink.

I tried to put a teaspoon of medicine into her mouth although I knew she hated the taste. This time she didn't have the strength to resist. I placed a wet cloth on her face to get the fever down, as well as the suppository I gave her. I left instructions to take her temperature every four hours, and if it didn't drop to under thirty-eight, to give her a bath in lukewarm water. "If she cries because she's cold, simply add some hot water, as long as she doesn't suffer."

I went down to my office to prepare Valentina a list of prescriptions for medicines as my stock was running out. While waiting outside her office, through a crack in the door I saw two women and a man sitting in front of her. I heard scraps of conversation and realized they were speaking Italian. One of the women spoke Russian with an Italian accent in a particularly shrill voice. Probably a translator.

"We want to adopt a child of your choice. The age doesn't matter," she said on their behalf.

Valentina asked if they intended to bring their own doctor or if they'd trust the orphanage doctor.

I heard murmuring and then again the shrillness, "They're not bringing a doctor. They have full trust in your doctor."

Valentina explained that the procedure entailed advance coordinating with the district adoption authorities regarding the affiliation of the parents to the specific child and that her role is to determine beforehand if they want a son or daughter.

I wasn't aware she had so much influence. I thought everything was dictated by the district. And then I heard chairs moving and realized they were about to leave. I think she told them to wait on the sofa as she had to find out several things. I waited for them to leave and then entered to give Valentina the envelope of prescriptions and ask permission to call the hospital to ask after Yana.

"Of course, call them," said Valentina.

I dialed and spoke to the nurse, who took a message for Dr. Petrov, who was busy and asked me to call an hour later. In the meantime, I went up to see how Olga was doing. She looked more comfortable, the suppository was beginning to take effect and her temperature was coming down. I wiped the perspiration from her forehead, and she enjoyed the attention she received.

I returned to Valentina's office; she was talking on the phone to the adoption authorities. She gestured for me to come in. I listened to the conversation in which she explained the situation, apologizing for her call and acknowledging that she was familiar with the procedures, but didn't have the heart to send the Italian couple away, telling them to return the following week. The conversation seemed to end to her satisfaction, after she concluded, "Thank you very much! We'll talk tomorrow."

An hour later, I again called Dr. Petrov. He told me that Yana had two more convulsion episodes during the night, the level of oxygen in her blood had dropped and her pulse was very high, over the top limit of the monitor. I realized she wouldn't be returning that day, but we were fortunate because she wouldn't have survived the night had she stayed at the orphanage.

I continued to examine all the sick or recovering children and go over the treatments and medication. At four o'clock, I asked Valentina for permission to visit Yana at the hospital. When I arrived, I immediately took her hand. She opened her eyes and smiled at me. When the doctor on duty was available he called me to his office, presented me with the data and let me read the results of the EEG. I looked at him. The situation wasn't encouraging. I choked and hurried out of his office and back to her.

Just as I arrived, she started to convulse again. Her left leg became spastic and her left arm rigid, rising and falling with extreme trembling. Her chest wasn't moving. I immediately called a nurse because I wasn't allowed to touch anything as I wasn't one of the staff.

The nurse put an oxygen mask on her and opened the tap on the balloon. Over the mask I could see the triangle of her graying face and as I knew – it would soon turn blue. The doctor arrived and I pointed this out to him. He didn't wait three and half or four minutes as I did at the orphanage and immediately injected her, relying on the color of her face and fingers and her pulse rate on the monitor.

I counted four seconds and waited to see the first signs of improvement. Yana started breathing again but remained unconscious. I sat beside her, looking at the hands of the clock on the wall. I counted the minutes.

On the other side of the curtain the nurses were taking care of another child. I heard one of the nurses say, "That little girl is so lucky to have someone sitting with her and holding her hand."

The other nurse said, "God sent that doctor to this baby because He knew she has no mother."

I was surprised and tears started to flow from my eyes. If only those nurses knew how much love there was in my heart for the children at the orphanage. But they're right, I thought to myself, Yana is truly in my heart.

As I wiped away my tears I remembered my grandmother from the village saying that "pity" is a word that is connected with terms like justice and morality in the relationship between a human being and his fellow man. It didn't make sense to me in this situation. How can one talk about justice and morality in the context of a baby who hasn't experienced parental love?

Eleven minutes passed. Yana didn't wake up. Once, it had taken her eighteen minutes to wake up. Gazing at her, I counted the seconds. Every time I got to sixty, I glanced at the clock. After twenty-two nerve-wracking minutes I went to the doctor's office and asked gently if he wasn't concerned.

Getting up from his chair, he went to her bed and began to shake her chest. "Yana, Yana, wake up…"

Again the convulsions began. Her left leg and arm, the blue triangle, her sunken eyes, the doctor waited two more minutes. Her pulse rate was over the monitor limit, Yana's limbs also began to turn gray.

"I'm not waiting any longer, I'm worried there might be brain damage!" he said and injected her, while I was angry with myself for not thinking of this sooner.

"I get the impression from the way you relate to her that you're her mother and not her doctor," he tried to encourage me.

"I'm her doctor," I said with difficulty. "And I am so sorry."

In the meantime, it was now evening. I remembered that since Klara's cookies I hadn't eaten a thing. The nurse offered me a cup of tea and a slice of bread and apple jam. I thanked her and joined her in the small nurses' room. I took large sips of tea and quickly chewed the bread. Brushing the crumbs from my dress, I left to call Yuri from a public phone to let him know I'd be late.

I sat down beside Yana again. My eyes were closing but I struggled to stay awake. At a certain point, there was suddenly light in the room. I observed a nurse and doctor next to me, and Yana was convulsing. Again, she stopped breathing. Again, the blue triangle appeared and spread over her face. My whole body immediately went cold.

The doctor injected her, the spasticity weakened slightly but the blue mark continued to spread. I noticed that her fingers and legs were blue.

I held her hand, crying, "Yana, my Yana, wake up!"

She didn't respond. Her hand grew cold and limp.

"Yana! Yana! You must wake up, open your eyes!"

The doctor put his hand on my shoulder. "Yana can no longer hear you, Yana is dead."

All at once, there was an explosion of pain in my chest and through my body. I felt like I was losing my balance. I leaned against the wall, but couldn't sit down. I didn't know what to do. For a moment I wasn't sure it was really happening. Not again! No!

The nurse removed the oxygen mask and infusion, covered Yana with a blanket and left her head and throat visible.

Approaching, I said, "Rest, my beloved Yana. Rest in peace. I really don't know what kind of life was waiting for you with your severe illness. And maybe the doctor was right, because I did feel a little like your mother." I kissed her forehead three times and, with tears in my eyes, left through the main door. Outside another day was breaking.

I went home to sleep for two hours, I was exhausted. When I arrived late at the orphanage, the entire staff already knew. I went at once to Klara's room, and the moment our eyes met, I burst into tears. She made me a cup of tea with sugar and told me to go and examine the children; that I had to go on. That many babies there needed me.

I knew she was right. It was hard for me to do it but there was no choice.

8

Tali

Udi's dialysis started to be problematic. The fistula created through surgery between the artery and the vein to facilitate rapid blood flow to the dialysis machine, badly affected his heart and Udi weakened. After each treatment, his strength diminished and he couldn't work the next day and, very often, nor the day after that.

The subject of a transplant now arose seriously and the feeling that there was a medical solution strengthened me, although one glance at Udi was enough to tell me there was no reason to be encouraged. His family suggested finding out if they could donate but they were all found to be incompatible. His energetic parents checked everywhere and registered him for a transplant at the hospital in Jerusalem.

We went through a difficult time. From being the spoiled daughter who had never taken a bus to the hospital, who had a loving boyfriend waiting for her in his American car to take her wherever she pleased, I became rather like a nurse at home as well. Suddenly, I had to cope with shortness of breath at night, with Udi who slept sitting up for lack of air and with connecting him to oxygen. Suddenly, all that preoccupied me was improving his present situation, and I didn't allow any thoughts of the future to penetrate my mind.

After about two months, they called from the hospital one Saturday and told Udi to come in for a transplant. We immediately got organized and all the way talked excitedly about a bowl full of watermelon chunks, which he'd been forbidden to eat for a long time, and about a hefty steak. Moolie drove fast up the hill and to tell the truth I was a little afraid. When we arrived I breathed with relief.

At the entrance, a doctor was waiting for us. Strange, why would he be waiting at the entrance? I wondered, although I didn't suspect anything. But he approached and told us directly, in a monotonous tone, "The family of the donor is sorry. They're now regretting their consent to donate." He stood with us for another minute, said he was sorry, and went back to work.

We were silent. My mouth was dry, our eyes were sad. We returned to the car in silence. Our faces were frozen. Udi never told me what he felt during those hours. His expression said it all.

Two weeks later, Udi and the professor, director of the hospital transplant department, were invited to a popular television program "Alei Coteret" hosted by locally famous television personality, Menny Pe'er. The studio was in Jerusalem and the professor suggested Udi meet him beforehand at his clinic.

His parents and I went with him. The professor, a large man with white hair, spoke about the low awareness of organ donation and expressed distress at the disappointment we'd recently experienced. Apart from the kidney disease, he concluded, Udi was a healthy young man and there was no reason for him not to get a kidney in the near future. His words encouraged me, I felt we could rely on him.

From there, we went directly to the television studio. The program was televised live. Menny Pe'er interviewed the professor from the transplant department first and then Udi. When the interview ended and Pe'er went onto another item, Udi remained, sitting beside the professor. Suddenly, we noticed that the technical team were helping the director disengage from his microphone and he left the studio.

I thought his early exit was planned in advance, for before the broadcast, he'd told us he was very tired.

We arrived home at about one in the morning and went immediately to bed. Two hours later we were woken by the ring of the telephone. "Come quickly, there's a kidney for Udi!" the hospital informed us.

We quickly got ready, got into the car and again drove fast to the hospital. Moolie didn't drive as fast, but I was still scared. I wasn't sure he was alert. This time there was no doctor waiting for us. We went inside, admissions, hospitalization – and swiftly to the operating room. We understood from the team that during the television interview, a young girl had been killed in a car accident and her parents had agreed to donate her kidneys. This was why the professor had left the studio in the middle of the program. It turned out that the whole country was talking about the story, and we were the last to hear.

Excited, each of us in turn ran to telephone the family, while other relatives stayed with us in the waiting room adjacent to the operating room, to ensure we wouldn't miss anything. Then the uncles from Jerusalem and Udi's friends began to arrive to keep us company. The commotion broke the tension and the atmosphere was festive.

Udi felt fine after the surgery, had a good urine output, his respiratory difficulty disappeared. A chest X-ray showed that his heart had almost returned to normal size. Two days later, on Friday afternoon, Roni, in her ninth month of pregnancy, arrived with a bowl of watermelon chunks. More friends and relatives came and I was already fantasizing about a visit to the kibbutz. I was longing for the privacy taken from us during the hospitalization.

Three weeks later, without any warning, his fever suddenly went up and a blood test indicated reduced functioning. We realized it was a rejection of the kidney. He was immediately moved into isolation in another room. Only his mother and I were allowed to visit him, wearing a gown and special coverings for our shoes. His father went abroad on a project for the Ministry of Agriculture once the doctor assured him that Udi's condition was stable and there was nothing to prevent his going.

Two days passed with neither deterioration nor improvement but I was optimistic. The doctors showed no particular concern. On the morning of the third day, I helped him get ready for a shower. After helping him into a wheel chair under the tap, I left for a moment to get the towel and shampoo I'd prepared on the bed, a meter and a half away.

I was gone for only two seconds but when I returned to the shower his head was drooping, and he was unconscious.

"Udi! Udi!" I screamed and called the nurse, who pressed the bell to call for resuscitation. Within minutes Udi was returned to bed, and the resuscitation team surrounded him with all their equipment.

It didn't help. My Udi was dead.

I stood at the side of the room, leaning against the wall. I was cold and my belly hurt and the cold and pain got worse until I bent over and fell to the floor. Not a word left my mouth. I realized that at a certain point his mother was standing beside me. Neither of us could speak.

I didn't know how much time passed and suddenly she pulled herself together. "I'm going to let them know," she said in a strange voice and went out to call.

A long time passed – maybe an hour, maybe longer – until Udi's two older brothers arrived. Noni took Debby home to Petach Tikvah while I decided to remain. They allowed me to stay with Udi as long as I wanted. Rami, his eldest brother, was busy making administrative arrangements and when he'd finished, he joined me in silence.

At a certain point the pain in my belly subsided. I stood beside his bed, stroking his beautiful face for the last time, then gestured to his brother that I was ready to go. When I managed to collect myself and my bag, I saw the stretcher they'd brought to take him away.

9

Ira

Lena lay curled up on the bed in a fetal position. This is how I found her. She told me she'd left school early because her belly hurt and she'd gone past the clothes store to let them know she wouldn't be coming that day. I tried to understand the problem and asked if she had nausea or vomiting, diarrhea or constipation.

"I don't have diarrhea or vomiting, but I've had nausea for some time," she answered.

"Menstrual cramps, maybe?" I tried.

She shook her head and seemed to be suffering. I made her tea with ginger, chamomile, and fennel seeds.

An hour passed and the tea hadn't yet eased the pain. An hour later, I decided she should see a doctor and it was easiest for me to call the brother of a friend from the residency, a neurologist who didn't live far away. He offered to drop by on his way home from the hospital. When he arrived half an hour later, hwe asked the same questions I had, and a few more, like how was her appetite.

"I had less of an appetite for several weeks or months, I don't remember, but now it's come back and it's all right," answered Lena.

The doctor put his hand on her belly. "It's hard to know," he said to me. "She's in so much pain. Take her to the hospital, maybe it's appendicitis."

He called the hospital and spoke to a colleague of his, telling him that I'm a doctor he knows and asking him to let me stay with Lena.

After I'd thanked him, we went out to the street where I stopped a taxi. In the emergency room, Lena lay curled up on the stretcher, and a nurse approached us, took her temperature, blood pressure, and noted it down. The pain did not subside.

After almost an hour, a tall doctor in green scrubs appeared from the operating room. I introduced myself as a doctor and he nodded and allowed me to remain.

"Lie down on your back, please," he said to Lena and examined her belly. When he finished, he said that the pain wasn't located on the right or on the left side, and it wasn't appendicitis, nor was it an acute abdomen requiring urgent intervention. He decided to refer her to a gynecologist.

I was surprised and alarmed. What could it be? An ovarian cyst, perhaps? I recalled that my maternal aunt once had an ovarian cyst and the pain was very severe, but only on one side.

Lena was exhausted by now and unable to walk. Her head lolled constantly on her shoulder, she didn't even have the strength to hold it up. A kind nurse understood the situation and brought us a wheelchair. I managed without a paramedic and pushed the chair to the women's ward on the third floor.

It was a relief when a female doctor came to examine her. She spoke quietly and gave us a really good feeling. She saw Lena was in a good deal of pain and was sure I was her mother. I got the impression she'd been told I was a doctor. She asked when Lena had started menstruating and when she'd had her last period. Lena was exhausted and answered very faintly. The gynecologist took notes, made calculations on the page, asked Lena to give a urine sample and told us to wait outside.

After close to an hour, the doctor called us back into the room and asked Lena to lie on her back on the examining table. For a whole minute she kept her ear to a wooden instrument placed on Lena's belly. It was a fetal stethoscope. I already suspected but refused to believe it.

The doctor finished, sat down and looked at her notes. And then she looked at me and Lena. "How old are you?" she asked her.

"Seventeen and ten months."

She looked into my eyes and said, "Your daughter is pregnant."

"What? How is that possible?" I tried to argue with the diagnosis, as if that would help. "And how does that work in terms of her last period?"

The gynecologist explained in a soothing, pleasant voice, "It's possible that Lena experienced pregnancy rooting bleeding that stems from the rooting of the pregnancy in the womb. It's a known and normal process. Most women think they're menstruating since it mostly appears around the regular time of the period."

I looked at Lena who sighed. I had no idea what was going on in her mind.

"I can give Lena a suppository to help with the pain," stated the doctor. "Something that won't hurt the baby."

Lena nodded and stopped sighing for a moment.

"Everything is fine, you're healthy, but from now on you mustn't smoke or drink alcohol or take medication without instructions from a doctor," the gynecologist said calmly. "You're very thin and should eat more meat and eggs because you're eating for two now."

Embarrassed, Lena nodded, still looking confused.

"I'll make sure of it," I told the doctor.

We slowly walked out of the hospital and took a taxi home. We were silent the whole way. How could I not have foreseen this? I was angry with myself. After all, they sleep in the same bed and what will happen now? How will we manage when I'm the only breadwinner? Maybe I'll suggest she has an abortion? It's too dangerous. There might be a complication and she won't be able to get pregnant again, or the possibility of losing a baby would be greater.

How I wish Slava was with me now. He would certainly know what to do.

Only when we got home, did Lena start to speak. "I'm afraid of what my father would do if he hears I'm pregnant," she said. "I don't want to go back to blows and bruises."

"Why? Do you think we'll throw you out now because of the pregnancy?"

She nodded, tearfully.

"Silly girl, have you forgotten that you're my daughter and the baby is my grandchild?"

I put my hand briefly on her shoulder. I felt her tremble. Yuri had just come in from the shower and looked worried. I hadn't called to update him. He only knew what I'd written in the note, that Lena was in pain and we'd gone to the hospital. He came to her, hugged her and asked how she was.

She cried and said, "I have something important to tell you. The doctor at the hospital told me I'm pregnant."

Yuri flinched slightly, half closed his eyes, took a deep breath and asked, "Are you sure?"

Lena nodded, stressed by his reaction. I could see that Yuri had paled although it was evening and our lights weren't bright.

"You're absolutely sure? Is it true?" he asked again, this time looking at me.

I nodded.

He filled his lungs with air, exhaled slowly and admitted, "And I was so afraid you had something dangerous…" And then he leaned toward her and kissed her twice, one large kiss on her forehead and the second on her belly, for "the baby."

I looked at my little man and filled with pride.

That night Lena cried out. Yuri and I woke up. I reached their bed. Her nightgown was damp with sweat and her breaths were short and frequent, she put her hand on her heart and made tapping movements like palpitations. I brought her a glass of water and after she drank it, she tried to sleep but couldn't.

Yuri fell asleep, and the two of us moved into the living room. I made her a cup of tea, but she said, "Only a glass of vodka calms me down, that's what my mother taught me."

That's all I needed, for the girl to drink. I made her tea and reminded her what the gynecologist had said. After sipping a little tea, she went back into the bedroom behind the curtain and emerged with a new nightgown in her hand. She told me that at noon, when she'd gone to tell them she wouldn't be coming to work, the owner of the shop had thrust a package into her hand and said he hoped she'd feel better soon. Only when she got home, did she discover a new nightgown in the package, a gift. "He and his wife are good people, Ira. I want to give you the nightgown as a gift."

I was touched. Since Slava's death, I hadn't received a gift. There was no reason to celebrate our wedding anniversary and I'd long forgotten my own birthday. It was no longer important to me. My life was devoted to Yurinka. And suddenly this young girl had appeared.

"Keep the nightgown," I said firmly." It was given to you." I didn't want gifts from Lena. My frustration at our new situation hadn't subsided yet.

Her face expressionless, she left her cup of tea on the table and returned to bed. The nightgown remained on the chair. I was left sitting there, with a cup of tea in my hand. I was filled with worry, but out of that dark cloud suddenly shone the knowledge – I'm going to be a grandmother!

10

Ira

The next morning at the orphanage, I was still affected by yesterday's events. I went to the same floor twice and couldn't remember why. I returned to my office, remembered and went up again. On the way, I noticed that the Italians were sitting in Valentina's office again. I was really curious to know which baby they were adopting but, as usual, Valentina was discrete.

At a certain point, I had to go and examine a baby in Yana's room. I allowed myself to fantasize that Yana was still there. Maybe she was alive and it was all a bad dream. I asked the caregivers not to put a new baby in her bed just yet. Against *Sglaz*, the evil eye.

Before going into the room, I stopped by a playpen at the entrance. Bending down to the infants, I gave them colorful balls that were placed in the corner. I got some chuckles out of them and smiled back. Just as I stood up, Valentina came in with the Italians and their translator. I nodded hello and gazed after them with curiosity to see which child they'd approach. They passed Yana's room and I couldn't see where they were going.

I went into Yana's room to examine the baby. The kind caregivers accompanied me, talking about Yana, asking what had happened. None of them had taken it in yet. Neither had I. She'd been with us a whole year. Each of them recalled Yana – her first smile. Her first tooth.

The convulsion. The joy at seeing her wake up. It hurt to hear them. The pictures from the last night with Yana were ingrained in my mind.

When I'd finished there, I stopped in Olga's room and she smiled. I took her with me to visit Klara. The treatment room was empty, I gave Olga a taste of Klara's cookies. The sweetness made her smile. From there I went down to the playroom, where Klara was treating Pavel and Jenia. Both of them were doing exercises to improve their crawling.

I sat Olga down in front of a board with lights and taps and showed her how to press the button that turned the light off and on. Each time she laughed, I felt a light go on in my heart. Klara signaled to me to pay attention to Pavel's movements, and I recalled how he was crawling last month. I knew that Klara was an excellent physiotherapist but now, I noticed again that she really had something special in her hands. A magic touch. We were very fortunate to have her on the staff, I thought.

I suddenly heard approaching voices – Valentina with the Italians. The man was holding five-month-old Alex in his arms. Valentina told the translator that they should spend time in the playroom with Alex, playing with him and getting to know him and, in an hour, take him back to his room on the first floor. The shrill-voiced translator translated for them.

They looked like a nice couple. The tall, slender woman wore a narrow, green dress and her hair was clipped back at the neck. Her husband wore a checked blue and green shirt with blue pants. They smiled at me and Klara and then put Alex down on the carpet, photographed him and tried to amuse him with a small toy they'd brought.

I caressed Olga, kissed her and approached Klara. I badly wanted to talk to her in private. At the first opportunity, when we were the only adults in the room, I told her about the pregnancy. I said I didn't know whether to be happy about it because Lena hadn't even finished high school and Yuri would only finish this year.

"How will Lena manage? Who will help her? I'm at work for hours and now need to be mother, father, and grandmother."

"Don't worry," Klara said calmly. "You'll manage. I know you. Like after Slava's death. Remember? You were afraid you wouldn't manage alone with Yuri. At first you were in shock and didn't believe in yourself and then you managed very well."

I knew Klara was right, but I suddenly felt broken inside. "Yana's death is still with me," I said. "Only now do I realize how attached to her I was."

"Naturally, I saw how devoted you were to her. Everyone here saw it. Now Olga and Vitya will smile at you. And soon you'll have a grandchild of your own. Think about it, the cycle of life."

I realized there was something in what she said. When I disengaged the little one from the switches and taps, she held out her arms and smiled for me to pick her up. I swooped her up and she laughed out loud.

At the end of my shift, on my way home, I thought about the wedding I'd probably have to organize. What troubled me was that I didn't know where Lena's identity card was. Without an identity card she wouldn't be able to marry. How would she obtain it if it was in her parents' home? Later on, I shared my concern with Yuri and he said he and his friends would take care of it. I was afraid to ask how. He murmured something about watching her parents' house and when they left, Lena would go in and fetch her passport.

Although he sounded confident, I was still very anxious, but didn't have a better idea.

We waited two months, until Lena turned eighteen, so she could marry Yuri. In the meantime, she became lovelier by the day. Her brown hair matched the color of her eyes, her cheeks filled out, but she remained thin, with narrow shoulders and hips, widening slightly only in the pelvis and thighs. We could already see a tiny belly peeping out.

Yuri obtained Lena's passport. I didn't ask how, I didn't want to know. The most important thing was registering their wedding at ZAGS, the registration hall for civil marriages and, of course, to choose their rings.

In honor of the wedding, I asked Slava's mother to prepare our favorite dish, an Olivier salad, which nobody knew how to make the way she did. She came to our home and peeled potatoes sitting down, a towel on her knees. Underneath, she put a bowl for the peels and on the table a bowl for the peeled potatoes.

When she was done, I asked Yuri to fill a pot with water and boil it on the fire. Every quarter of an hour I checked the potatoes weren't overcooked and watched the carrots and peas. In the meantime, Grandma chopped up a fresh cucumber, a pickled cucumber, hard-boiled eggs, chicken, meat, and an apple.

I waited for the potatoes to cool a bit before slicing them. Afterwards, Grandma mixed everything together in a bowl with mayonnaise and secret spices she brought from home and let me taste.

"Grandma, this is the best salad I've ever eaten," I said. I covered the bowl with plastic and put it in the fridge.

I asked Slava's brother, Yifim, Yuri's uncle, to take care of the sausages and vodka. He knew where to buy and what to choose. The owner of the store also gave them excellent bread, and butter as a gift. Aunt Fanya, Yifim's wife, and their daughter prepared more salads and brought a cake with white cream in a separate bowl – to spread on it just before we left for the ZAGS.

I brought chairs from the neighbors, blew up two balloons, one red and one white, and decorated the apartment with flowers. A lot of flowers. In every corner I put a vase of flowers. Only when the house looked ready, did I make time to dress.

Lena was happy to wear my wedding dress, after I suggested several changes and added lace, which refurbished the dress and hid her belly. Lena tried it on and smiled a little. She looked tired. I sent her to bed so she'd be able to stand on her feet at the ceremony. Yuri was supposed to wear the white shirt and black pants I'd bought him last *Novy God*.

Grandma and the uncle and aunt had already gone home. The plan was that the following day at twelve noon, we'd meet at the hall and after the ceremony we'd go to our home. My belly constricted, my feet were tired, and my head was pounding.

On the morning of the wedding, Lena rose refreshed, put on the dress and I helped her to gather up her hair behind and insert a small ball of wool to add volume. It was the fashion, and Lena wanted to be like the brides she'd seen in magazines and on television. I so wanted her to be happy, not so sad all the time.

At the church, she smiled a lot, which made me happy. Finally, I felt some joy.

I wore a festive dress I'd kept in the closet for special occasions. There hadn't been festive occasions for years. I also put on red lipstick and high heeled shoes. The uncle and aunt came directly to the ZAGS with Grandma. The government official called Yuri and Lena's names and asked them if they wanted to marry. Once they answered in the affirmative, he instructed them to put on each other's rings and finally declared them husband and wife.

At this point we gave Lena flowers and the ceremony was over. Once the tension subsided, we became hungry and hurried home to celebrate. I took the salads out of the refrigerator, sliced the sausages and yellow cheese, made sure there was an abundance of butter next to the bread, and added golden, canned sprats. Naturally, we also drank a lot of vodka. Maybe too much. Lena didn't drink and sat quietly to one side.

At some point, I stood beside her and hugged her. "A mother's hug," I said and we both teared up.

11

Ira

Valentina seemed restless. She was talking a lot on the telephone, every now and again going outside to smoke, then coming back in. I had to give her a list of additional medicines to supplement the previous list, but felt it wasn't the right day and decided to go in the next day, but she saw me and called me inside. She took the list and promised to make the order soon.

When I left the room, a young man and woman entered. They appeared to be Russian and, later on, from the corridor, I heard them speaking Russian. By their appearance and voices, I felt I'd already seen them here at the orphanage.

I went up to the first floor. I thought that before going to check up on the two sick children, I'd spoil Vitya a little. He hadn't had any special attention from me in a long time. Since the story with Yana, I'd been reluctant to become strongly attached to another child. With Olga, it was different – she was a special child born with a genetic impairment, which anyone could see. To this day, I haven't met parents who wanted to adopt a child with Down's Syndrome.

I spoke to one of the caregivers and decided nonetheless to start with the sick children. One of them had a rash and I wasn't sure if it was an allergy or not. I gave instructions for him to receive porridge with a milk replacer for a few days and observe the spread of the rash.

I knew I had to use the vegetarian milk replacer sparingly because it was very expensive, but I really didn't have a choice. I diagnosed the second baby with a virus and left instructions to observe him. I planned to return to him before the end of my shift.

I then washed my hands and went to Vitya. He held out his arms to me, straightening them urgently, it was impossible to refuse them. I was glad to pick him up and play a little. A few minutes later, lunch was brought in, puree and ground meat soaked in soup. I mixed everything in a bowl and fed him with a spoon. What an appetite he had. Suddenly, I heard a voice behind me, "What a sweetheart. Papa's here. Look at Papa. How you've grown."

I turned my head to discover the woman I'd seen with Valentina. She was holding Alex in her arms and speaking to the man with her. I got up and went to the caregivers, although Vitya hadn't yet finished eating.

"What's going on? What's happening? Doesn't he belong to the Italians?" I whispered, concerned.

Natalie the caregiver talked with other caregivers who had gone out to another room and for five minutes all the caregivers on the floor came in and out, wanting to see. I didn't understand what was happening. I finished feeding Vitya, returned him to the playpen and went downstairs to Valentina. I wanted to make sure she knew what was happening on the first floor.

"Yes, Ira, I do know. Didn't you see how pressured I was all morning, constantly on the phone? After we'd finished with all the paperwork for the Italians who were happy to adopt Alex and had photographs with him and showed me the clothes and toys they'd bought him…"

I couldn't understand what had happened. Why was she so stressed? It was great that the adoption had worked out for Alex and the Italians.

And then she continued, "Something good happened, but I don't know what to do with the Italians who were so easy and pleasant and they also bought a lot of toys for the orphanage. 'For the ones who remain there,' they said. Such nice people."

"I don't understand, Valentina, if something good has happened, what isn't good about it?"

Finally, Valentina realized she'd confused me and slowly, like a teacher, she explained, "What's good is that Alex's biological parents have decided to take him, but I feel very uncomfortable regarding the Italian parents."

I suddenly understood and put my head in my hands. That really is unpleasant. I felt great compassion for the Italians, while knowing that by law, Russians are always first in line to adopt, before the overseas families coming to adopt.

After a few moments, I realized that Valentina needed support. "I believe that it will all turn out all right. Invite them, appeal to their hearts. You know how. You're good at it. Tell them the truth," I told her.

"The adoption case was supposed to come to court in about three weeks' time, the Italian parents planned to come to us a week or two beforehand so that Alex could get used to them. Well, I must call the translator and explain the situation to her so she can inform the parents."

I looked at her, my heart going out to her. I wouldn't want to be in her shoes. Before leaving the room, I said to her, "Good luck, Valentina. I trust you. You know what to say. You always find the right words."

I then returned to the first floor, thanking God I'd chosen to be a doctor and not a director.

12

Ira

Lena's pregnancy lasted four and a half months after the wedding. Her belly grew but no-one at school knew because it was winter and she was wearing large clothes. She also continued working at the clothing store. Every ruble helped us. At night she'd wake from bad dreams and I caught her drinking vodka several times. I didn't want to hurt her, so I said nothing, but I was curious to know where she got it from. Maybe she bought it with the money she earned at the store. The drink wasn't expensive, but I hoped she wasn't stealing it.

Then one day at dawn, she woke me – the contractions had started. I asked her to time them and in the meantime to prepare a bag with a toothbrush, sandals, and a new comb. I asked Yuri to help with the bag but he seemed alarmed and confused, managing to help only after receiving clear instructions. I hurried the two of them out to rodinný dom, the maternity hospital. I had time in the taxi to explain to Lena that the first birth can take hours sometimes and she must be patient. I suggested she fast from then on and that if she gets thirsty, to take a teaspoon of water every half an hour.

Outside the hospital a lot of people were waiting. Families were forbidden to enter and Lena went in through the main door. A paramedic sat behind the door, glanced up from the counter and gave a telephone number they could call to find out about the birth.

I stood outside with Yuri and explained to him that the birth could take many hours and since he'd started a new job at a metal factory, he shouldn't take time off right at the beginning and we should both go to work. We decided to return to the hospital after work.

When we returned, Lena still hadn't given birth and every half hour we approached the paramedic to ask if there was any progress. At half past eight we were told Lena had given birth to a son weighing three kilos, one hundred grams. We hugged and hurried home to tell the neighbors. Excitedly, I called my parents and Slava's brother.

The next day we waited with all the families outside the building and the mothers inside came up to the windows to present their babies. The families clapped and pressed up against the windows, examining the resemblance of their baby to Papa or Mama or Grandpa.

In my heart, I laughed, after all, they all look the same: small, wrapped in a cotton diaper, and a hat on their heads. What could anyone see? But when Lena showed us our baby through the window, I said to Yuri, "I feel your father has sent him to us from heaven. He is so like him."

Yuri nodded and opened his eyes wide as if in agreement and murmured something indistinct with shining eyes.

The following day, in honor of my grandson, I bought an enormous cream cake at a cake shop on the way to work. It had raspberries, which Valentina particularly liked. Luna the cook kept the cake in the refrigerator and promised to cut it and hand out plates at a quarter to ten. I also asked Klara to join me in Valentina's office. When we arrived, her door was closed and we waited on the sofa in the corridor. I put the cake on a round, glass table in the corner.

After ten minutes, I listened at the door and heard Valentina talking, but couldn't work out if people were sitting with her or if she was talking on the telephone. Klara couldn't wait any longer and went off to get Olga for hydrotherapy. Five more minutes went by. I considered leaving and returning. I was expecting new babies to arrive and had to see sick children first. I took the cake and when I was in the middle of the corridor in the direction of the kitchen, Valentina came out of her office and called me inside. I sat down opposite her with the cake, and she congratulated me and gave me a gift.

Through the cellophane I saw a thin cardboard box inside which was a smart, white baby outfit – wool trousers, a sweater, hat, and tiny slippers. The gift was tied with a blue ribbon, my favorite color. I hugged Valentina, kissed her, and thanked her very much.

She tasted the cake and nodded in pleasure, turned to a corner of the room and began to make us instant coffee from abroad. Adoptive parents probably brought it for her. I'd never tasted coffee like it. After a few sips I felt energy in my entire body and the taste was strong and dizzy-making.

Valentina politely asked after Lena and if she was managing with the breastfeeding. But I sensed she didn't have the patience to listen. I was uncertain whether to stay or leave and began to get up from the chair. Valentina gestured to me to sit down and asked me to complete Alex's file by noon, when his parents would come to pick him up.

A simple file, I mused. The child was healthy, developing well, eating well, no allergies. "Did you know Alex was intended for Italian parents?" she asked.

"Yes, you told me, remember? And then I visited Klara in the playroom while she was working with Pavel and Jenia, and they came in with Alex."

Valentina suddenly looked up from the papers on her table, looked me straight in the eye and asked, "Ira, were you alone? I mean, were only you and Klara and the two little boys there?"

I didn't understand the meaning of the question or why her tone had changed. "Yes, I was there with Klara and the two boys and—"

"Tell me everything, what exactly happened!" she demanded.

I went on while my blood pressure rose in the direction of two hundred, "I took Olga with me, you know I worry about her because I don't believe anyone will want to take her. You see, she's already been here for two years, she's among the older children."

"Ira, you don't have to justify yourself. It's all right. Olga isn't the only child to remain with us for a long time. There is also a group of older children in the other building. I kept Olga with us because of her pace of development."

I didn't understand why she said that. She stopped talking and looked irritably at the papers. After a few moments she said, "Thank you, you can go, you have a lot of work today."

With a sense of despondency, I hurried to my usual morning rounds. I saw the sick children, gave instructions for treatment and then went downstairs to finish Alex's file.

At noon I went up to the first floor with a plate of cake for the staff, where I met Alex's parents who were dressing him in festive clothes and I congratulated them with all my heart, hoping they would enjoy raising him. I went on to the second floor and then stopped to see Klara. I gave her some cake and shared what had happened in Valentina's office.

"I don't understand," she said, shrugging. "It seems strange to me, too."

When I reached my treatment room, the caregivers were already waiting with the new babies I had to examine. It was three o'clock by the time I'd finished. I went in the direction of the kitchen to ask if there was a cup of soup left. Out of the corner of my eye, I saw the Italian parents accompanied by Valentina. I thought she'd said they were supposed to come in a week's time, before Alex's adoption court case, which had now been cancelled. They went up to the first floor, continuing up the stairs to the second floor.

I went back to my treatment room to complete the paperwork and instructions for the new babies, when suddenly the door opened – Valentina stood in the doorway.

"What's wrong?" I shivered.

"Can you come outside for a moment?"

I went out and saw the Italian couple with Olga in their arms. "They fell in love with her," said Valentina excitedly. "When they saw you and Olga in the playroom, with Klara and the boys."

I was so happy for Olga, I didn't believe she'd ever be adopted and was afraid of what would happen to her in a year or two. But now, when this couple actually chose and wanted her, I felt distressed. I wanted this for Olga, but not for myself. I loved her and was attached to her and feared imagining my daily routine without her hug and rolling laugh.

I stood gazing at them, my eyes filling up in silence.

13

Ira

Lena and the baby came home from the hospital four days after the birth. Lena chose the name Mikhail and we at once called him Misha. We prepared the house before they arrived. Yuri blew up and hung balloons and I baked the white cake Lena liked and decorated it with mocha cream and sweets.

At home, I held my grandson for the first time. What a beautiful face and blue eyes, I thought. I moved the wool hat slightly off his face to see the puff of fair hair. I gently hugged and kissed him and put him in Lena's arms. I could see she was nervous. She'd never held such a small baby. My Yuri was moved in his own way. Tried to amuse him. It didn't really work.

"He's still small," I explained.

All at once, Yuri and Lena's sleeping corner became a family room, three in one corner. The orphanage gave me an unused crib, which was very lucky as we didn't have one. In the makeshift closet among my clothes, I kept a tin hidden where I'd saved a few rubles. Since the wedding, I hadn't bought any expensive sausage. I'd been saving for the baby.

After about an hour, I took the baby back from Lena, put him on a clean sheet and began a neurological examination.

Yuri drew back the curtain with a worried expression. "What are you doing?" he asked.

"A grandmother has to make sure her grandson is healthy."

And indeed, I found that our Misha was healthy.

Lena, despite concern, turned out to be a responsible mother. She changed Misha's diaper whenever necessary and fed him. We gave him his first bath in a tub together, and I felt she could be trusted. I saw she was happy with Misha, though her eyes became sad again.

All in all, Misha was a good child. Lena usually woke to nurse him once a night but she herself would wake crying out from nightmares at least once.

When he was three weeks old, I noticed that Lena began to withdraw into herself. She didn't speak or smile and she wasn't happy.

One evening, when I came home, I found Misha in a dirty diaper, she probably hadn't changed him since the morning. I immediately filled the tub with water for a bath. His bottom was really red and after I'd washed him with soap, I changed the water and prepared him a bath with Cali water – to soothe the red skin on his bottom. The poor little thing was half asleep, he'd probably cried a lot and was tired.

When I asked Lena, she couldn't explain what had happened to her, but promised it would never happen again.

I put Misha in his crib in the living room and went to clean my bedroom and theirs. Under their bed, I found a bottle of vodka wrapped in brown paper. I didn't say anything, although I was worried, and not only because of the money, but because of the breast-feeding. It wasn't good for Misha.

I assumed that Yuri didn't know, because after he came home from work, he played a little with Misha and fell asleep. Depending on his shift he sometimes left for work before I did. There were days we didn't have time to talk at all. I became increasingly worried. What would happen when Yuri enlisted the following month? He'd be in the army for a whole year. Clearly Lena and Misha would have to remain living with me and could only move to a separate apartment when Yuri was released.

And this is what happened. When Misha celebrated his fourth birthday, I packed up the cake I'd baked, put my gift in my bag, and after a quarter of an hour ride on the bus, I got off at the bus stop. Misha was sitting on the steps, waiting for me. He was glad to see me and, rejoicing, we went up together, hand in hand.

Only after I'd put down the cake and the bag, did I get a huge hug from him. Afterwards, he didn't let go of me. The birthday table was ready, the balloons were hanging up, and we started singing a birthday song in Russian. "*S dnyom rozhdeniya tebya!*" Misha was happy with my gift – a set of small colorful cars, and gobbled up all the chocolate sweets.

That evening, he asked me to tell him stories. I told him about my childhood in the village, about the animals, and fruit trees. I was astonished by his intelligent questions. I didn't always know what to answer. He understood many things by himself. When it was time to go to bed, he asked for another story.

I allowed him to take the little cars I'd brought him to bed and he created a car track on the blanket and moved them one after the other. I got up for a moment to straighten my skirt, and three of the seven cars fell. I bent down to pick them up and found only two. I looked under the bed and could also see under the curtain separating his room from Lena and Yuri's. It was already dark but I was sure I saw the corner of a bottle peeping out of a paper package. I pulled out the third car and went on with the story. I then parted from Misha with a kiss and promised to come again the following Sunday.

When Yuri accompanied me to the bus stop, we had an opportunity to talk privately. "Everything is fine, Mama," he answered when

I asked how he was. "Fine at work. Fine at home."

"And Lena, how is she?" I persisted.

"Lena tries very hard with Misha, and when I come home she makes food, everything is fine."

"I'm glad to hear it, Misha is a delightful child."

I kissed Yuri goodbye but I was uneasy. All the way home I wondered how my Yuri, who had grown up a sensitive, caring child, hadn't noticed that Lena was drinking again. And maybe she wasn't? I thought, maybe that bottle has been there a long time and she's simply forgotten it?

14

Tali

"The fetus has stopped developing," whispered the doctor as we looked at the ultra-sound together.

This was the first disappointment after several weeks of joy and excitement – not only had the first treatment succeeded, but my body was also healthy and fit. I was afraid that my termination two years previously had harmed my ability to fall pregnant again.

I may not have liked the termination, but I did initiate it. My partner at the time couldn't bear it, we weren't married and hadn't discussed the matter of a child together. He already had two young children of his own with his divorced wife, when she showed signs of deep depression and he supported her. I didn't feel it was appropriate to keep the pregnancy. I felt it would be too much for him. At the same time, he became grave and sad and his response to me was occasionally confused. We spent more time together, he grew closer, but the sadness remained in his eyes and there was a constant sense of the weight on his shoulders.

My gynecologist was a friend and colleague from my days at nursing school. We met when he was in his first year of residency. Now, disconcerted, he scratched his head and said that a pregnancy that wasn't developing is common and doesn't necessarily have implications for the future. "This is the first attempt and we're just starting fertility treatments. Statistically, quite a few first pregnancies end spontaneously at an early stage," he went on.

"Thank you," were the only words to come out of my mouth. I dressed and quickly left the clinic to go to my car. I didn't want to be seen with tears in my eyes and questioned in the corridors. I'd worked in each ward at the hospital for close to twenty years, everyone knew me, from the director to the orderly.

In my small apartment, I closed the blinds and sat down on the gray sofa. I didn't want to listen to the noise of the outside world, particularly not to children's games in the basketball court at the adjacent school. Sad and frustrated, I stared at the walls and furniture. After drinking coffee, I got into bed, then got up, had another cup of coffee and again got into bed.

The issue of motherhood had begun to stir in my mind three years previously, even before I turned thirty-seven. At every opportunity, I thought about a child; I gazed at parents and their children when they played in the park. I imagined what I'd do if my child lay on the ground screaming, while people were walking past, that he wants a candy now, and I won't buy it for him, and what would other parents in the park think of me. Every time I met a toddler with his parents, I imagined what I'd do instead. Since my work filled my life and gave me great satisfaction, the time to think about a child was restricted to when I drove between hospitals and it didn't usually take over my daily routine.

By then, I was the Director of the National Transplant Center for the Ministry of Health. My main role was to establish a new national system for the coordination of transplants. I couldn't have found a more successful role, which includes a winning combination of influence in two areas: logistic management and therapy, particularly accompanying families in situations of traumatic loss. The role also included appeals for organ donations and facilitating support groups for families for many years after they'd experienced a tragedy.

After two days of grieving the loss of the first planned pregnancy, I began to plan the next pregnancy, which evoked joy of life and motivation. I checked to see how much rest my body needed and, at the first opportunity, I reported for treatment.

I loved the excitement, the tension waiting to find out if I'd conceived. My life divided into two sections – two weeks until ovulation, and another two weeks from ovulation until the end of my period. For the first two weeks, I was busy counting the days until the injections, the days of the injections and ultra-sound follow-up until the signal for the treatment itself. The treatments were easy for me. Some of these included an anesthetic and I'd fall asleep chatting with the staff and wake shortly afterwards in recovery, energetic, positive, smiling, and hopeful. I drove to work after resting.

Every day, I counted the minutes until the moment I was supposed to call the ward to find out if fertilization had taken place, if a fetus had formed. The answer was frequently negative but instead of hurting, I somehow learned to make friends with the disappointment, to give it space, while making sure it didn't control me.

I allowed myself time for my disappointment and immediately afterwards set up another transplant and waited for the next treatment. But in a certain sense, I became "addicted to treatments;" I became a machine focused on the following week, when I'd begin a new treatment cycle and another one after that. Turbo-like. No-one tried to stop me, not even the staff at the fertility clinic.

There isn't anything I haven't tried to aid the success of the treatments. The blind reflexologist Ora, for instance, was known for her success with fertility cases. I saw her once a week. Her blindness conveyed a unique ambiance; I attributed to her qualities of channeling and expertise in the field on levels I couldn't see or understand. I also tried a Haredi expert on healing herbs. I left a few hundred shekels with him and the remedies he recommended arrived by special delivery, in dark bottles, so they wouldn't be affected by exposure to light.

One Wednesday, when I was at a crowded convention at a hospital up north, the break lasted until eleven o'clock and I was forced to slip away from all the participants to find a quiet place for my telephone call to the fertility unit. The line was busy.

One of the participants at the convention went by and asked how I was.

"Fine, and you?" I responded impatiently and redialed. The two minutes before the line was free seemed like eternity. Tensely, I prepared for a negative answer but the moment the employee at the fertility recognized me, she cried out in excitement, "We have a fetus!"

"What, really?" I wanted to hear it again, to be certain.

"Yes! Yes!"

I tried to be cautious with my happiness. It's only the beginning, I told myself.

A few days later the fetus was restored to the womb and a few days after that a blood test confirmed the pregnancy. At this initial stage, everything was a secret. Only my boyfriend and I knew. I intended to raise the child as a single mother and not obligate my partner, if he didn't want to be a part of raising the child.

I took care of myself, avoided intense sport sessions, took folic acid to lower the risk of birth defects in the fetus, and made sure to eat healthier foods than usual. The pregnancy was stable, but I continued to hide it until I was sure. Fortunately, I gained very little weight and apart from constant itching in the area of my back and hips, everything seemed normal.

In my seventeenth week of pregnancy, as part of a routine follow-up examination, I saw a doctor privately who was an expert in ultra-sound and fetus defects, who had a good name. In the prenatal screening test, he noted three different, indistinct signs: one was related to fluid in the area of the neck, the second was a weakness in the kidney, I didn't hear the third.

It was clear to me that Down's Syndrome was suspected.

I immediately understood that this pregnancy too would be lost.

Upon leaving, I called my gynecologist. He tried to calm me, saying that the test isn't always precise, that he knew many women whose ultra-sound revealed signs of the syndrome, but this was ruled out by an amniocentesis. Eventually, after gaining experience in delivering bad news, I thought to myself that I'd like to return to that gynecologist and suggest additional ways of coping with the possibility of fetal problems. Certainly not to start with sentences that create hope and illusion. Even if he really did have positive experiences, he should describe the picture in full, without embellishment.

Within two days, I had the amniocentesis procedure and two weeks later the doctor called me. When I saw his number on the screen, I already knew. After all, amniocentesis results take four to six weeks and if they've arrived after two weeks, it means they've found something, it's all clear.

The test confirmed Down's Syndrome.

Within a day, I had an appointment at the hospital. Before the pregnancy termination procedure, I had to endure the punishment of the "pregnancy termination committee" – an unnecessary and embarrassing procedure during which I had to meet with the committee members, all employees at the hospital. The secret I'd kept would now be revealed. Everyone would know, and I also had to endure all the looks of affection and pity from the staff as well as the gossip, just like kibbutz.

On the committee itself sat a gynecologist with whom I was acquainted, another doctor, the deputy director of the Department of Internal Medicine, where, eight years before, I'd been Head Nurse, and the social worker with whom I worked closely in the Department of Internal Medicine. Throughout the interview, I looked for dirt on the floor. Out of embarrassment, I dared not meet anyone's eyes. My answers were brief and laconic, yes or no. It passed quickly. I waited outside and it was speedily approved, except that a termination in the nineteenth week required complex intervention with hospitalization.

The next day, I was hospitalized in the women's ward, a room with three other women, and given the bed nearest the door next to the sink. I closed the bright curtain around the bed, put on the floral gown that tied around the neck and left the back exposed, because the cord around the waist hips kept opening. I wanted privacy and quiet while I wondered about the procedure itself – would it hurt? How much would it hurt? What would happen? I felt great stress that perhaps pushed pain and disappointment aside.

At noon, I was called to a treatment room to one side of the maternity ward complex. The first thing I saw was a large syringe in the doctor's hand, pointed straight at my belly. Under an ultra-sound, the substance that caused contractions was slowly injected into my uterus.

I realized that during the contractions my baby was supposed to die and then be born. Die? What, is the baby dead already? Did we kill it? I repeated to myself.

I was then taken back to the women's ward to wait for the substance to work. It sometimes took twelve hours, sometimes twenty-four, they explained. I waited for hours in the hospital, until the contractions. My partner sat beside me and his face revealed greater suffering than my own. Only late that night did the contractions start and I was taken to the delivery room. They put me in one of the cubicles near those where women had come to give birth to healthy babies. Screams of pain have no smell or taste, from a distance they're the same.

I began to count the positive things, first of all there was Rina, the midwife who attended me, whom I knew and liked. The pain was terrible. I didn't understand the policy of not giving pain killers. After all, there was no fetus to protect.

After the procedure was over, I was taken down to the operation theater to complete it. It was almost morning when I was taken back to my corner in the women's ward, exhausted, in pain, crying.

By that afternoon, I was home and my feeling was mentally and physically unbearable. I weighed myself and noticed that I'd put on two kilos because of the hormonal changes. I put cabbage on my chest to stop the milk and mainly cried uncontrollably and non-stop.

After a few days, my partner and I decided to go out to a movie, to get some air, experience other people's story, but even inside the cinema I didn't stop crying and in the end I didn't even see one minute of the movie.

I needed a few months to recover and afterwards there were two more attempts. On a visit to the clinic one evening, the doctor turned to me and suggested, "Maybe you should start to think about egg donation or surrogacy."

It took me a moment to digest what I'd heard. I was confused. Not sure what I answered. I went home, sat on the corner of the bed and wept. What did the doctor mean? That I'd never have a child of my own? That there was no hope? Dreams? Was it possible that my body, going on forty-one, is signaling that it is too late? How could my body, which I'd nurtured with healthy nutrients and work-outs, betray me like this?

I couldn't fall asleep. The more I dived into myself, the things the doctor had said became less hurtful and more logical. Why not in fact? I thought. It isn't that my body has betrayed me, but simply that I'd put it through unusual torment and maybe it needed to rest. Maybe if I continued this path I'd damage it and my health. I think it was only toward dawn that I came up with a decision – to attempt adoption. I immediately made a list of the people I knew in this area, and only after I'd completed it, was I able to fall asleep.

With energy and renewed strength, I began to meet with the leading figures in the field in Israel. I quickly learned that I wouldn't be able to adopt a baby as a single mother here. At the same time, I met a couple, doctors at the hospital, who just two months before had adopted a two-week-old baby from Vietnam and who agreed to share their accumulated knowledge and experience with me. Very quickly, I became an information-collecting machine and within several weeks I completed the endless collection of documents required by the adoption authorities in Russia, including a Certificate of Integrity from the police, a permanent employment permit, and my earnings from the Ministry of Health, etc.

In addition, an introductory meeting and fitness assessment was arranged with a social worker, who came to visit my house to ensure there were appropriate conditions for raising an adopted child. I wrote a family resume, got a letter from a doctor confirming my health, and underwent a psychological evaluation to assess my parental fitness.

When I wondered why the hell I had to go through all this, I answered myself that it was "all for the sake of the child" – a new concept that served as a calming remedy.

15

Ira

It happened at noon. I was suddenly called to the telephone in Valentina's office. Who could it be? When I picked up the receiver and heard Yuri's voice, I was immediately stressed. "What's wrong, Yuri? Is everything all right?"

He sounded pressed for time and asked when I'd get home.

"At five, but what's happened?"

"Everything's all right, Mama, don't worry too much. I'll see you in your apartment at five."

I continued to work as usual, trying to suppress the conversation and his voice. Fortunately, there was always something to do at the orphanage, but at four o'clock I was already starting to glance at the clock. I began to count the minutes until the end of my shift.

He was already waiting for me at home. I sat down at the table, we sipped the tea I'd made and nibbled on cookies I'd happened to bake yesterday for him to take to Misha.

"What's going on, Yuri? You worried me."

"Mama, Lena isn't right," he shared. "I don't know what's going on. Something isn't right, she's very nervous. Maybe she needs a doctor."

I put my cup down on the table, finished the cookie in my mouth and asked for details, I wanted to understand more.

He responded, "When Misha comes home from school, Lena's in bed. He's already learned to be independent and heat up his own food. Sometimes she wakes up and gets angry with him. I saw him tremble, he's afraid of her and constantly tries not to make her angry."

I continued to drink my tea, but it didn't taste sweet anymore.

"She also gets angry with me for no reason, truly for no reason," he stated. "She's always irritable. Then she shuts herself up in bed behind the curtain and shouts whenever I try and approach. I'm sleeping in the living room."

I stroked his head and said, "My Yurinka, you don't deserve what you're going through. You're so good-hearted."

I poured out the remains of the tea and put my cup in the sink. Once I'd sat down again, I said, "Tell me the truth, is Lena drinking vodka again?"

"I think so."

Sighing, I looked at him with compassion.

"Mama, how can we help her?"

I suggested I'd call Kiril, a friend from the residency who had gone on to specialize in neuro-psychiatry. He'd certainly know better than I what to do in a situation like this. I imagined that the drinking was connected to the trauma she'd experienced at home. "Is she still crying out at night?" I asked.

By his face, I realized she'd never stopped and that he'd grown used to it. Had Misha grown accustomed to it? I hoped the cries didn't wake the child. Maybe he woke up and didn't say anything?

"Very well, Yurinka, it's late now. Maybe you should go home?" I suggested worriedly. The sudden thought that Lena was drunk there with Misha made me nervous.

He rose reluctantly. I hugged him and pushed the box of cookies into his hands, promising to come the following day. After he left, I called Kiril and gave him as many details as I could.

"There are all kinds of treatments but the best thing is to come to me at the clinic," he responded.

The next day, when I went to visit them, Lena was in her bed. When I told her about the appointment with the doctor, "to help her with her nerves and give her the strength to get out of bed," she merely shrugged and stared with indifference.

"I'll come to take you, "I said. Before leaving, I stroked Misha's head; he was gobbling down the cookies. And I left with a bitter taste of despair in my mouth.

A few days later, while we were waiting at the clinic, Lena ran to the bathroom and vomited. She immediately came back to sit with Yuri and me. She looked pale, exhausted, and weak. When her turn came, the two of us went in. I was glad to see Kiril and shook his hand.

He asked us to sit down, noted down several things, and took Lena's blood pressure – 80 systolic. "For how long has she been vomiting? Has she lost weight?" he asked me, not her.

"For two weeks now," she herself answered. "I've been vomiting for two weeks and seem to have lost weight."

His face grew grave, and he put his hands on the table and said, "Ira, I can't continue. I need to know that Lena isn't pregnant. Do a test, and if the result is negative, come back to me."

For a moment I felt I couldn't breathe. How come I hadn't thought of that? That's all we needed.

"Ira, are you all right?"

"Yes, I'm all right. Thank you. We'll do a test tomorrow and come back. Thank you. How much shall I pay you?"

He wouldn't agree to take even one ruble.

"Are you sure?"

Kiril nodded.

When we left the clinic, Lena again vomited, this time on the pavement. I went back inside to get her a glass of water and then we split up, me to my home and Yuri and Lena to theirs, picking up Misha who was waiting with the neighbors.

The next day, the urine sample confirmed the doctor's suspicion – Lena was pregnant again.

I was mentally and, apparently, emotionally unprepared for it. I couldn't smile. Couldn't feel any joy.

She very quickly got into the habit of lying in bed most of the day while Misha was in school and he spent the afternoon with his friends in the playground. In the evenings, when Yuri was working, I'd come to be with Misha. Lena wasn't functioning at all, but at least she wasn't drinking vodka because of the nausea, so I understood from Yuri, who told me he'd thrown out the bottle that was under the bed.

On these evenings, I'd get home rather late, tense and needing my own glass of vodka.

At the beginning of the fifth month, Lena began to feel better and even began to work at a laundromat. I warned her not to start drinking again. I told her about a baby who had come to us at the orphanage with Fetal Alcohol Syndrome. The first moment I saw him I suspected he had the syndrome. I saw that the bridge of his nose was flat, his upper lip really thin, and even the circumference of his head was small. I explained to Lena that apart from the unusual, external appearance, he also didn't develop like other children.

When he was two years old, the first signs of retardation appeared. And, in addition, since all babies at the orphanage developed more slowly, it was difficult to diagnose in whom the delay was developmental and in whom it was caused by disease or other syndromes.

"In any case, these children grow up with cognitive impairment and become nervous and difficult," I concluded.

I saw she didn't really understand me. "But what's the connection to the alcohol the mother drinks?" she asked.

I sighed and gave her a "semi-medical" lecture. I explained that the alcohol passes from the mother through the placenta into the blood of the fetus, so when the mother drinks – the fetus does too. The difference is that the impact on the brain of the mother passes, whereas the fetus might have problems with development and growth, as well as cognitive and emotional problems.

Lena didn't respond, but I think she understood.

I wanted to frighten her, although I knew that the most dangerous period for neural damage was between the second and fourth month, and Lena, after all, felt so bad she didn't drink. Despite this, I made it clear to her rather firmly that "A woman shouldn't drink while pregnant. If you drink, you will cause your baby damage for the rest of his life! Do you understand?"

She nodded in alarm, but I still wasn't a hundred percent sure she'd manage to avoid drinking until the end of her pregnancy.

"Lena, please promise me," I asked.

She nodded again, but didn't say a word.

16

Ira

I sat beside Yuri's bed. My friend's brother was a neuro-surgeon who worked at the hospital and he made sure they let me in to sit beside my son. He'd just come out of the operating room with an infusion in his arm and was still drowsy.

An hour before, they'd called me at work. Told me there'd been an accident with a crane and a large steel container had fallen on him. I'd come as fast as I could.

The surgeon, by his green gown, called me to his office. "Your son's lower back vertebrae were injured," he told me at once. "I performed spinal fixation, but now we need to wait and see that there is no nerve damage. It's still too early to know. We'll know in the coming days. Do you have any questions?"

I had many questions, but was afraid to ask. He continued, asking if I know of any heart problems.

I was alarmed. I immediately ruled out heart disease in Yuri, but was horrified and wanted to understand why he'd asked. And then I remembered that Slava had also probably had heart problems.

"He had cardiac arrhythmias during surgery. It might be related to the anesthetic. Don't worry," he said. "It's probably nothing, we'll find out tomorrow."

I went out to look for a public telephone to update Lena. She was at home with Misha. The evening before, I'd noticed that her legs had swelled up and that she was generally edematous and had trouble walking. The moment I told her what had happened, she started to cry. I'd never heard her cry out like that.

"When will he be home?" she asked pleadingly. "And what will happen to me?"

"Yurinka won't be back soon. He's had major surgery. He might remain in hospital for a month."

She sighed, sniffing.

"How's Misha?" I asked.

"He came back from school and went down to play with his friends."

"Good, try and rest and don't forget to give him a meal. I'll call tomorrow."

On the second day after the surgery, toward the end of the visiting hour, Yuri began to wake from the anesthetic. When his shoulders rose and his neck straightened and became rigid, I realized he was about to vomit and immediately put a bowl under his chin. He vomited a lot, only green bile, and I wiped his face. Once he calmed down, I gave him a teaspoon of water to take away the bitter taste. I asked a passing nurse for anti-nausea medication. The vomiting passed and he remained drowsy.

To my surprise, he didn't complain of pain. "Isn't he supposed to feel pain?" I asked the nurse.

"The anesthetic may still be working," she answered rather indifferently.

When I saw he was fast asleep and that the visiting hour was almost up, I went home. The minute I got home I changed my clothes and put on a nightgown. I turned on the television. There was nothing to see.

I switched it off. I poured myself a vodka and drank until I fell asleep.

The next day at work, I updated Valentina and she allowed me to leave at noon for the visiting hour. I immediately started my round of sick babies and gave instructions for their care. I finished rather quickly and thrust a neurological hammer into my bag.

I was very tense. I kept asking myself if they'd damaged the nerves during surgery and what about his heart. Scenarios of disability, paralysis, and heart disease ran through my mind. I counted the minutes until noon when I left for the hospital.

Yuri was awake and not in pain. I immediately made sure none of the staff were around and took out the neurological hammer I'd brought. Gently, I touched his foot, once in circles and once in straight lines, along and across his foot. I got no response. I tried again, increasing the pressure, but nothing moved. Maybe I wasn't pressing hard enough, after all I was used to infants.

I tried again, with the other foot.

Nothing.

I felt like I was about to faint.

"What are you doing?" Yuri suddenly asked, and for a moment I was sure he'd felt the touch.

With a big smile I asked, "Yurinka, what did you feel?"

Yuri didn't really understand what I meant and what I was trying to do and answered indifferently, "Nothing, Mama. I saw you were arranging the blanket for too long."

I choked for a second, but immediately pulled myself together and said quietly, "I've finished with the blanket. Everything is all right, Yurinka."

I felt as if a sharp knife had penetrated under my chest into my back through my spine. A channel of pain formed inside me. Hunching, I felt I couldn't get up. He was only twenty-four and a half, my boy, why did he deserve this?

At some point I managed to stand. Holding onto the wall, I recognized the nurse. I asked her if they'd done an ECG for Yuri. She went to find out. When she returned she asked me to talk to the doctor. I knew nurses, they were forbidden to give information, and her response made me even more fearful. They've probably found something in the heart, I thought.

The doctor confirmed what I already knew, "There is no response in the limbs. It might improve once the edema passes. In the meantime, I've started treatment with hydrocortisone. We'll wait." He said this in a tone of optimism, which enabled me to breathe normally. I thanked him and asked about the ECG.

"The cardiologist will be here tomorrow to interpret," he answered.

The optimism his words evoked in me dissipated in a second. I returned to Yuri's ward. I sat down and looked at him. Holding one hand in mine, I stroked the back of the other hand, back and forth. I felt the dryness in my mouth increase together with the worry.

"Hey, Mama, where did you go?" he suddenly asked.

I didn't even have time to think about how I'd explain the situation to him and would it perhaps be better for the doctor to tell him? But I didn't hold back and said, "The doctor said there is edema in the area of the surgery and that's why sensation has vanished in your legs."

Quiet tears flowed down his cheeks when he asked, "So, am I paralyzed, Mama?"

I continued to stroke his hand at an even pace while tears ran down my face. I didn't know what to answer. I opened my mouth but no words came out. He closed his eyes, and after a few moments I realized from his breathing that he was asleep. For a moment I thought of calling Lena but as I left the hospital and passed a public phone, I felt unable to do so.

After a month of rehabilitation, the hospital announced that we could take Yuri home the following week. He'd learned to move about in a wheelchair with the help of his hands and even felt his legs, but they remained weak and flabby. Fortunately, he had fairly good control of his sphincters. They also taught him where to press to help him empty his bowels. He lost weight because he barely ate. He had no appetite. He also barely spoke. He seemed despairing. When I helped him in the bathroom, I saw tears in his eyes. Maybe he was ashamed in my presence. Maybe he felt humiliated. We didn't talk about it, although my own eyes were full of tears.

We never spoke about what we were feeling, not even with our Slava. Each one of us was alone with what was in the heart. It was the same with my parents.

We discovered that Slava, who left Yuri at such a young age, also left him an inheritance: the cardiologist said that Yuri was developing heart failure and prescribed medication.

That evening, I got to Lena's home to talk to her about the release. I found her sprawled in the living room. A bottle of vodka was on the table. Her entire body was edematous – legs, arms, face. I woke her up and made her get up. She wasn't steady and I had to accompany her along the corridor to the shower. I had no idea of whether it was their day for the shower but she had to wash. By her smell and the state of her hair I guessed she hadn't showered in at least two weeks. Fortunately, nobody was in the corridor and we weren't seen. I was afraid she'd fall so I stayed to bathe her.

When we came back from the shower, I noticed that the apartment was neglected. I started to clean and tidy up. By the time Misha came in from playing with his friends, I'd had time to put a pot of soup on the stove made from all the products I'd found in the fridge. Most of the things were old and spoiled and I threw them out. Afterwards, I set the table and we sat down to eat. Lena ate only soup and went back to bed.

"How is school, Misha?" I asked.

I heard with satisfaction about his successes. We both ate hungrily, I hadn't eaten since the morning. After dinner we parted with a kiss and I left.

On the way home on the bus, I realized that there was no point in talking to Lena as I'd initially thought. I didn't even think about it. Yurinka wasn't going back to his home. He'd die there. I'll bring him home to me, I decided.

17

Tali

The flight was planned for the end of May and I counted the days. Despite the workload, despite the obligation to alertness and willingness throughout the day, I devoted every available minute and second to thinking about the adoption, preparing the room, the bed, and all other issues. I booked the tickets and took care of the visa and suitcases two weeks in advance. At work, nobody knew the purpose of my journey. I made up a story about an invitation to London to celebrate a cousin's milestone birthday.

In restful moments, I remembered the photograph Dr. Pachkowski had shown me. I met him for the first time at the Tel Aviv School of Medicine. I had just finished lecturing at the nursing faculty in the adjacent building and he was about to start a lecture for pediatricians a quarter of an hour later. We sat in a large, empty lecture hall and he handed me a photograph of the baby girl I was going to adopt.

The baby was wrapped in a blanket and photographed against a pale blue background. The picture was blurred and I couldn't even make out facial features. I had indeed asked for a girl and in time I learned that most first adoption requests were for girls. Although I couldn't see the face clearly, after such a long time of yearning, I saw in her the perfect little girl. Her face stuck in my mind.

One day, at noon, I was called to Soroka Hospital in Beer Sheva due to a suspected spontaneous cerebral hemorrhage in a woman in her fifties. During the journey I went over the clinical details with the local donor coordinator: blood pressure, oxidation of the lungs, liver and kidney function. Everything was normal. The patient's husband had died of cancer several years previously.

At the hospital, I met the son, twenty-five, who spoke fluent Hebrew, and her sister, who spoke poor Hebrew. They'd been in Israel for seven years after emigrating from the Ukraine. I asked about her life, supported them, and clarified the severity of her condition for them.

"But Mama is breathing. Look, her chest is rising and falling, and the monitor shows that the heart is working. When a person dies there's a straight line. There isn't one here. She's alive!" said the son.

I nodded and answered, "That's true, Mama appears to be sleeping, but what you see is being artificially done. If we switch off the machines and stop treatment, she will collapse. Two specialists will soon be here who will examine the functioning of her brain. Do you want to call other family members?"

They didn't want to.

The specialists, members of the Committee for Determining Brain Death, carried out all the tests required by the Ministry of Health and, finding no neurological response, were forced to determine the patient had died.

We gave the family the bad news. We waited. Silently. My telephone rang on silent and I didn't answer. I told the family about their right to donate organs. My telephone rang again.

The son asked how they'd do the surgery, "What will my mother's body look like after they remove the organs?"

I explained to him that because the organs are internal, nothing will appear different.

He asked to think about it. My telephone vibrated again. I glanced – an unidentified call. I didn't answer.

A quarter of an hour later, the son announced, "All right, we'll donate."

I expressed my great appreciation and accompanied them to the office to receive a death certificate and guidance with regard to the funeral. We returned to the ward and approached his mother's bed, I drew back the curtain and left them to part from her in intimacy. Again the telephone in my pocket vibrated. Who was bothering me all the time? I went out into the corridor.

"Yes? Who is it?"

A woman's voice answered, "From the hospital."

"Well, all right, I'm also at the hospital. Who is this?"

And then I heard Dr. Roitman, my doctor, shouting joyfully, "You're pregnant!"

At first I didn't believe it could be true and asked, "Are you certain it's my test?"

He thought for a moment that I was joking with him. "I'm serious, Tali, you're pregnant, I checked twice!"

I was afraid to be happy. I had known so much disappointment, but the doctor infected me with his joy and the quantities of adrenalin that filled my arteries provided me with a cheerfulness and freshness during the hours of the night in the operating room and continued on the drive home.

A week before my flight to adopt, the third week of my pregnancy, Lisa, the Director of the Adoption Association in Israel, scolded me when I told her.

"Didn't you know that anyone who starts the adoption process has to stop treatments?"

I stammered that the professor had forbidden me to fly during the coming weeks, to prevent atmospheric changes in takeoff and landing from harming the rooting of the fetus in utero.

She was still angry. I understood her, she'd worked hard to find me a baby, everything was organized and settled overseas, and now I'd spoiled the plan. I wanted to tell her that in my job most of the activity is unexpected and difficult to plan, but I didn't dare.

"In my experience, the pregnancy won't hold," I tried unsuccessfully to console her.

In any case, it was clear that my baby would be given to another family. My adoption process was frozen.

At the end of May, three Israeli families boarded the flight to St. Petersburg for the adoption. At the orphanage, Israeli Dr. Pachkowski presented the baby intended for each family separately. He presented Anat and Eitan Blumberg with the baby in the photograph, the one intended for me.

The moment Anat heard the date of her birth, April 14th, she understood it as a sign from her father who had died the previous year on the same day. She had no doubt it was he who had sent her the baby.

And just as I'd had no doubt – the pregnancy didn't last. I lost it in the sixth week.

I informed Lisa, who expressed her condolences, but I wasn't interested in condolences. I demanded she return to the adoption plan as soon as possible. I knew I had to have the process to hold onto to avoid sinking into disappointment because of the miscarriage.

She said I'd have to wait with several other families who were waiting for a first adoption journey. I already knew that a group of parents travel together for the first time, because it's easier to coordinate the visit to the orphanage and accompanying administration, so we all waited impatiently for the return of the first three families who had gone. We met when they returned, still without the children. We heard about their experiences and the excitement, we saw pictures, received guidance about the place, the daily routine, and dealing with the mediators and director of the orphanage.

When Anat Blumberg showed the baby intended for them, I went to the toilet. For some reason I couldn't see them – not the baby or the beaming Anat. She didn't know her baby had been intended for me. Naturally, I didn't say a word. I returned a few minutes later. The picture had already been returned to her bag.

In the course of the week, following information we'd received, we prepared a list of things to arrange for the children, from toys to various toiletries that would fill three suitcases at least, and, naturally, all sorts of gifts for the caregivers, such as makeup, creams, and nail polish. We received a detailed briefing from Yevgeni, our Russian mediator, regarding the special brands of cognac we had to bring. Each bottle cost between eighty and a hundred dollars in duty-free. All for the sake of the child, I told myself as I swiped the credit card.

18

Ira

I woke Yuri early in the morning and took him to the toilet. The neighbors hadn't woken yet so there was no queue. Then I gave him porridge. He didn't want to eat it and said he didn't want to live either. I got angry with him when he talked like that. I left him alone, as usual, with a plate of lunch covered with a napkin on a tray at the edge of the table. He drank very little so he wouldn't need the toilet before I came home. I organized the possibility of help from a neighbor who worked evening shifts.

I was tired, but I needed to go to work. I closed the door, took a deep breath and went on my way.

When I entered the orphanage, one of the caregivers said to me, "What's wrong? You've really lost weight."

I didn't know what to say to her.

I looked at myself and noticed that my clothes were hanging on me. Luna recognized me from the kitchen counter and came out with quick steps to push a bowl of porridge toward me.

"Thank you, Luna," I said. I ate several spoonfuls and put the bowl aside. As usual, I started examining the new babies, giving instructions and guidance, then joined Klara for a cup of tea. She was the only person in the world I ever talked to about myself. I told her how much I missed my mother. "She could have helped me a little, particularly with Lena about to give birth, actually, she's due any day now."

"And why isn't she coming?" asked Klara.

"Yuri won't agree. I think he's depressed. I don't know what to do, give him an anti-depressant? Is that allowed with heart medication? I don't know."

In fact, Yurinka managed to smile only when Misha came to visit. I realized this was his medicine.

"So, how can you get him to come more often?" asked Klara.

Although he wasn't seven years old yet, I began to teach Misha how to get to us by bus. I knew he was too young to travel alone but thought it wouldn't do him any harm. I encouraged him to tell his father about school and play board games with him.

He was glad to come to us. A week ago I heard him quietly asking Yurinka so I wouldn't hear, "When are you coming home, Papa? Mama shouts at me a lot. I don't understand what she wants. I'm a good boy, I do everything she asks."

I saw how Yuri stroked his head and told him, "You really are a good boy, Misha." My heart broke.

I suddenly realized I'd stopped talking to Klara and that my eyes were full of tears.

She stood behind me, massaging my shoulders and saying, "You're completely stiff, Ira, you've taken too much on yourself."

I dipped a cookie in the sweet tea. I knew she was right but I didn't know what to do. I couldn't divide myself into so many parts. "You know, Klara, it's only here that I get any rest."

"You need to learn to ask for help and think who could help you, Ira."

"Yes." I sighed.

At the end of the day, I managed to make myself call Slava's brother and ask him to visit Lena and help her with the shopping. He promised to go on Sunday and I was so happy. At that moment, I really wanted to give Klara a teaspoon of red jam, as she'd give the children who succeeded in doing complicated exercises.

On Sunday, uncle indeed did the shopping and aunt helped Lena take a shower. Afterwards, they all came to visit us. It had been two weeks since Lena had been to us. She came in her slippers because her feet were so swollen she couldn't get them into her shoes.

I set the table for lunch and took the chicken out of the oven. Aunt helped me, whispering that she'd seen a bottle of vodka in Lena's apartment. "And she smelled bad," she added.

I didn't even want to think about where she'd gotten the bottle from. I was afraid she might have asked Misha to get it for her. Or stolen it.

At the end of the meal, I served the torte I'd baked that morning and the compote I'd prepared two days before. Misha thoroughly enjoyed the cake. I promised him that in a month's time, when his summer holiday started, he'd come to me and we'd bake cookies together.

After everyone had gone, I tidied the house and dropped onto the sofa. Yuri was already asleep. Taking the vodka bottle out of the closet I found there was barely any left.

At dawn, Misha called to say, "Mama has a sore belly and she wants to go to the hospital." It took me a moment to understand, because with all the pressure and taking care of Yuri, I hadn't noticed that the days had passed and it was her due date. I quickly organized Yuri, took him to the bathroom and within forty minutes I got to them.

I found Lena sprawled on the sofa in the living room. The contractions didn't seem very strong to me but I didn't want to take a chance. I packed a bag with a gown, a comb, and a wash bag, asked Misha to prepare his school bag and I called a taxi. It was a bit expensive but there was no choice. On the way, we dropped off Misha at my apartment to be with his father.

At the hospital, Lena barely managed to get out of the taxi she was so edematous. As expected, the orderly outside the door wouldn't allow anyone but the mother inside. I assumed it would be many hours before the birth and hurried home.

When I got home I fried eggs and sausage for breakfast because I knew that Yuri would eat together with Misha, and I poured them tea. After the meal we parted from Yuri and ran to the bus stop. Two stops later, Misha got off to go to school and I continued on to work.

I enjoyed traveling by bus, I had time to rest and think, but that morning all I could think about was what would happen now: How would Lena take care of a baby, Misha, and herself? I felt I was drowning. Valentina must have seen this and when I entered, she told me to rest for an hour.

I asked Klara to come to my room and I lay down on the sofa. She sat beside me and pressed on points in the middle of my eyebrows, then above my lips, close to my nose, behind my head, on my shoulders. I don't remember anymore. I must have fallen asleep.

After a while, she lightly tapped my shoulder.

I opened my eyes and said, "You saved me from drowning, Klara."

She continued to massage the muscles in my shoulders and asked me what was troubling me.

"Everything, Klara, everything."

I looked at the clock. In five minutes the hour Valentina had given me would be up. I rose, and on the threshold, looked down at the floor. "I'm afraid with regard to Lena's baby," suddenly came out of me. "She won't be able to raise it. She's drunk all day, and I won't be able to take care of it. Neither can I bring the baby to us. I have to work."

Klara took my hand in hers, looked me straight in the eye and said in her benign voice, "Are you thinking what I'm thinking?"

We remained standing there ten more seconds and then our hands dropped. We both seemed to be thinking the same thing. Sudden fear filled me.

Toward the end of the shift, I went to Valentina's office, asked to use the telephone and dialed the hospital – for maybe the tenth time that morning. I was told that Lena had given birth to a baby girl who weighed two kilo and six hundred grams.

"Congratulations!" said the nurse.

Something in me was glad and nonetheless I was terrified. I left Valentina's office, my shoulders hunched and my eyes flowing with tears of happiness and sadness.

Misha was already at my house after a long walk from his school. He was sitting beside his father and the two of them were watching television.

"Congratulations, Misha, you have a sister. Congratulations, Yurinka, you have a daughter," I said tiredly.

Yuri smiled. I saw by his response that he didn't know whether to be glad or not. Misha had a similar response, and I wasn't able to interpret my feelings. Was I glad? Maybe, but I didn't feel it was real happiness. I went into the kitchen and took out the cookies I'd baked several days before.

A quarter of an hour later I went to the maternity hospital. Dr. Korzhikov, with whom I'd gone to school in the village was on duty and allowed me into the ward. Lena looked weak. Her face was expressionless. Everything was quiet. I sat down beside her and stroked her head. "How are you feeling, Lena?"

She shrugged.

I wanted to ask if she'd organized her release but suspected not.

She took my hand and put it on hers. "I'm trembling. I'm nauseous. Will you take my pulse?"

I took it and it was indeed far over a hundred. I immediately realized that Lena was suffering from withdrawal symptoms. I hadn't realized she'd drunk so much.

"You're actually addicted to alcohol," I whispered in her ear. "Do you think you'll have the strength to take care of a baby and Misha?"

Again she shrugged.

"My Lena," I said gently, holding her. "Do you remember when you ran away from home when you were a girl and Yuri brought you home to us? It was hard for you and you have nightmares to this day. You are suffering from Post-Traumatic Stress Syndrome, Lena. You're often angry with Misha. Even when he's good."

Lena began to talk and weep at the same time, "It's true, Ira, everything is true. I don't know what to do. It's stronger than I am. Only the vodka helps me calm down."

I continued to hold her. She looked so lost.

"You know, my Lenka, that I love you like a daughter. From the day I saw you I decided you would stay with us. I didn't even say so to Yuri. I saw your extinguished eyes and your body tense with fear and anxiety. Like it is now. You haven't been happy for weeks. You aren't happy with the new baby either. You're huddled and sad."

I don't know if it was a good thing to tell her that. I didn't want to cause her further unhappiness.

She raised her head and asked, "Help me, Ira, I can't. I'm unhappy. Suffering."

I promised to help and do everything I could but that I needed her cooperation. She looked at me questioningly.

"Your life is hard, like your mother's, but I don't want your new baby to continue this chain. I want us to help the baby to have a better life."

Lena seemed to begin to understand. She straightened her back and sat more attentively in bed. "Is it possible?" she asked.

"It is, Lena. If you want to, it's possible. You can sign that you're giving her to parents who can give her a good life. Like I gave you."

I didn't plan to say it. I felt the need to re-organize my breathing. I examined her face. She didn't appear to be astonished, but mainly confused.

"It's a hard decision, Lena. You don't have to decide now."

It was late, but I didn't want to leave her. I felt that the conversation was half suicidal. I continued to hold her hand until her eyes closed.

Before leaving the hospital, I went into Dr. Korzhikov's office and confided about Yuri's medical issues and his living with me. I tried to discuss Lena a little. The doctor already knew that Lena was drinking. She had a lot of experience with withdrawal syndrome. She also knew about men who exploited the situation and smuggled in vodka to the mothers.

"What do you do in these circumstances?" I asked.

"You know, Ira."

"Help me decide, please…"

"You know, Ira, when there is no grandmother who can raise the child, you know…" She considered her words and then after a brief silence, she said explicitly, "We suggest to the mother that she sign a waiver."

"Yes, I know."

When I got home, I found Misha asleep on the sofa and Yuri drowsing in front of the television. I took him to the toilet and then helped him to bed. My back was finished. When I settled his legs in bed, I saw the beginnings of a pressure sore on his buttock. I put on cream and covered it with a plaster. He barely felt it.

Afterwards, I sat down on the sofa and remembered I'd forgotten to buy a new bottle of vodka.

19

Ira

The following day, as I entered the orphanage, Valentina called out loudly, "Congratulations, Ira!" She smiled. "No cake today?"

I dragged myself into her office, closed the door and sat down, my eyes downcast. She realized I wasn't happy. "No, Valentina, no cake. Not in the mood. You know Yuri's situation. You know he's living with me. Lena can't raise the child. She's ill."

Valentina opened her eyes in surprise. "I didn't know that Lena is ill. So, who will help her with the baby?"

"There isn't anyone who can help. I'm taking care of Yuri, and we have no contact with her parents. I'm mother and father to her."

I wasn't able to say what I wanted. I hoped that Valentina would hint or suggest, but she asked, "So, what do you want to do, what are your thoughts?"

I was silent. I couldn't answer. The tears began to fall, and I left her office and went to Klara's room, where I could relax and weep.

Klara held me and stroked my head as if I were a child. "Why don't you bring the baby here to us and then you'll have time to decide?" she suggested.

I looked admiringly at her. Without another word I went back to Valentina, burst into her office without knocking and asked, "May I bring my granddaughter here until we know what is happening with Lena?"

She looked at me in surprise.

I sat down, I didn't feel so heavy after I'd gotten it out, but Valentina said, "I'm not sure it's permitted to bring her here because of the family relationship between you. I'll have to talk to the adoption authorities." The hope and excitement that had filled my heart drained, making way for despair.

"But, Ira, I will fight for you, I'll do everything I can." Valentina restored a little hope. I thanked her and left her office.

Dr. Korzhikov asked the nurse in the baby's ward to show me my granddaughter through the window. I looked at her and smiled. Sweet little thing. Her eyes were brown, like her mother's, likewise her nose. Her forehead might have been like Yuri's. I was afraid of falling in love with her, so after a few minutes I went to see Lena, who'd just had a shower and looked better. Maybe I was wrong yesterday. I thought. Maybe she'd be able to care for her baby after all?

"I feel better today," she said, but after a few minutes the trembling in her hands returned. "I have to drink."

I sighed sadly. "My Lena," I said. "This trembling is probably a withdrawal symptom. If you go on as you have for the last two days without drinking, if you make an effort for a few more days, you will be able to get over it and stop drinking."

"I'm sorry, I simply have to. Can't you do anything?"

She started walking restlessly around the room.

"'I'm sorry," I said and I left. I noticed Dr. Korzhikov but didn't feel able to exchange a word with her. I left the building, crossed the street to the bus stop, and when the bus arrived, I sat by the window and looked at the entrance to the hospital.

I saw Lena so clearly, wearing her nightgown, but I gasped when I noticed a strange man beside her. Who was it? He wasn't a doctor or an orderly. She thrust something into his hand and he gave her something wrapped in a brown paper bag. The bus started to move.

The following day, Valentina told me that the baby could come to us only after I signed a document with several guidelines. The first guideline was that I wouldn't be responsible for her medical treatment. The second was that if the baby were to be adopted, I wouldn't be present on the day she left the orphanage.

I was overwhelmed by tears and couldn't read the other sections. Klara, my support, entered the room and stroked my shoulders. With a trembling hand, I signed the document and handed it to Valentina. "Thank you very much," I said, feeling suffocated.

After work, I went to release Lena from the hospital. I found her sprawled drowsily on the bed, smelling of alcohol. When I collected all her things from the cupboard next to her bed, I discovered the brown paper bag.

I woke her and helped her shower. After she was refreshed, she sat in in the armchair beside the bed, whereas I found a wooden chair in the corner of the room and sat down beside her. I tried to discover whether she'd thought about raising the baby after our conversation the day before. It seems my expectations were too high.

"I don't know," she said again and again, once verbally and once shaking her head and waving her hands.

"You realize that if you drink and sleep like this, you won't be able to raise her? And you also have Misha to take care of."

Her expression was half frozen, her speech was slow and monotonous. "I don't know. Maybe I won't drink."

I felt myself losing patience. "Lena, you know I won't be able to help you, I have to take care of Yuri and work. Please sign the waiver!"

Suddenly, she sat up straight in the chair, opened her eyes and asked loudly and with emphasis in contrast to her speech until now, "What? Give up my baby?"

"Yes, Lena. If you want her to have a good life, give her up. It's for her. That's how you'll help her."

"And I'll never see her again?"

Her question pierced my heart, but I managed to answer, "I don't know. Perhaps. When she is eighteen. If she asks."

"Perhaps," she said. "Perhaps I'll agree."

I held her hands in mine for encouragement.

A few moments later I got up and went to Dr. Korzhikov's office. I asked her to call the welfare representatives. She understood and hugged me. In an attempt to make it easier for me, she hastened the procedure of the waiver document. I asked her to maintain discretion.

"Of course," she promised, and then she told me when welfare would come and said she'd prepared them ahead of time and conveyed the message that it wouldn't be right to talk to Lena again.

At a certain point, Lena and I went into a room where a doctor I didn't know was sitting with an advocate from the hospital and a welfare representative. On the table was the waiver.

Lena wrote in her own hand that she was giving up her daughter Svetlana of her own free will because she couldn't raise her. I stood on the side. I didn't hear everything, and I didn't want to hear. The doctor signed, the advocate signed, adding the hospital stamp, and asked me to sign too.

I did it with a heavy heart and a trembling hand, while wondering what to tell Yuri and Misha.

At noon I returned with Lena to her home. Their shelf in the refrigerator was empty. By the time Misha came home from school I'd managed to clean and buy some food. I made soup, meat balls, and mashed potatoes. If I'd had more patience, I'd have made some cookies, but I made do with my white cake, which Misha loved so much.

An hour later, he came in and immediately ran to his mother, who was lying drowsily on her bed, kissed her and asked where the baby was.

I felt the blood drain from my body. I called him, asked him to sit down, asked if he was hungry. He shook his head, but when I cut him a slice of cake, I saw his eyes glisten.

While he ate slowly, hungrily, I told him that we'd taken the baby to a convalescent home until she was stronger.

"All right, Grandma. And when will she come home?"

I couldn't bear it. Again I felt I was drowning. "I don't really know," I murmured, hugging him. I felt the tears fill my eyes, but I managed to stop them, at least until I left.

20

Tali

In mid-July, four families boarded a Russian Transaero flight from Tel Aviv to St. Petersburg. Dr. Pachkowski accompanied us as he was very familiar with adoption medicine and the language of the place from which he'd emigrated to Israel.

Waiting for us at the airport was Yevgeni, representative of the Israeli Association in Russia, who helped us register at the Hotel Moscow. To the left of the huge entrance foyer with its tall ceiling, youngsters were playing billiards. The hotel was large although it only had six floors; the length of each floor was about four hundred meters, and each corridor was divided into several sections. Because of the length of the hotel and large number of rooms, there was a café-restaurant in each section. Next to the elevator was a shoe stand. Each color – black, brown, and transparent – had three revolving brushes to clean, color, and polish.

The hotel may have been impressive, but all I could think about was that the following day I would become a mother. Tomorrow everything would change. That evening we couldn't sit quietly and left the hotel, we exchanged money for rubles and looked for a restaurant.

The locals didn't speak English and we had to point at photographs of the dishes we wanted on the menu. We didn't know what we'd ordered, didn't notice the taste, and we had no appetite. It was already late and the light of the famous white nights of St. Petersburg showed us the way back to the hotel. I was glad that the next day was coming closer.

In the morning, Yevgeni took us in his car to the orphanage. On the way we learned that he was born in Russia and today lives in Israel with his wife and three-year-old son. We had no choice but to rely on him. Everything was supposed to go through him. He also had two local assistants, Vadim and Ilya, who had lived in Israel for several years and were fluent in Hebrew.

After a while, the car stopped and, from this moment on, despite the warm weather, my shoulders and hands shook slightly. Before us was an iron gate painted the pale green of operating rooms. To our right stood a guard in a special building, on our left was a wall that encircled the area of the orphanage up to the guard hut. Apart from this, we could see nothing of what was happening inside. It reminded me of a prison, without the barbed wire.

Inside the compound were three large buildings connected in a u-shape. Around these was a yard with green, leafy trees and wild-growing vegetable patches. At the end I noticed a covered area with a sand box and a bench. We walked toward the central building and went up four steps to the entrance. We turned left, Yevgeni entered the director's office and we waited in the corridor.

I couldn't speak and the shaking continued.

Beside me, on a round table standing on one leg, was a round white tablecloth with a green, potted plant made of plastic. The small windows were covered by white lace curtains and on the walls was a crowded display of photographs with children of different ages in varying frames. Apparently, past joyful adoptive parents sent mementos to the staff.

Moved, I fantasized, promising myself that when I got to Israel with my baby, I'd also send a photograph to the orphanage. Soon I'll touch the dream. Soon I'll be the mother of a real baby.

The trembling stopped with the appearance of a sudden belly ache I'd only felt on the day my Udi died.

After about an hour we were called to the second floor that housed the children's rooms. Dr. Pachkowski, our doctor, stood next to a diapering table and examined the babies intended for us. We were allowed to wander through the rooms. In a playpen were six or seven babies of approximately six months old and only a few toys.

I gazed at the babies, surveying them one after the other. Will that one be mine? Or maybe the second one? Or the third? I wanted to hug and adopt them all. They all seemed full of charm, holding out their arms to each adult who stood in front of them, hoping someone would pick them up. I felt bad for those who would remain without adoptive parents or a loving hug.

The youngest children were on this floor, which was divided into groups according to age. Later we were shown into the babies' room, and then I was called to see the baby intended for me. For a moment, I seemed not to hear well, while knowing they had indeed called me.

My legs were simultaneously heavy and light. My eyes opened wide, and then – just like the cliché – love at first sight. She was only six weeks old, a normal birth, thirty-seven weeks, birth weight two kilos and six hundred grams, birth date 15.6.1998.

She didn't have blond hair and blue eyes as I'd imagined, but a thin layer of light brown hair and brown eyes, exactly like my nieces, and so I thought she belonged to our family. The "parting on the side" hairstyle, as we called her in childhood, made her appear similar to babies in the pictures my sister Efrat hung on the bedroom wall after the birth of each of her four girls.

I will also photograph her, frame the pictures and hang them up, I thought to myself.

I stood at the diapering table while Dr. Pachkowski removed the shirt and diaper and examined her: motor examination, muscle tension, primitive reflexes, symmetry of arms and legs, and communication function classification. I watched intently while gazing into her face. I knew what to expect from her responses. Gradually, the belly ache diminished and disappeared.

During the psychological pregnancy I went through until the trip to Russia, I met an Israeli pediatrician, the husband of a good friend, who also dealt with adoption medicine. From him, I learned that a baby of about two months, who grows up with parents is expected to make eye-contact and that the smile, until then activated as a reflex, will become a social smile and will beam at the sound of a familiar voice or the sight of a familiar face. Likewise, it is expected to make gurgling or humming sounds, when alone as well as when interacting.

So I breathed a sigh of relief when the baby passed the communication test with flying colors. She focused on any movement, smiled at every attempt to amuse her or make a special sound. At the end of the examination, they dressed her and put her in my arms. I lifted her, a little confused, still not digesting the fact that she was my baby. She was tiny and alert, on her head was a white cap made of fine thread, and she gazed at me non-stop.

The other babies intended for adoption were drowsy most of the time, and only my baby smiled, responded, and followed my every movement with her eyes. She seemed so extraordinarily active I was afraid to leave her on the chair for a moment to photograph her.

The care-giving staff didn't bother, whether deliberately or not, to tell me her name, but I understood that at the orphanage they'd chosen the name Sveta, short for Svetlana, "light" in Russian and in Hebrew – Ora or Orit. On the way from Israel, I'd thought about many names, but after seeing how tiny she was, it was clear to me that the name I'd choose would end in an open syllable. To express flow not closing. To enable her to grow. To thrive.

So I chose – Ella.

Near the exit, at the door to the building, stood a local woman, wearing a blue uniform with a belt and a white apron, who looked like one of the care-giving staff. I smiled at her and she returned the smile. I noticed that two upper teeth were missing on each side of her mouth.

Ilya stopped to talk to her and introduced us. "Her name is Irena and she's a doctor here."

She didn't at all look like a doctor, I thought, but the main thing was that she appeared sympathetic. They spoke and Ilya translated. He told her that I'm a Health Ministry nurse, which pleased her. I went toward the exit to the car waiting outside, and the doctor continued talking to Ilya. When he parted from her, I asked what she'd wanted, and he said casually, "Nothing much, she asked which baby you were going to adopt. I told her it was a female baby but I don't know the name."

I smiled proudly. "You could have told her, I know. Here she's known as Sveta."

Ilya turned round to the doctor who was still standing in the entrance, gazing after us, and shouted to her, "Sveta."

She smiled a huge smile that revealed her missing teeth and waved goodbye to us.

That evening, after excited calls to my mother, sister, and brother, there was one especially important call to make, to those who hadn't shared in the secret of the adoption: Debby and Moolie Ben Dror, my Udi's parents. Debby almost fainted in the middle of the conversation. Her excitement traveled the entire distance from Petach Tikvah to St. Petersburg.

In the coming days, we were allowed to visit for only three hours each day. For the visit our children were dressed in fine clothes, "presentation uniforms," for the adoptive families, which were kept solely for this purpose. Without noticing, every day the caregivers exchanged the "presentation uniforms," which made us smile. Every morning, on the way, we'd try and guess which one would be wearing which suit.

We spent most of the visit with our babies on the ground floor, in a special area that looked like a daycare. The floor was covered in soft Russian carpets with small chairs, suitable for two – or three-year-old children. Next to the wall was a dark brown grand piano.

Our babies lay on the carpet, enjoying the attention they got and the age-appropriate toys we'd brought from Israel. They allowed us very little time in the baby room on the second floor. They didn't really like us wandering around. Maybe they were right because we were vocal and excited.

In the baby room, we also found the babies of the three families who had come to adopt in May. They had already filled out the official forms here and returned to Israel until the court date, after which they could return to Israel with the babies. It wasn't difficult to recognize them, they had begun to make the baby room "Israeli" and we continued this. The children's cribs were equipped with colorful mobiles and decorated crib bars.

From members of my family who work in education, I learned that in the first weeks of their lives, children don't distinguish colors, and so I chose a black and white mobile. On the wall we hung a tape recorder that played the childhood songs we all grew up with, like *gina li, pilpilon,* and *ima yekara li.*

On the diaper-changing table, which was almost empty, we put disposable diapers and baby cream to relieve rashes and in the table drawer we put a long-term supply of these items. On the little white tray next to the table I put tiny bottles of Vitamin A and D and Ilya translated my explanation to the caregivers regarding how to give the vitamins exactly as they give them to babies in Israel.

The children's room was colorful and nurturing once we'd put our stamp on it.

On the second day of our visit, we met Klara, the physiotherapist, whose job was to take care of babies born with disabilities like muscle weakness, orthopedic impairment, congenital motor disabilities, or those created from birth complications.

Klara began to take care of our children. We all crowded into her small room and watched each movement of her hand with astonishment. At a certain point, she removed Ella's clothing and I followed her closely, also to learn which exercises she did for Ella's shoulder and hip joints.

Ella laughed out loud when Klara rolled her back and forth on the plastic ball. Every time I heard that laughter something inside me softened and I filled with pride.

At the end of each treatment, Klara would hold the baby upside down by the feet, head down, for about half a minute. When she did this to Ella, I was alarmed for a moment, but the smile that appeared on Ella's face taught me that there was nothing wrong with the exercise, and that we had something to learn from the treatments in Russia. By this stage I was mad about my Ella; outbursts of love went through my heart and penetrated every artery and vein in my body.

Like the other Israeli parents, I also fell in love with Klara. The next day we brought her a box of butter cookies. On the third day, our mediators hinted to us that an additional hundred rubles a month would ensure our babies receive ongoing treatments without a medical reason.

As far as I was concerned, this was a wonderful way to ensure that someone would touch Ella, stroke her, and give her personal attention, at least once a week, for approximately twenty minutes. Without hesitation, I gave the liaison officer the required sum for several months in advance.

That day, as I left Klara's treatment room, I looked at the other toddlers and babies in the place. Nobody approached them when they cried or complained, when they were hungry or suffering from gas.

I'd read while I was preparing for the adoption that this reality would cause children to lose trust in adults while growing up as well as causing difficulty forming relationships with a constant figure. I felt the pain of the little ones pressing on my chest for a time.

I photographed her constantly. I didn't want to lose even a piece of the puzzle of Ella's life, already missing a large piece anyway.

During the remainder of our time during the long days and white nights, we studied the city and all its broad streets. We visited the wonderful Hermitage Museum and the huge plaza in front of it. One evening, we went to the Mariinsky Theater. The building, foyer, seats, the gilded walls, and shining crystal chandeliers hanging in every corner were impressive, and the audience was elegantly dressed, just like the movies. With all the excitement, I don't really remember the performance.

We were accompanied everywhere by at least one of our liaison officers. The custom, which we speedily internalized, was that after a visit to the orphanage, we went out for a meal at our invitation. The liaison officers never offered to share the cost. There was also a fixed daily rate for the liaison officer's service as well as a fuel rate. Every action was priced. Although we were in Russia, our liaison officers usually chose Georgian restaurants and I learned to enjoy the Georgian style of serving and cooking.

On Saturday morning, our last day there, we entered the orphanage and met local parents with their three-year-old son. They'd come to visit their one-year-old son. We learned that there was a special arrangement for families in economic distress: they could leave their child at the orphanage and come to visit until the age of three, when they had to decide if they could raise him by themselves or give him up for adoption.

A considerate and humane option, I thought to myself, but also a sad one. If the parents cannot economically raise their child after the age of three and decide to give him up for adoption, what happens then? In most cases, older children are less "desirable" for adoption and are simply transferred to another orphanage, a kind of boarding school, until the age of fifteen. They will then most likely find themselves on the street.

The distress I felt evoked the thought that maybe I'd adopt two children, my Ella and another, older child, who was no longer considered desirable. But I very quickly realized that the Russian method works precisely, without improvisation. Everything is black or white, as determined in advance and according to the rules.

We knew that in the course of our visit we had to complete administrative arrangements with the Russian education department and prepare documents for local authorities for the court case, after which we would finally be able to take the children home.

It was explained to us that the Hague Convention to which both Israel and Russia have acceded, allows parents who have given up their children for adoption to revoke consent during the first six months, thus it is impossible to adopt babies from Russia who are under six months old. However, the older the child, the more possible it is to distinguish severe development and health issues that are not noticeable in the first weeks.

It was uncomfortable for me to admit that I was looking for a healthy child. After all, that's why we brought a doctor from Israel. And the Welfare Ministry in Israel sets tough requirements regarding international adoption and required tests for infants and toddlers in order to prevent the entry of infectious diseases into the country, for example.

One day, when I took Ella down to the playroom, I met an Italian couple who were playing with a baby on a linoleum surface placed on the carpet. They spoke English and the father said that their new baby had been infected with syphilis by his mother and they'd take care of him in their country, where they'd do all they could to ensure his health and avoid the complications of the disease. What saints these parents are, I mused, sensing unpleasant contractions in my belly.

Before the flight back, I packed test tubes with blood samples taken from Ella in order to bring to a lab in Israel. We were told it was preferable to rely on labs in Israel. This is of course forbidden and I had to hide them well. I wasn't concerned because I heard about other families who had managed the flight from Russia to Israel with test tubes.

During our last hour together before I returned to Israel, I hugged and kissed Ella and sang to her all the time. I repressed the thought of the parting from her as long as possible. I didn't want to leave her alone. I imagined her in the playpen with all the children, no-one holding her when she cried or when she had gas. If only I could take her with me now.

"Soon," I whispered to her. "Soon I will come and take you with me."

When I landed in Israel, I hurried to the Medical Center, a private lab in Herzeliya, left the test tubes and asked when I'd receive the results. And then, even before I went home, I stopped at Photo Negba to develop the photographs.

In the course of the coming days I was preoccupied with thoughts about her, wondering what she was doing, when she slept, when she ate, was anyone holding her? I was told I had to wait until she was six months old and hope her mother wouldn't regret it and take her.

I counted the days until my next visit to Russia and I marked the New Year.

21

Ira

Dizzy, I returned to the complex of children's rooms. All the Israeli families had gone, they'd apparently left before with Yevgeni and the doctor. I immediately went up to Sveta's section, to have as much time with her as possible. The sand in our hourglass was beginning to run out. I picked her up, put her on the carpet, played with her, and she chuckled at me. I wondered if she recognized me. My voice.

Were these my last moments with her? For a moment I was terrified. I held her close, pressing her to my heart. She showed signs of wanting to be released to play. I put her down and gazed at her, wanting to imprint everything about her in my memory: eyes, expressions, movements, laugh, and smell. Before it all fades. For they could take her at any moment and I was forbidden to be with her when this happened.

My shift was about to end, but I stayed another moment, another minute, with her, until the caregiver came and said she had to change her. I stood in the doorway for a moment and sniffed, hoping there would be one more time, just one more time.

At home, I told Yuri that someone had recently come from Israel who would probably adopt our Sveta. He smiled a half smile. I didn't know if he was glad or if this was his usual half-smile. Maybe it was just a reflex. I didn't know what to feel either.

I knew that it would be better for Sveta not to stay here, but I couldn't imagine the parting from her. How will I manage without her? I thought. What will happen if I come tomorrow and she's no longer here? After all, I came straight to see her every morning. Zina would save her lunch so I could feed her. On my breaks, I always took her out into the sun. When I was busy receiving new babies, Zina herself would take her into the sun with the caregivers who went outside to smoke. I couldn't imagine a single day without my Sveta.

I poured myself a glass of vodka and considered talking to Valentina. Maybe the adoption could be postponed a while. I swallowed the vodka in one gulp. I poured another glass to blur the pain of regret that had begun to surface along with doubts that Valentina could help.

I had gotten myself and my family on a track of no return. I felt lost and poured another glass.

The next day, after work, I went to visit Lena and Misha. I didn't know whether to tell Lena that a family had arrived who was interested in adopting her daughter. I feared her reaction. Maybe it was better not to say anything. Maybe, I thought, I'd tell her only if she asked.

Lena was spreading a tablecloth on the table in my honor and she'd made tea and taken out cookies. I was touched by her welcome. She looked better, less pale. She was clearly more herself. She told me she was trying to be a good mother to Misha and had found a job as a cashier in a little store across the road.

I was glad to hear it but my happiness faded at once – she suddenly began to cry.

"What's wrong, Lena?"

"I wasn't good with Misha," she said, weeping. "I was constantly mad at him and shouting, and he wasn't at all to blame and didn't do anything wrong."

"But you'll be fine now, Lena, and Misha will understand that you weren't well and he'll forgive you."

She stopped crying, sniffed and continued, "It isn't only about Misha. I want my baby back. She comes to me in dreams, crying for me to pick her up. I can't bear it anymore."

I didn't know what to say to her. I felt confused. I also wanted Sveta to stay with us, but didn't really know what to do about it now.

"I want her. I want her! You took her out of my arms!" she declared loudly and burst into tears. I squirmed and didn't know what to say.

"Lenushka," I responded apprehensively. "I don't know what we can do now. I really don't know."

"Give her back to me!" she said resolutely.

I couldn't admit to her just how much I identified with her maternal feelings. I was forced to tell her, "It no longer depends on me, Lenushka."

Fortunately, Misha came in at that moment because I couldn't bear it any longer. If only she knew what a delightful baby she had brought into the world. A sweet little doll. I held Misha and stroked his face still sweaty from playing outside. Despite my longing for him, I couldn't stay. How fortunate it was that I hadn't told her a family was interested in adopting her baby. I left there in pain, regretting the visit.

The next day, when I arrived at the orphanage, I went into Valentina's office and closed the door. I got straight to the point and told her that Lena had taken herself in hand and had begun to rehabilitate herself. She was looking well and had begun to work. The house was tidy and I'd even found food in the refrigerator that she'd prepared for Misha.

Valentina politely said she was happy to hear it. She apparently didn't understand the hint. So I dared to say more clearly, albeit in a pleading voice, "Maybe Lena is able to raise her baby after all."

Valentina's expression hardened at once and, in the style of an authoritative director, she reminded me that a family had recently come from Israel, the nurse who worked for the Ministry of Health.

I didn't want her to continue. I knew it would be the end of my request. "But maybe Lena really can raise her," I pleaded. "She's changed. She's rehabilitated herself."

Valentina explained that on one hand, the ideal situation is for the parents to be able and willing to raise their children. "And on the other hand, Lena has been addicted to alcohol for many years, barely managing to work, she can't even take care of Yuri, her husband. Do you realize what you're asking?"

I tried to protect Lena. I said that looking after Yuri was difficult with the toilet and the wheelchair. "She wouldn't be able to do it alone, she's so thin and small. I'm a mother and a doctor and I decided it would be easier for me to take care of him. I believe that Lena will manage to maintain a healthy situation. I'll help her and go to her every day after work."

"And who will take care of Yuri when you're with Lena?"

I didn't know what to say. "I'll think of something."

I suddenly felt great hope penetrate and fill my arteries. I smiled.

Valentina didn't smile but said solemnly, "I'm not sure that Lena could raise the baby."

"I think she can," I said confidently, but for a moment, the thought of that nurse from Israel came to mind, and I was filled with great sadness.

The next day when I reached the orphanage, Yevgeni's car was outside. Another family from Israel? I wondered. I went inside and very quickly realized that two more families had arrived, accompanied by Dr. Pachkowski. They were waiting on the black sofas next to Valentina's office.

I invited Dr. Pachkowski to my room for tea and cookies – several remained in a box that Klara had brought the previous day. We chatted about common friends from the pediatric residency and I filled him in about those with whom I was still in touch. Most were working at the pediatric hospital in the city and I occasionally contacted them to get advice regarding the hospitalization of a baby, for instance.

He asked about me and I told him about Yuri's situation, but not about Sveta. I deliberated, but in the end, didn't hold back and asked about the nurse from the Ministry of Health who had been here at the beginning of the summer.

"I heard from the Association that she really misses the baby and will come during the Jewish New Year holiday, tomorrow apparently," he said.

His words were like a blow. I continued to smile, but couldn't wait for him to leave the room. The minute he left, I went to tell Klara. She didn't understand why I was stressed. "If the doctor said she was missing the baby, then she's coming for a visit," Klara said, soothingly.

"It's a good sign that she loves my Sveta and it's a bad sign that she'll be taking her soon."

"I don't understand, don't you trust her to be a good mother?"

"It's not that, Klara. I simply don't really want anyone to adopt my Sveta."

Klara still wasn't sure she understood. "Ira, what's wrong with you? After all, it was your idea, and what choice did you have?"

I was silent. What could I say?

"I remind you that you wanted the best for Sveta, and she'll receive the best. What is in her best interests, to live with Lena and Misha?"

I didn't know what to say. I began to feel my stress increase.

"Ira, I don't understand, are you intending to cancel the adoption and take Sveta home?"

"I think that... yes. I think so," I responded, my feet carrying me out of the room, away from the mirror Klara was holding in front of me.

"My Ira, you can't. You know you can't. Think again."
I didn't answer, just closed the door.

After work, I went home and took care of Yuri as usual until he fell asleep, I was confused, but on the other hand determined and sure of myself. Yes, I wanted to cancel the adoption, I had no doubt, but a heavy stone still weighed on my chest. I couldn't eat.

This stone had only one solution – vodka.

After two glasses I dropped onto my bed and fell asleep in my clothes.

The next day I got up. Fortunately, it was our shower day. Afterwards, I felt physically fresh, but inside, the stone was relentless. I organized Yuri and went to work. I did the usual treatments and examinations and gave the usual guidelines, but the whole time I was watching the main door.

Valentina didn't talk to me about our conversation the day before. I went to see her again but she was constantly busy on the phone to people. I was sure it wasn't random, she was avoiding me. For my part, I was avoiding Klara. I passed her room but wasn't able to go in.

At noon it happened – the nurse arrived.

I couldn't breathe for a moment. I examined her from a distance. She seemed to have green eyes and she looked a bit Russian. I tried to behave as usual as I followed her. I saw how she took Sveta in her arms with confidence and strolled with her outside the building. Even from a distance I could see she was enthusiastic about my Sveta. She was attached to her and this really stressed me. Other adoptive parents were usually reluctant to touch the babies and feed them. On the other hand, I liked the fact that she might have experience.

I continued to do my usual chores but didn't take my eyes off her.

That afternoon I dared to approach. She smiled at me and seemed to remember me from her previous visit and knew I was the doctor there. I had no choice but to return a smile. As I was gazing at them, envious for myself and Lena, I thought there were many babies here who resemble her more, with blond hair and blue eyes. My Sveta had brown eyes and honey-colored hair, like Lena's. She didn't resemble the nurse in the slightest so why did she specifically want her?

I wasn't able to talk to her, because she didn't know Russian, I gave up. I also didn't know if I liked or hated her. Inside, I wanted to pity her when they took Sveta from her, I wanted Sveta to remain with me. She was mine, after all.

At the end of the visit, after she'd gone, I immediately went into Sveta's room, stole a quick kiss before the caregiver returned, and only then did I go home.

22

Tali

Yevgeni picked me up at the airport in St. Petersburg and on the way explained every site and large square, as befits someone who was born in the city and lived there until he was twenty. Later, I realized that the "tourist tour" he took me on was to soften the atmosphere.

"The biological mother of your baby is stressed. Her family is pressuring her and she is considering raising her after all," he suddenly said.

I wasn't sure I'd heard right. He'd spoken about it over the phone when I was still in Israel, but now I saw his round face looking very serious.

"I won't give her up," I said forcefully. "No chance. Do you know how hard it was for me to come?"

Since I'd been appointed Director of the National Transplant Center the year before, I hadn't felt comfortable leaving the country for a whole week. The transplant coordination system was in the process of being established, built, and developed; the procedures were being integrated into teams and the rest was in stages of learning and acquiring skills. However, the transplant coordinators encouraged me to go, promising to support each other while I was away.

He shrugged and sighed. "I don't know if you have a choice."

I was astounded. I didn't think it was real. During the phone conversation I convinced myself that it was just words. I tried to repress it throughout the flight, but I couldn't help wondering what I could do if the mother really revoked her permission. I had no idea. What could I do apart from saying I wouldn't give her up?

Yevgeni took me to another orphanage, Orphanage No. 6, to introduce me to another little girl. The small place, surrounded by trees and plants, was located right in a bustling urban compound. I waited a minute or two in the entrance and was then taken to the children's room where a little girl with blond curls, blue eyes, and snow-white skin was presented to me. Again, I felt strange pains in my belly.

Although she was very sweet, I couldn't connect with her. I was angry with myself for feeling like that, but apparently there was no other way. I didn't stop thinking about my Ella for even one minute. Fortunately, the visit was a short one and then we drove to Orphanage No. 10.

I was excited by the fact that I'd soon be seeing Ella. The minute we arrived, I quickened my pace and when I saw her I couldn't help myself. I immediately gathered her into my arms, I couldn't stop hugging her and examining her face. Her eyes seemed less brown than I'd thought on my previous visit, maybe a little greener, and she'd also grown a little.

Suddenly, as if everything that had happened was forgotten, I surrendered without worrying about my love for Ella and the relationship with her.

The caregivers remembered me from the first visit. Most smiled at me, and for the remainder of the day they let me go up to the second floor and feed her and even take her outside for a walk. Later, I received permission to take the other Israeli children outside. They were a little older than Ella. I made sure to follow the community custom we'd established and photographed all the children, as other

Israeli parents did when returning from a visit to Orphanage No. 10.

When my walk with Ella was over, I met Dr. Ira at the entrance to the building. I felt she really liked me, but until this point wasn't really sure. There was something odd in her behavior toward me. She made sure the director, Valentina, wasn't around, then she grasped my hand and said a few words in Russian. What I managed to understand was *malinka* and *spaciba*. I gathered she thanked all the adoptive parents who save the children from this place, promising them a better future. Ilya had told me that up until a few years ago, international adoption was forbidden in Russia.

In the babies' bedroom nothing was left of the extra supplies and equipment we'd brought. I suppose it was just a matter of time before the inequality was discovered between the "Israeli" babies and other children, and an instruction from above came to confiscate the products, or distribute them to everyone. I felt a momentary discomfort at the privatization of the supplies, equipment, the objects, and remedies we'd brought for our children, while also feeling compassion for the children who hadn't gained parents to take care of them and spoil them. Ultimately, I came to the conclusion that actually a kind of justice had been done for the sake of the whole.

On the way back to the Hotel Moscow, Yevgeni told me he'd talked to Ella's biological mother and tried to convince her to give her up. He told me she wasn't married, that the father had disappeared and she had no way of providing for her daughter, but members of her family had promised to help her.

This conversation was my first lesson in understanding the series of messages, reports, and vague updates. In time, I learned that none of the information was certain and that the liaison officers weren't always accurate or detailed. They'd sometimes change the story completely, maybe not to weigh us down with details regarding local bureaucracy. Maybe they'd been given information that wasn't clear.

The more I explained to Yevgeni that I had no intention of giving up Ella and the more I realized that the law was not on my side, so his message became clearer: I understood that if I paid five thousand dollars, I'd manage to silence the biological mother and she'd give her up.

Yevgeni gave me the feeling he was on my side and didn't pressure me to make a quick decision. What's more, the final word had not yet been said, certainly not about the money. Not on his part and not on mine. Either way, even if I decided to pay, I could only do so after I'd returned to Israel.

At the hotel, I met two new couples from Israel who'd come to adopt. After a brief conversation, it turned out that one of the women and I lived on the same street in Ramat Gan, she at No. 10 and I at No. 17. Both families were observant Jews and upon the start of the Shabbat, a kosher meal they'd brought from Israel was set on the table.

The door to the hotel room remained open and my neighbor, Rinat, from Ramat Gan, lit the candles and, her lips moving, made the blessing, her palms covering her eyes. Our singing could be heard clearly in the hotel corridor: "*The Angels of the Sabbath, the angels of peace, the angels of the Most High.*" My heart filled with joy.

The next day those who observed the Sabbath remained at the hotel most of the day, touring on foot a little, and I went with Yevgeni to the orphanage to visit my Ella. After the visit, he took me on a pleasant trip outside the city, and we finished with a traditional meal at a restaurant, where I invited him. He then took me back to the hotel. Not a word was said. Not about the money or about Ella's biological mother.

On Sunday, the Israeli couples returned home, and another group of parents arrived from Israel. It was nice to guide the new people, and to learn from the experienced. Two days later, we dressed up and gathered in the square of the Great Synagogue with its white stairs leading to the door. Prayers for the Jewish New Year began.

I'd never been abroad for the Jewish New Year, let alone in a synagogue. I promised myself that from next year I'd make sure to take my daughter to the synagogue for New Year and we'd join in the holiday prayers and the blowing of the *shofar*.

Afterwards, we had a holiday meal at a restaurant, blessing and singing from the holiday tractate I'd brought with me from Israel along with candles and fireworks, as befits the daughter of a kibbutz cultural coordinator.

Over the coming days, I spent many hours at the orphanage. I connected with the caregivers without language. I gave them little gifts and they indulged me with more hours with Ella.

After the visit I went for a walk along the great Neva River that crossed the city. It was near a telephone. I took care of a donation from a young soldier killed in an accident, and his parents asked for another opinion to make sure he was brain dead. Once another specialist confirmed the diagnosis, there was no question – it was clear to them that they'd donate.

After the present group of parents had returned to Israel, I had one more day before my flight. The caregivers allowed me to spend long hours with Ella and I made use of every minute with her. I kissed, hugged, sniffed her, played, and just prayed these moments would last. However, the visit evoked frequent emotional upheavals and the joy that overwhelmed me was bitter and frightening.

I was afraid they'd take my Ella from me.

23

Ira

It was terribly cold. Everything was frozen. Yuri wasn't feeling well and I didn't know how to get him to a doctor. I was afraid he'd get pneumonia on the way. He didn't have a fever, but when I tried to take his pulse, I wasn't sure I was doing it right. The result was thirty. Impossible.

I called a friend from medical school and he asked about heart disease in the family. After hearing about the family background he suggested I call an ambulance. I dialed 03 for an ambulance, which arrived rather quickly. The *feldsher* carried out an ECG for Yuri that showed irregular heartbeats. We were immediately taken to the hospital, he was connected to a monitor and medicated.

It was so cold on the way back that I decided not to call in on Lena to tell her, but to call from home. One of the neighbors on that floor answered and went to call her, but it was Misha who came to the phone. I was glad to talk to him but didn't tell him his father was in the hospital. I asked to speak to Mama.

Misha said she was in bed and couldn't answer. After drawing him out, I realized that recently he'd found her in bed every day. He'd eat his dinner alone, bread and sausage or anything he found in the fridge.

I couldn't bear it, I put on my coat and went there.

Misha opened the door and I went inside with a container of soup and palamini dumplings in one hand and a box of cookies in the other. I heated up the soup at once and Misha gulped in down. I'd filled the palamini dumplings with ground meat that he barely chewed, almost swallowing them whole. He then asked for another helping. I realized that he was starving and hadn't had a cooked meal in a long time.

"I think Mama is tired. Maybe she's sick. She's in bed a lot," he said while gobbling down the palamini.

"How long has she been like this?"

He shrugged.

I stroked his head. "Maybe she is sick. That's why I'm here. I'll take care of her, Mishinka."

I went to Lena's bed behind the curtain. What I saw was enough; I left her a brief note and asked Misha to prepare his backpack and take clothes with him. I told him he was coming with me for a few days until Mama recovered. On the way I told him that Papa wasn't feeling well and was in the hospital for tests.

In the morning, I informed Valentina that I'd be late because Yuri was in the hospital, but I went to Lena. Most of the house residents were already at work. I dragged her to the shower, although I had no idea if it was their shower day. If residents came along because it was their day, I'd apologize and tell them she was ill and had vomited.

She smelled bad and I gathered she hadn't showered for more than a week or changed her clothes. It was hard to know when she'd last combed her hair. Her face was yellow.

When she'd finished showering and before she went back to bed, I made her eat the porridge I'd prepared. She recovered somewhat. I asked her about her work and she muttered indistinctly. I went to change her sheets. Fearing the worst, I bent down to clean under her bed – brown paper bags and cigarette butts. I felt suffocated.

"What's this, Lena? Where did this come from?" I asked with difficulty, feeling unable to look at her.

"Someone at work gave me the cigarettes," she answered, adding that she hadn't worked in two weeks.

"Why not? Since when do you smoke?"

"It made me feel good. Floaty, my troubles disappeared. It was good. I felt the baby was with me."

It took me a moment to understand. "Lena, were you smoking drugs?" I asked angrily.

Lena, who wasn't used to hearing me like that, responded rudely, "Don't interfere. It's how I feel the baby is with me. It's good."

The blood boiled in my veins. "It's bad," I said to myself out loud while getting up with difficulty from the chair. I picked up my bag and tried not to look her in the eye.

"I'll be all right, I promise," she said suddenly, pleadingly.

I'd already heard that so many times and didn't really believe her. I was filled with despair.

"I promise. I'll go back to work tomorrow," she said as I opened the door. "I'll be all right. I've finished with vodka. There isn't any at home. You can check. You'll see I'll succeed. I promise. Don't be angry with me."

I didn't answer. Just closed the door and hurried off to work.

The moment I arrived, I went into Klara's room to sweeten my day with cookies. When she asked what was new, I updated her about Yuri, he'd be all right, relatively.

"They gave him medication for his heart rate and in two or three days, they'll release him." And then I shared what had happened with Lena. I told her about the neglect, about Misha's hunger, about the brown paper bags, about her not getting out of bed, about the drugs, and her pleading. "I don't have the strength," I admitted.

Klara looked at me and said she'd never seen me like this. "You've always stood resiliently on your own two feet and known what to do. Maybe it's just a bad day. Maybe you should go home early and have a good sleep."

I so loved the fact that she was concerned for me, but it had nothing to do with tiredness, not this time. It was something else, much bigger, more despairing. I was so looking forward to taking Sveta home. I couldn't bear the idea of her being adopted and never seeing her again. I badly wanted to believe that Lena had really given up the drinking, that she was going out to work, but reality smacked me in the face.

I don't actually remember Klara's question, but I went on telling her about Yuri's situation, about Sveta's forehead, identical to his own, and how she'd taken Lena's colors, her eyes, and nose, and I said I'd never forgive myself for raising the idea of adoption.

"But what choice did I have? I wanted Sveta to have a good life. I wanted to save her. I knew what kind of a life she'd have with Lena. But what will I do now, Klara? Tell me. How can she raise another child? And how can I agree and allow my granddaughter to grow up with her?"

I felt my head was splitting.

"What will you do?" asked Klara. "Will the adoption process go on as planned? Will you give her up?"

I looked at her and didn't know what to answer. I tried to think, maybe I could take both my grandchildren, together with Yuri? But how will I take care of all three of them?

I suddenly had a bright idea: maybe I could ask Slava's brother for help?

I enjoyed the hope for only a few moments, until I realized that even if Slava's brother and his wife could help, it would only be on weekends.

"So what will you do?" Klara asked again.

I sighed. "I don't want to give her up, but it appears I have no choice."

24

Tali

The three families who traveled to Russia in May 1998, the same trip I was supposed to be part of but that was canceled because of the pregnancy, began the adoption process before the Associations Law was enacted in Israel, and they were helped by Dina Golan, an experienced attorney who had herself adopted two children.

A short time later, the Adoption Act was amended following which Golan established the association "Bayit l'yeled", home for a child. I chose her to lead the adoption process for me because I trusted her and her word. For years, she was well-known in this field in Israel, many years before the State began to regulate it. Even my brother, an economist on the kibbutz he moved to with his wife, turned to her for families who adopted children from South America.

Since I didn't go to Russia in May, I was required – like other parents who applied to adopt afterwards – to act in accordance with the new regulations, according to the Adoption Act. Accordingly, international adoption had to be carried out only through an association that specialized in this subject, and that received special permission, met the conditions determined, and was recognized by the Minister of Labor and Welfare and the Minister of Justice.

Every recognized association is supervised by the Central Authority for International Adoption, a body under the aegis of the

Ministry of Labor and Welfare, which is supposed to supervise the activities of the association both socially and financially. The recognized association is responsible for all the procedures related to adoption and must determine if the applicant is fit and suitable for this; it must contact the responsible authority in the State and request information regarding the child intended for adoption, ensure that all the procedures have been observed, and all the permits and documents given by the State with regard to giving up the child for adoption; take care of the child's entry permits into Israel, and follow up his/her absorption into the adoptive family.

We, the future parents, constantly re-discovered that in all the adoption processes, more was hidden than visible. However, the head of our association, even though orderly and meticulous management was not her strong suit, knew how to reach the right people abroad, talk to whoever was necessary, manage, smooth things out, and advance procedures, particularly procedures that frequently included secret or open gifts.

But there were rumors that something had happened in our association. Apparently, the head of the association's conduct didn't conform to the new procedures and international agreements. Without explanation, the International Adoption Unit of the Ministry of Welfare suddenly informed us of the appointment of a new CEO for the association and Golan remained active but without an official role with the Israeli authorities.

I met with the new CEO for the association, a pleasant, good-looking man who gave the impression of being trustworthy, a man who knew what was going on and spoke the truth. After the introductory meeting, we remained in phone contact only as I was already in the middle of the process.

In October 1998, soon after my New Year visit to Russia, it still wasn't clear if Ella would be mine. I got the money, emptying out my savings and after exchanging it for dollars, I arranged a meeting with Yevgeni, who took a vacation from work and came to Israel.

On a Friday afternoon he waited for me at a café in Herzeliya, dressed rather formally in a pale blue buttoned shirt and dark trousers. He smiled and was particularly polite. Why not, he was waiting for my money.

I sat restlessly at the beginning of the meeting and very quickly dispensed with politeness. "Yevgeni." I fixed my eyes on his. "I don't understand. Has the biological mother revoked her permission and does she want to raise my Ella?"

"Yes, that's what's happened. Family members pressured her, told her she couldn't give her baby away and she must bring her daughter back."

My right foot moved nervously forwards and backwards. "So what does this have to do with money?"

"Of course it's connected. She's a young woman, unmarried, in a bad economic situation, and this money is a lifeline for her entire life. Do you have any idea of what this sum will mean to her?"

I wasn't convinced. "Wait a minute, are you saying that on one hand she wants her child back, and on the other hand, she is willing to give her up for five thousand measly dollars?"

"Yes. That's the situation. It's hard to judge her."

"But who will promise me that after she receives the money, she won't ask for the baby?"

"That won't happen."

"Who will promise me that this procedure will work?"

"Don't worry. Trust me."

"I trust you, but what if she does revoke her permission?"

"Don't you trust me?"

Even before the coffee arrived, I left the envelope of dollars and got out of there, filled with doubt and the desire to trust him, just as long as Ella was mine.

At the end of October, the three May families returned, bringing Lilach, Iris, and Noga to Israel. They gave me photos of Ella in a bubble bath, the upper part of her body peeping above a pink inflatable ring, beside her Klara, who was apparently moving her joints with circular movements. All this for the hundred rubles we made sure reached her every month. I hoped she indeed received regular treatments, and not only when Israeli parents were present or when photographs were taken.

After the babies arrived in Israel, my Ella and other babies were next in line. After a month, I called the association.

"Shalom," they responded. "Galina speaking."

"Hi, Galina. What's happening with my Ella? When is the court case?" I got straight to the point.

"Don't ask. The Director of the Education Department was ill and everything was postponed until next week."

"Ah… you told me that two weeks ago."

"Yes, everything has been postponed. They're now waiting for district elections. It depends on who is elected."

"I don't understand, what does it matter to us who is elected?"

"It's extremely important. If it's someone with whom we have connections or not."

"And if there aren't any connections, that's the end of it? And the person from the Education Department who's been ill, is she no longer connected?"

"The district director determines who receives the children," answered Galina.

I sensed she wasn't telling me everything. "So it's not a done deal that the children are ours?"

"Sort of a done deal, not formally."

I felt she wanted to end the conversation, but I was still uneasy. "Tell me, Galina, I don't understand what it has to do with the

Education Department, and when is the court case?"

"We're now waiting for the district elections that take place in February, and then I hope the court cases of our children will take place in March or April."

"What? So long?"

"Yes," she responded. "I'm sorry."

I ended the call and felt my belly contract. I felt cheated, not by Yevgeni or the association, but by something far bigger, my fate. But in the same breath, I straightened up and told myself, it will take as long as it takes, I won't give up my Ella.

The more time passed, the uncertainty grew. I decided that February would be a good time to go again to see what was happening first-hand and, of course, to see Ella. This time I went reinforced by a local businessman who had emigrated to Israel and continued to run his business in St. Petersburg. The purpose was to make sure that Ella was still mine and hadn't been transferred to another family who had asked for her.

It wasn't clear whether her family had asked for Ella, as Yevgeni told me, or if other parents who came to adopt a child had seen her and offered "more." We'd heard of situations like this. It was likely that others wanted her, she was after all the caregivers favorite. Every time they went out for a cigarette break, they took her with them in their arms.

In any case, I didn't know what was really going on behind my back, and as time passed, I assumed it wasn't Ella's biological family because in mid-December, the six months during which the biological family could revoke permission, had passed, and on the other hand, maybe not. After all, I'd also heard that in Russia families who had given a child up for adoption were allowed to revoke permission whenever they wished up until the adoption court case. I also wasn't sure to what extent our mediator had reported everything to members of the association in Israel.

Thus, the questions only increased and the fact that I didn't understand the language only thickened the fog. Nothing that happened in Russia was really clear and the businessman was supposed to help me clarify the uncertainty a little with the help of his contacts.

Preparing for a trip to cold, Russian February was no simple matter. Israeli stores had no suitable clothing for that weather. Friends were recruited to help. From my friend Keren's mother, I borrowed a fur coat she'd bought in St. Petersburg; Ittai, the husband of my class mate Ayala, who'd been an emotional support throughout the adoption process right from the beginning, came all the way from his kibbutz, Sdot Yam, to bring me the high fur boots he'd acquired for me. In the middle of the day, at the busy Arlosorov/Derech Namir intersection, he got out of his car, as usual taking no-one else into account, and simply came over to my car to give me the box.

"Ittai, you're great!" I shouted as he hurried back to his car.

At home, I discovered the boots were a little too big for me. Room for socks, lots of socks.

Upon landing, the coat and boots were of no help at all, the cold was terrible. Minus forty degrees!

I stayed at Hotel Moscow, which was familiar to me and the businessman stayed at the elegant Hotel Astoria. I knew his lovely wife, who told me about their son who was studying medicine in Bologna and their daughter who had recently married and moved to live in the United States.

On the first night, I met two Israeli women in a café at the hotel. Their flight back to Israel was a few hours later, but they were so excited after their first meeting with their babies that they felt completely awake. Conversation flowed between us and, at a certain point, the name of my childhood kibbutz came up. One of the mothers, a psychotherapist with chestnut hair, noted that her husband, currently asleep in his room, has family on the same kibbutz. After a brief inquiry, it turned out that the father of her husband, who was an architect, was my mother's cousin.

The baby girl of my relatives whom I didn't really know, was brought to the orphanage in a small crib by the woman who had given birth to her. She put her down at the entrance and disappeared. The infant appeared to be about two months old. It actually sounds like a fairy tale. We parted very late with a good night and a promise to meet in Israel to complete the details of our experiences.

The following morning I went with Yevgeni to meet the businessman with whom we'd arranged a meeting in the city before leaving Israel. His office seemed stately and was furnished with heavy, dark wood furniture. The arrogant dignity of the security man and director of the bureau radiated a sense of awe on all who entered. Yevgeni spoke in Russian, and the businessman appeared severe and unsmiling. In the office he was cold and unpleasant. They spoke sharply and directly.

Twenty minutes later, we parted from him, left the building and got into Yevgeni's car. "Well?" I asked impatiently. "Tell me what he said."

"Didn't say much. He wanted to hear what it was about."

I was stunned. "What do you mean? Didn't he know what it was about? Did we come for nothing?"

Nonchalantly, Yevgeni continued to drive. "To me he seems connected with all kinds of influential people and he'll talk to whoever he needs to."

There was nothing to be done. It was too cold to walk and I wasn't allowed to visit the orphanage; it wasn't a visiting period, due to the replacing of the district director. I returned to the hotel and read a book, but was worried the whole time.

That evening I arrived in the foyer of the elegant Hotel Astoria at the request of the businessman. When he recognized me he asked me to come up to his room. I was very uneasy, not liking the idea at all, but neither could I allow myself to refuse. I had to be polite and grateful. I hoped his room also served as an office.

The room was large, and in the center of the ceiling a gold chandelier was suspended, like those covering the ceiling of the foyer. There were also gilded chairs and a marble table with rounded edges decorated with gilded metal. The businessman went immediately into one of the suites and came back wearing a white vest over his large belly and a pair of shorts down to his knees. I was overwhelmed with confusion. Although I wasn't a little girl and I'd seen things in my life, and what I hadn't seen I made up for in movies and books and the stories of friends, but for a moment I stood there frozen.

He came over to me. I choked. Did I have to give him my body or give up my Ella? Was that what was happening? I couldn't do it. I tightened my coat around me and closed it like a wrap around my body. My mouth went dry. It wasn't easy for me. I couldn't even shout. I don't even remember if I said the word "no."

But I remember him instantly filling with rage and throwing me out of his room. He actually threw me down on the floor.

I felt great relief and hurried away. I didn't want to arouse the attention of hotel guests in the corridor. I got into the elevator and arranged my messy hair in the mirror. Fortunately, they spoke English in the foyer and I asked them to call me a taxi to my hotel.

A few minutes went by until it appeared that felt like eternity during which I didn't stop looking at the elevator and hoping he wouldn't come out of it. I couldn't look at him. I could still smell him, still feel his hand grasping mine and it hurt from the fall. I might have been in shock, but I was still in control.

When the taxi arrived, I ran out, and only when I was sitting inside did my breathing return to its natural rhythm. I couldn't speak; the sense of revulsion and fear filled me right to my throat, making me feel nauseous. At the hotel I wept myself senseless and, nonetheless, the fear remained. I was afraid of him, afraid he'd take revenge, make sure I wouldn't receive Ella. I needed a glass of wine to fall asleep.

The following day was my last before returning to Israel. Yevgeni promised to arrange a special meeting with Ella. That afternoon we went out to buy a bottle of excellent vodka for the doctor on duty.

At nine o'clock that evening we passed the guard hut at the green iron gate and went on to the entrance to Ella's building. It was pitch black. After the four or five steps leading to the door, I already remembered the way by heart: a long corridor, left to the administrative offices and right to the kitchen. Near the steps to the entrance were more steps leading to the second floor, the location of the baby's room.

Ella was about eight months and no longer considered a baby in the terms of that place. I heard she'd recently been moved to an older group, where the infants were a year and four months. I knew each group had different rules.

Yevgeni signaled to me to remain quietly in the entrance and hide. I stayed close to the wall under the staircase that lead up to the first floor and I started singing to myself *Givat Hatachmoshet*. Pictures from the clip of our soldiers seen hiding from the enemy on their way to conquer Jerusalem went through my mind. My heart beat fast in the knowledge I'd see her soon, my Ella.

After ten long minutes of *Givat Hatachmoshet*, Yevgeni motioned for me to come and I went into the doctor's room with him, and he gestured at me to wait hidden. A few minutes later that felt like an eternity, one of the caregivers came in, carrying my Ella wearing a red dress.

I gazed at her, trying to see if she recognized me, but the doctor signaled for me to be quiet. He asked to examine her. She will recognize me the moment she sees me, I thought to myself. The caregiver probably wondered why the doctor had to examine her at such an hour, but she didn't say anything.

I waited for her to leave and only then did I come out of my hiding place and take her in my arms, my little one. She smiled and laughed at me as if she hadn't been woken from her sleep and as if she recognized me. Yes, she recognized me, I was certain of it.

I managed to take only one photograph of her when I handed her back to the doctor. I felt like I was Ella's mother right from our first meeting, and had no doubt that even this brief meeting tonight was worth the trip here.

On the way back to the hotel, Yevgeni told me that the doctor was Jewish and it was he who had allowed us this stolen visit. In my heart I was glad that the excellent vodka I'd bought that afternoon, when I went out with Yevgeni, had been given to the doctor, whether to ensure the visit or whether in gratitude.

At the hotel, before I fell asleep, I told myself out loud, "My Ella, this evening, you filled me with quantities of love and joy that will keep me above water until our next meeting. They will give me the strength to fight for you. Undoubtedly. It's clear. I'm finally bonded with you forever. I'm not giving you up."

I returned to Israel and continued my work. March was at its height, winter was almost over, and still no new information. I missed Ella fiercely. I didn't stop thinking about her. Imagining her. Sometimes I felt her face growing blurred and I'd take out one of the photographs and cling to the image of her face.

One Friday, I invited over the adoptive parents-to-be, whom I'd met on my trips to the orphanage. We were a rather large group, sitting in a circle, and each one shared information, more relevant or less relevant, they'd heard from some official. One of the parents told us he'd recently met with the CEO of the association, and he'd been attentive and promised to promote our cases.

A few days later, we received sudden and horrifying news: The CEO of the association had died. We immediately began to talk among ourselves to find out what had happened. We listened to the radio, checked in with representatives from the Welfare Ministry, but nobody knew the details. The next day an item appeared in the newspaper: "The CEO of the Adoption Association has committed suicide, waiting couples left without an answer."

I was astounded by the headline. I continued to read the item. It said he'd been attentive to the distress of the parents and always responded pleasantly and patiently, but it went on to hint at entanglements with overseas agents who conducted a sting and it was also suggested that the association was heavily in debt and perhaps his conscience and mental stress broke him.

I felt for his wife and three daughters while wondering what would happen now, who would make sure that our children wouldn't be given to other parents?

On the same day, I was summoned urgently by the Unit for International Adoption in the Welfare Ministry to a meeting at a Tel Aviv hotel near the beach, along with all the other "parents-to-be." We entered a rectangular room and sat round a long table, in partial lighting. There was tension in the air, along with confusion and uncertainty. We all seemed afraid to speak. They offered only water there. At the end of the table stood the head of the International Adoption Unit, an older woman, whose life experience and wrinkles were etched deeply into her face.

"Since you are all in advanced stages of the adoption and in light of the distressing circumstances, I am transferring you to the responsibility of another association, that will make sure your children are brought to Israel," she said.

Then she introduced Lilit, the head of the new association, who told us that she had been born in St. Petersburg and had lived for close to a decade in Israel. In fact, she and her husband had themselves adopted a child from Orphanage No. 10.

I heard that and my eyes shone. What a relief. I wondered where they'd found her and what she'd done before. But the meeting wasn't festive, which was an understatement. After introducing herself, she began to impose guidelines and administrative and logistic instructions in a tough, uncompromising Russian style, as if to say: this is the situation. Without our help, you won't get the children.

We all felt we had no choice, but it was nonetheless encouraging despite her tough exterior and formal conduct that was a little frightening, she showed determination and said she intended to provide the goods no matter what.

So, an hour later I left the meeting afraid yet encouraged.

Since the first meeting at the hotel with the Head of the new association I didn't hear a word about my Ella and didn't know if she'd been taken from me by another family or remained mine. I decided not to ask so as not to rouse doubts and bring about an examination, which might be damaging.

In April, several families left for St. Petersburg, a date had been set for the court case that would determine the final adoption, after which they'd be permitted to return to Israel with their babies. Mellie and Nissim from Be'er Sheva, Sharon's parents, were among the travelers and they sent me photos of Ella.

For me this was another sign that she was still mine, otherwise Yevgeni would have told them not to send me the photographs. In all of them she was dressed in a gray representational dress, with a design of a dog on her chest. Underneath were embroidered the words *my happy dog* in pink, the color of her wool tights. Her hair had grown but was badly cut. Simply chopped off. Was it the risk of lice? I wondered.

Around April 20th, I was also summoned for a court case in Russia and my joy was unbounded. I had trouble falling asleep the night before. I kept fiddling with the clothes in my suitcase. This time, I'd formally be Ella's mother, I told myself. It's about to happen, it's final.

Among other arrangements I made, I also prepared a declaration regarding the baby's future in the event of anything happening to me, God forbid. It wasn't particularly pleasant to think about it and, on the other hand, it was the right thing to do. I appealed to my good friends who lived nearby and although they were touched by my request, they asked me to check with my family first, to avoid unpleasantness.

They were right. My sister thought it a family concern and signed under the statement whereby: "I know that my sister Tali Chaikin is about to adopt a baby girl. If, for any reason she is unable to take care of the child, I will take full responsibility for her care."

I thanked her, looked at the document and for a moment was gripped by fear.

25

Ira

I went up to the first floor and from under the stairwell tried to get a good view of the second floor corridor. I stood on the tips of my toes but couldn't see. Neither did I want to be seen like that.

When I went down to my room, I met Zina, who was carrying bottles of porridge on a tray up to the second floor.

"Can you look and see if the nurse from Israel is here?" I asked her.

"Who?"

"The one who looks a little like a Russian woman."

She nodded.

I already knew that several families had come to my Sveta's second floor that morning. It wasn't hard to recognize them. The parents constantly spoke loudly and noisily and carried large backpacks. They were also very nice and smiled, bringing us candies and cookies.

I went up with Zina to the first floor and before she went on to the second floor, we coordinated where I'd be so she could see me from above and signal to me.

I waited nervously. Two minutes later, Zina nodded and called out, "*Da.*"

I was suddenly stressed. What is going on here? I wondered. Why is she here again? Could the process of Sveta's adoption have progressed without my knowing? Is she about to take her today?

Since she'd promised to rehabilitate herself, Lena was really trying. She attempted to return to work but someone had already taken her place, and maybe they didn't want her because she frequently arrived late. Recently, I'd been going to her home almost every day to help her. The house was clean, there was food in the refrigerator. Even Misha had started smiling again. I was sure we were on the right path.

I decided to check with Valentina and knocked on the door of her office. Something inside me wanted to burst out and slap her: How could you not tell me that they're taking Sveta? But the words wouldn't come out of my mouth. All the anger dissolved, replaced by great sadness.

"Irinka," she greeted me tenderly. "I've been the director of the orphanage for many years and I truly haven't seen anyone like you. The effort you've made to help. You're very special in your giving and your love for others, but understand that not everything depends on you. Our first obligation and responsibility is to take care of our children. Just as you are devoted to your Yuri and take care of him."

She was right. I had nothing left to say.

"Lena has to take care of her children," she went on. "One child is hard for her, and you help a lot with Misha. She won't manage to raise two. Yuri was only released from hospital two weeks ago with heart medication. If he were healthy, you could raise her in your home. As a doctor, you understand only too well the meaning of an addict's promises."

Sighing, I answered despairingly, "Every time Lena took a step forward, I believed she'd manage to save herself. I wanted to believe it. It's true I don't know any addicts who have really rehabilitated themselves, who have put alcohol behind them. Lena grew up in a terrible home…"

I didn't finish the sentence, and Valentina continued, "Until you saved her. You have a big heart, Ira. You succeeded in giving her a life.

She has a home and she has a child… and a sick husband. What kind of a life is that in which to raise an infant?"

I didn't know what to answer, but remembered that until the court case the mother can revoke her consent to the adoption, which comforted me. "Thank you, Valentina," I said. "For everything."

Leaving the room, I stood in the corridor and, for a moment, didn't know what to do with myself. See what's happening with Sveta? Go back to work? Drop in on Klara?

Although I wanted to see a continuation of the positive change, deep inside I knew nothing had changed in Lena. She lay in bed most days and when I asked her about the drugs, she ignored me every time. Again, the smiles were erased from Misha's face.

Soon afterwards, shrunken and frozen, I returned to Valentina's office. "Go on with the adoption."

The words barely left my mouth. It was only after I managed to say the sentence, that my eyes filled with tears.

Valentina got up from her chair, came over to me, hugged me and said in a maternal voice, "Ira, I will never forget this day. It's been hard for me too, and for the staff. You can't imagine how loved you are by everyone here. I think you've also seen how everyone loves you, spoils Sveta, holds her…"

I had seen and I did know. Our staff were wonderful. "You've seen how delightful she is, my granddaughter?"

"Ira, I think it was right not to tell you in advance. For your own good. But you came in, so you should know that the court case is in four days' time. Be with her all morning and then, when her mother arrives, you should go home."

I agreed with her and asked her to let me know in advance on which day she'd be leaving for Israel, because I knew that sometimes the adoption goes into immediate effect and sometimes the court allows it only after ten days. Valentina agreed, but asked me to think hard about whether it would be right for me to be here on that day.

I was afraid to think of the parting, but felt it coming. It could happen in a few days' time, I told myself. So on the coming days I stayed close to Sveta, holding her at every available moment, leaving salty kisses on her face. I felt how each moment with her was my last. Every moment almost brought me to tears.

26

Tali

On Tuesday, April 20th, we landed once again in St. Petersburg, this time for the court case on Wednesday, which fell on Israel's Independence Day.

On the morning of the court case, we went to the courthouse with Yevgeni and representatives of five other families who had come from Israel. Before that we'd bought a considerable quantity of beer bottles for the judge, enough bottles to last the entire courthouse for a month.

Valentina, Director of the orphanage, and the judge were seated in front of a representative from the St. Petersburg District Department of Education. The hall resembled an empty theater with glass lampshades suspended from the ceiling. Families were called in one by one, while the other parents, those whose adoption had been approved by the judge and those whose hadn't, waited in an adjacent room.

At a certain point, my name was also called. I felt tense, both in body and mind. I respected the occasion with formal dress and I may have looked like an advocate in the black pants and jacket over a white shirt. I didn't understand a word. The court case went on for about ten minutes and at the end I dared to ask the handsome young judge if I could have a photograph taken with him. He was tall and slim, with a short beard; his pants and gown were black and the collar of his white shirt illuminated his smiling face. However, the ease with which he agreed to my request seemed strange to me.

At the end of this part of the court case, the adoptions were approved for all parents in the group and we progressed to the next stage. In an excellent mood, we walked to the Ministry of the Interior to receive the formal stamp approving parentage of our children. We waited in a room used for weddings and to pass the time until Yevgeni came with the signed documents, we dressed up as brides and grooms with the help of veils, hats, and dresses we removed from hangers.

After leaving the Ministry of the Interior, we went down in the elevator with a couple. They were Orthodox Jews from Jerusalem, new parents like myself. When I asked them why they hadn't been with us, they responded that they were concerned about our cameras, particularly the video documenting the adoption process of one of the mothers, a well-known singer. They explained that they were concerned about an arranged marriage for their adopted daughter in the future and that if their community knew they'd adopted a baby from Russia, they might doubt her Jewishness. Their situation touched me and I decided to remain with them, so they wouldn't feel lonely.

After all the administration and permits required for legal adoption, I went with Ilya in his car. I knew he loved Israeli Elite black coffee and so with every trip to Russia, I made sure to renew his stock. Moreover, Ilya didn't talk a lot.

According to the accepted custom, we went to the best cake shop in the area of the orphanage. The moment we entered, the display of cakes caught my eye. Most were high, tortes, spread with cream, the colors of which indicated their taste: mocha, chocolate, or vanilla, with blueberries, cherries, or white cream with chocolate flakes.

Ilya told me which cakes were Director Valentina's favorites, I paid and the sales lady began to pack them. I asked to buy for the caregivers and Ilya went along with me. When we reached the orphanage, we put all the cakes on the desk in Valentina's office. I hoped some of it would reach the caregivers.

Valentina thanked me for the cakes and admired them, but didn't seem surprised. I shook her hand warmly. She was dressed in a matching, speckled silk blouse and skirt with gold-colored shoes.

The adoption document was already in my hands and I felt I was at the finishing line with only a few small arrangements left to make. The main obstacle was to get a visa for Ella, a Russian citizen, on Israel's Independence Day. Without a visa for Israel, not only could I not buy a plane ticket for her, but I couldn't bring her into Israel, and Independence Day was a holiday for our embassy in Moscow.

What did one more day matter after everything I'd been through? I said dismissively to myself.

A minute passed and I was suddenly overwhelmed by resistance. No! I couldn't bear any more, I couldn't stay in Russia even one more day. I wanted to go home.

I asked permission to use the telephone and started trying to activate friends and acquaintances in Israel. The ambassador graciously responded at once, instructing the relevant person to open the embassy especially for me. Yevgeni and Ilya boarded a quick internal flight to Moscow. Only later did I discover that they'd indulged in business class at my expense. All for the sake of the child. The main thing was that I had a permit to enter Israel and could finally call my friend Na'ama, in charge of the desired role of "coordinating the adoption flight," and order a plane ticket for a baby girl called Ella Chaikin.

Toward evening, I parted from the caregivers at the orphanage. Valentina and the doctors on the morning shift had already gone home, so I couldn't say goodbye to Ira. I dressed Ella in clothes I'd brought from Israel and gave her a new toy, a light brown kangaroo.

I then went downstairs to the kitchen window and gestured for them to fill the bottle I'd brought with porridge from the orphanage. I didn't want to try new food on the flight – I'd learned this from adoptive parents who had experience on the journey to Israel.

On the night of April 23rd, we took a taxi to the airport. Ella didn't take her eyes off the window, examining the traffic on the road. We boarded an internal flight to Moscow accompanied by Ilya, who wanted to make sure that the authorities didn't hold us up for some reason and that the transition through passport and visa control went smoothly.

I listened to Ilya's advice and put fifty dollars inside the passport. To be on the safe side. I was glad to find there was no need. The official saw the money, but ignored it, as if it was there by mistake.

I waved a final goodbye to Ilya and was swallowed up in the airport, from which there was no way back. No-one could stop, ask, or search. Although everything was legal, I felt nervous and unsure until I reached the El Al terminal.

We boarded the plane, in one hand I had a traveling bag with changes of clothing, diapers, and other things we might need on the way; in my other hand, I carried a handbag and Ella was in a sling wrap on my belly, face to face while she gazed, examined, and touched.

On the plane, Ella was on the seat next to me. She refused to lie in the cradle. I suddenly realized how tense I was, how much I was waiting to hear the engines, be in the air, as if while on Russian soil something could go wrong, suddenly someone could come and demand another document, another permit.

Why is that man still fiddling with the overhead compartment? Why aren't the flight attendants sitting down? Why aren't we hearing the voice of the pilot telling us to prepare for takeoff? Thoughts raced through my mind and I got hot. The belt was too tight.

Only after long minutes, when I felt emptied of oxygen, was the sound of the engines heard and the plane began to move along the runway, speed up and take off. And only when we were in the air, a few moments afterwards, did I begin to feel the blood returning to my body and enormous, euphoric relief overwhelmed me.

It's happening, I said to myself, I'm going home to Israel, with Ella, my daughter.

At that very moment, she began to cry. I caressed her until she fell asleep and I soon followed.

27

Ella

A new baby in the Land of Israel. The bed was new, the language was new, the sound and touch were new for her, everything was new. And yet, this little baby already carried with her many lines in the book of memory. She'd also been given a new name, Ella. She had to learn that this combination of letters was indeed directed at her.

Weeks passed before she learned to cuddle up to the woman who had adopted her, before she grew accustomed to falling asleep in her presence, until she discovered that every time she cried, the same woman came to her. She would test this eight times a night.

Gradually, she became used to the woman's voice, her scent, and touch. Despite this, she continued to smile at anyone who passed and hold out her arms in an attempt to attract attention, so they'd pick her up.

Within two months, she stopped this behavior and began to prefer the woman close to her. She later learned to call her "*Ima*," Hebrew for mother, and she learned that she belonged to her.

In and outside the home, and at playgrounds, she looked for hiding places, getting inside anything that looked like a box or a large carton, in which she felt safe and protected. In between, she enjoyed the freedom of walking barefoot on the earth, crumbling green or dry leaves in her hands.

When her first steps grew secure and steady, she began to hop and skip and roll around. Everyone who saw her said she had a future in sports.

At the age of two, she already participated in sports lessons for four-year-olds and impressed her environment with her motor skills. She enjoyed her successes and mainly the love of those around her. That year she started wearing glasses.

"Ont milk," was the longest sentence she managed to say. The sounds and words from the first period of her life were few and flat, so she spent a lot of time with speech therapists.

She was a nurtured child, and not only in terms of warmth and love, but she was also dressed in the height of fashion. She categorically refused to wear the winter tights and dresses her mother brought her from brief trips to Milan. This is how her aversion to certain fabrics was first discovered. Once she learned to speak, she expressed this with the words "don't like it" and "scratches." After that, she was dressed only in clothes made of soft, smooth, caressing fabric.

At the age of four, she appeared with a group of six-year-olds in a performance hall and when she lost her focus and forgot a particular exercise, she ran to the front of the state, burst into her own dance and brought the audience to its feet in applause – not only because she was the smallest in the performance, but because of her beauty and the charm of her movements, which would accompany her in the future, for better or for worse.

Her loss of focus became more prominent in kindergarten, when she was incapable of sitting still in the morning meeting for longer than five minutes at a time. Although she disturbed the kindergarten teacher, her smiles and cuddles made her hug Ella and forgive the disturbances.

28

Tali

On Ella's first day in Israel, she woke early and we went out to a neighborhood playground with a sandpit. I knew that one of my most immediate and important tasks was to expose her to tastes, smells, various fabric and material textures, and earth.

From the sandpit, we went on to the slide. After a while, we were joined by Nitsan, the son of neighbors on the seventh floor. He was in first grade and had woken early that morning. I allowed him to swing Ella. While he was gently and rhythmically pushing the swing from behind, he asked the new baby's name and where she came from.

I told him that I'd adopted Ella from Russia, and he marveled. "What, you bought her like they buy stuff from the grocery?"

I smiled and explained what I could to him and said that, no, I didn't buy her from a grocery.

On Sunday, we went to the baby clinic. At the clinic, I met mothers with their children and to my joy I was immediately accepted into the community. The clinic nurses enquired whether Ella had been vaccinated and examined her vaccination booklet. It turned out that the Ministry of Health dictates precautionary measures and Ella had to receive all the vaccinations babies usually receive at birth, although she was already ten and a half months old.

Before building a vaccination program, the doctor examined her ears, eye movements and her gaze, and carried out a full general examination. He asked the nurse to put her on the scale.

"Six kilo and four hundred grams!" declared the nurse.

A tiny little thing. Was it genetic? I thought. Was it connected with the orphanage food? I immediately made several operative decisions regarding nutrition and the following morning I began to give her white cheese, each day a different taste, one day with bits of onion, the next day with sweet paprika or fresh tomato paste, and other supplements. In the following days, I tried hummus and two weeks later I was glad to discover that Ella particularly liked avocado and smoked salmon.

Like Ella, I also discovered new tastes – the taste of motherhood and the taste of joy and the responsibility that came with it. The burst of energy evoked by motherhood was mingled with extreme tiredness. With regard to work, the moment I landed, I was given the legal ninety-four days of maternal leave.

I very quickly realized that this was special leave, where waking naturally was a mere fantasy. That the hands of the clock move by themselves and at the end of the day the systems collapse. The night was divided into six or eight parts, not including coordinating donors, and I understood that in relation to leave, Elijah the Prophet wouldn't come and neither would the Messiah, son of David.

While bedtime with Ella went fairly smoothly, she would wake up at night, sometimes seven or eight times. I'd jump up at the slightest cry, teaching her that in her new home there was someone who heard and responded.

Even after the third week in Israel, the signs of the orphanage were still felt. Every friend or relative who came to visit and held out their arms, Ella would hold out her arms in return, as if asking to be picked up and so she passed from one to the other.

Aunt Mira was really irritating, constantly saying, "Look, she really wants me," as if I wasn't there, but I forgave her. I was happy. Tired and happy.

I was glad when Sarit from the kibbutz I grew up on came to visit me. Her name preceded her as the "mother of adoptions in Israel." After we sat down on the carpet to play with Ella, I found the courage to ask, "Ella has been clinging to me for some weeks now, but she's still holding out her arms to everyone else, just like she did at the orphanage, why?"

Sarit smiled.

"Be honest with me," I said. "Is there something I'm not doing right?"

"It's a well-known phenomenon and it's natural. It will take Ella from ten to fifteen weeks before she prefers you above anyone else," she explained patiently.

"So long?" I wondered.

"Yes. Until she came to you she was exposed to many caregivers and many constantly changing faces. She didn't have one, consistent figure."

"But why so long? After all, I've been with her day and night for almost three weeks." I had difficulty grasping this.

"You have to understand the world she was born into. You can't imagine how many papers and research studies have been written on the social and communication development of babies in orphanages and on the creating of an attachment figure."

"I realize this is supposed to comfort me," I said, doubtfully.

"Ella is one of the fortunate ones who were adopted as babies and not older children."

I nodded, that was true, and just at that moment, Ella held out her arms – to Sarit.

After Sarit's visit, I decided to lessen the visits of friends and relatives in order to avoid embarrassment. I'd say I was tired and that I hadn't slept well. People understood me. Days and weeks passed and to me it seemed that the theory was somewhat delayed, because only in the sixteenth week did Ella come solely to me and her nanny and not to strangers.

During this entire period, my work prevented me from being fully on maternity leave and the mobile phone became part of the family. Day and night I continued to coordinate donors. Between one teaspoon and the next at a meal, in the middle of a walk, and all hours of day and night.

There were two critical times I wouldn't permit them to disturb me. The first was the session before bedtime. "I'm putting Ella to bed," I would say to anyone who called. Those were words I'd heard from caregivers in the daycare on kibbutz, when they put us to bed at night, after the parents had finished telling bedtime stories.

The other time was bath time. Ella always splashed, played around, blew bubbles, and squirted water with the help of a plastic chick she received from grandma. I couldn't take my eyes off her even for a second. I'd vowed never to be in a situation I encountered at the hospital – when parents left the bathroom for a second or just talked on the phone for a "minute," and the toddler slipped. I knew that only a little water was enough to drown in.

I added subsections to this vow, like avoiding eating sausages or candies, or playing with small round objects like the lid of an Acamol bottle. Behind every subsection of my vows stood a toddler or two whom I remembered, who hadn't survived and whose noble parents had donated organs to save other children.

Among all the absorption issues to take care of in Israel, which included social security and health insurance, I also began Ella's conversion process. My first telephone call was to the secretary of the Rabbi at the Shapira Center. After filling out the initial guidelines, an appointment was made for our first meeting.

I was required to prepare a letter to the conversion Rabbis, describing my way of life with regard to *kashrut*, the food laws, keeping the Sabbath, observing the laws, attending synagogue, and so on. And what was all this for? Since the toddler wasn't yet independent, and couldn't commit to the life of a kosher Jew, the parents had to do it for her.

As far as I was concerned it wasn't a problem. My mother came from a religious home and loved to tell us that we were descended from the family of Baal Ha Tanya, Rabbi Shneur Zalman from Liadi, who wrote "*The Tanya*," and established Chabad-Hassidut in 1772. From her we learned about *kashrut* and separating meat and milk. I absorbed a lot of respect for traditional religion from her.

As a ward nurse at the hospital, I maintained the separation of meat and milk dishes. I knew the patients trusted us and I made sure that tea served after a meat meal was in white, not blue plastic cups, which were intended for a dairy meal. I kept my eye on the staff so they wouldn't make a mistake.

Batia, grandmother to Iris who had been adopted that Fall, drafted a skeleton letter to the Rabbis at the Rabbinical Center, which was passed around to all the parents as a model, to which their family content was added. Someone included the name of a distant uncle who was a Rabbi, another wrote about his mother who kept kosher, and so on and so forth.

For our next meeting at the Rabbinical Center, I brought along the Family Tree of Baal Ha Tanya, where my mother, my sister, my brother, and I are mentioned. The Rabbi and his two aides approved this section of the process and I also committed to raising Ella in a religious educational framework.

The trips to the Rabbinical Center and writing the letter were rather wearying, primarily because I didn't feel comfortable committing to Rabbis about things I wasn't sure I'd maintain. I did these things because it was necessary.

Thankfully, only the mikveh, the ritual bath, was left to complete the process. Conversions weren't carried out at every mikveh and we had to coordinate it ahead of time so that the *Rebbetzin* would be there to observe, supervise, and sign. I was supposed to go in with Ella, who had to be completely dipped in the water, including her head.

We arrived at the mikveh at the appointed time and I entered the water dressed in a long cotton shift lent by Ricki, the social worker for donor recipients at Ichylov Hospital. Fortunately, Ella loved the water and accepted the "dip" as a kind of game, which completed the process.

Although I placed no value on ceremonies of this kind, I was nonetheless enveloped in a special festivity. I couldn't explain to myself whether or not the sensation was connected with Ella being considered Jewish from now on.

At the exit to the mikveh, Ricky was waiting with a beautiful pair of candlesticks, a wonderful and perfect gift on the special day when Ella finally became Jewish.

29

Tali

I was on my way to a guidance meeting for adoptive parents endorsed by the Ministry of Welfare's International Adoption Department. I didn't understand the invitation or why I needed guidance. At the hotel in Tel Aviv were many parents who had adopted children from other countries. I didn't know most of them. The hall was rather dark.

The facilitator opened with an explanation about how important it is to make an "adoption book" for the child – a small children's book in simple language, even starting with words like, "a baby didn't grow in Mama's belly, so…"

I whispered to the mother sitting next to me who seemed sympathetic, "What a shocking sentence, is this what I left my daughter with a babysitter for?"

She smiled a forced smile, which said nothing.

The facilitator continued, saying that in the adoption book it's important to enhance the place from which the children came. Anyone born in St. Petersburg doesn't need this – after all, the city is beautiful and rich in the culture of theater, music, and ballet. She emphasized that we should always use the words "children's home" in front of our children and not mention the term "orphanage," which carries fears, discomfort, and stereotypes.

I didn't understand. Sometimes, the world of adoption seems to me like something out of a movie. Only the week before, I'd gone to a party for one of the girls whose parents were part of the group who had flown with me to St. Petersburg the first time. While tasting the food on the excellent buffet table, I heard guests and relatives chattering. I understood from the various comments that this event was for the birth of the couple's biological child and not their adopted daughter.

How is that possible? I wondered, and even if she'd suddenly fallen pregnant, was it a miracle? After all, nine months had to go by. I walked away from the guests and stood in a corner next to the members of our group with the toddlers we'd adopted from St. Petersburg.

After several enquiries, we managed to put the story together, albeit with more than a few holes in it. We understood there was a method we knew nothing about and never imagined was possible: mediators in Eastern European countries encouraged poor women to fall pregnant, and toward the end of the pregnancy, they'd be brought to Israel to give birth and give the baby to adoptive parents. The adoptive father would arrive at the delivery room and declare himself the biological father of the baby. In this way, adoptive parents apparently received a day-old baby. The birth mother was flown back to her country, probably with a handsome sum.

The facilitator continued to talk about the adoption book. I barely knew anyone at the meeting, but felt uncomfortable with regard to the facilitator and the parents with me around the table.

At a certain point they handed out paper and pencils and each one was asked to draw a triangle and at each point to write down one of the three: child, birth mother, and adoptive mother.

I quickly finished the task. I sketched a triangle with more or less equal sides and wrote down the words as asked. After this there was a discussion and only then did I grasp the attitude of the adoptive parents to the birth mother.

I glanced at the drawings of my neighbors and noticed that they'd drawn a triangle with a narrow base and two long sides that met at the apex. On one side of the base was the child, on the other side the adoptive parent, and at the apex, in the distance, the birth mother.

One of the fathers argued with the facilitator, an experienced social worker in the field of adoption, saying the birth mother had no place in his life, the life of his wife, or in the life of his adopted son. Several other parents agreed with him, whereas I realized I had nothing in common with these groups.

I became impatient with those who attempted to erase the significance of the birth mother in the adoption triangle. On the spot, I decided I didn't want to listen to their opinions and I left.

It was the last time I attended a meeting of that kind.

When Ella was about two, I began to tell her about my journey to Russia to find her. I told her, when she asked, about the bottles and diapers and clothes I packed for her in the suitcase before I brought her to Israel. She loved hearing the story every night, particularly asking to hear about the moment we reached Israel.

Very quickly we reached the story where the beginning became much shorter and the end much longer. I had to emphasize the names of all the family and friends who came and, most important of all, give details of the gifts she received in honor of her arrival. The gift from grandma was the most beloved of all – a doll in pink clothes that she herself had knitted and sewn, clothes that could be put on and taken off.

My mother had been a kindergarten and first grade teacher in her youth. Her educational skills and approach to children seemed to strengthen the relationship with Ella, and I tried to visit the kibbutz as often as possible. On one of these trips, a train went by. "Look, there's a train!" I said enthusiastically.

Ella, seated in her secure car seat attached to the back seat, turned her gaze to the window and immediately turned back. After a while, I noticed a plane in the sky.

"Hey, look, there's a plane!" I called out again.

She turned to look but didn't react.

I suddenly began to suspect there might be a problem. Maybe she didn't see well, or maybe there was some other developmental problem, after all apart from a few words, she still wasn't talking. I decided to take action the following day and find out if something was wrong with my little girl.

Fear filled my heart.

Fear she had problems with vision turned out to be valid and after the required tests, we went to a store and chose cute Harry Potter glasses. The doctor who examined her emphasized that as long as she wore her glasses, the chances of being able to discard them within five to seven years would increase.

The neurologist at the Department for Child Development referred us to occupational therapy for diagnoses related to language and Attention Deficit Hyperactivity Disorder, ADHD. Ella was diagnosed with "light to medium" ADHD.

When I asked exactly what this was and what I was supposed to do about it, I didn't receive a serious explanation and so I relied on the word "light" and told myself it probably wasn't serious.

The language diagnosis revealed disability and Ella was referred to a speech therapist. I didn't know if all these disabilities were connected to her life in the orphanage or to the genetics of her birth mother.

I asked myself what else awaited Ella. I feared some hereditary disease, God forbid, yet to be discovered, or some other rare phenomenon. I had no way of finding out or getting information.

I felt helpless.

30

Ella

I remember how much I loved lying in bed with Mama sitting near my head, caressing me and telling stories. From the age of two, I remembered things that weren't only from photographs. What I loved most of all were the stories about Russia. Every night before going to sleep, I asked again for the story about her flight from "Peterbur" – how hard it is to say that word – the city where I was born.

Mama told me that when I was a small girl I'd hold out my arms for anyone to pick me up and everyone would say, "Look, she wants me." Ima told me they competed for me.

When I grew up, she explained to me that this is how children who came from the children's home behaved. They didn't understand what Mama and Papa meant, and until children feel who their parents are, that they'll take care of them and look after them, they always checked to see who would agree to pay attention to them.

When I grew older, Mama read me stories from books, like, *A Tale of Five Balloons; Where is Pluto?* and *Let there be Evening* by Fanya Bergstein, which I particularly loved. *"In blue evening skies, in clear evening skies, sails a bright, round moon,"* is how the story begins, with a little girl who goes into a chicken coop at night and isn't at all afraid.

Mama said I spoke very few words. I didn't speak in sentences. "Didn't build sentences," is what she said. I didn't know what that meant. She talked to Aunt Efrat about a woman who would teach me. That woman loved me. She also came from Russia. I enjoyed being with her.

She told Mama to tell me a story from a real book. Many times. That's how I'd learn. She said I didn't understand "language patterns," because in Russia, they didn't read me stories when I was a baby and didn't talk to me, and that's why it was hard for me to build sentences. Mama did what the woman told her to do and, every day, she read me the same story. I liked that.

Even when I grew up, Mama didn't stop correcting my mistakes, which was annoying. She said I was lucky that the youth don't know how to speak Hebrew properly and so my "language discrepancy" was less noticeable.

I understood from what I heard adults say that maybe it was because until I was a year old, nobody spoke to me the way they speak to ordinary babies. So it wasn't my fault and I didn't care.

31

Tali

"What do you think about adopting another child?"

It was late afternoon on a Saturday when the question was asked. We'd just celebrated a second birthday for Noya, the daughter of a well-known singer who had also been adopted from Orphanage No. 10. The sun was sinking into the west and the two girls were playing on the lawn in floral dresses that flew up as they ran after each other with peals of laughter.

The singer described the oatmeal porridge she made for Noya every morning and her love of sour Grand Alexander apples. I was disconcerted because of the simple food I gave Ella: tomato, egg, cheese.

"Well, what do you think?" she asked again.

I wasn't ready for a question like that and didn't know what to answer. "The truth is that I haven't thought about it. I am so busy caring for Ella on a daily basis, busy with my new motherhood, and with the transplants…"

I fell silent for a few moments and then went on, "You know what? Let's do it."

She laughed and we decided to do it together. I wasn't sure she was serious. I wasn't sure if I was serious. We parted at the end of the party and said we'd talk soon.

During that entire evening and into the middle of the night, I continued to think about it. Would it be possible? Did I really want it? Did I have the energy for those journeys? Did I have enough money? And did I have enough love in my heart for another child?

I was still not completely sure the following morning. This time, I decided to ask the advice of people whose opinions I respected.

"The first child is like a key chain," explained my friend Anat. "You take him everywhere with you and he adapts himself to your daily routine. A second child means a family."

How so? I wondered. What does that mean? How could it change the life I've made for myself and Ella? I remembered research studies indicating that a child with siblings adapts to social life better than an only child. I remembered other bits of the conversation with Anat: an only child gets all the attention and has less experience competing for it, less experience with fighting, conflict, jealousy, or confrontation. He or she is less equipped for real life.

But how will I manage with two? I was afraid. I was afraid I'd fail as a mother. I was afraid I'd fail at work and my career and I didn't want to give up my dream of a doctorate. I was also afraid of doubling my bank overdraft.

I suddenly thought of the future, of the fact that at some stage I wouldn't be here and Ella would be left alone. Alone again. Abandoned again. She didn't have a father either. After all, she'd already experienced enough of that in her short life. I suddenly felt an external pressure on my throat. As if someone had wound a scarf around my neck and was tightening it.

I felt like I had to thrust off the pressure, I had to free myself, I couldn't leave Ella like that, it was suffocating me. I won't do it to her. No, I won't!

In fact, I must give Ella a brother. I will bring her a brother.

The pressure on my throat relaxed rather quickly. This idea suddenly sounded like the most logical thing in the world.

This time, things progressed faster once I applied to adopt a boy. It turned out that most parents asked to adopt girls and the queue for boys was shorter. I wanted a boy from Orphanage No. 10, so his and Ella's starting point would be similar. I was already experienced with the stages of the process, the forms, and period of time each stage took, as well as the amount of money required.

Time passed, November approached and I prepared for a two and a half day trip to meet my intended son. In the meantime, I organized Ella's daily routine. In the morning she'd be in daycare and in the afternoon she'd be with my neighbor, Rinat, who had adopted Niv, and she'd also sleep there. The children got on very well together and I felt Rinat was doing it wholeheartedly.

I parted from Ella with a hug, telling her that I was flying to see a baby who would be her brother, she seemed happy. I wasn't sure she completely understood what it meant. It was the first time we wouldn't be sleeping in the same home.

When the plane took off, I again felt the scarf tightening around my neck. My breaths became quick and shallow. I imagined the plane falling and Ella being left alone. Who would take care of her? Who would look after her? Would my sister, who had signed the letter for Russia, take her to the kibbutz?

The woman sitting next to me tried to make conversation and asked questions that restored me to reality and regular breathing, but I didn't really attribute importance to this or pay attention to what I answered. However, I noticed that the notion of another child had been raised by the singer, Noya's mother and, ultimately, only I went ahead while she decided to give it up.

Upon landing, I met Ilya and we went at once to the orphanage, even before going to the hotel. The caregivers, Ira and the director Valentina – all remembered me. I showed them pictures of Ella in an album I'd put together. It was mainly Ira who looked at them, paying attention to each photograph, asking if she liked water and why she was wearing glasses. Valentina glanced at her several times but she didn't notice and continued to hold the album as if it were a baby, and then caught herself and was sorry. I noticed that her eyes were slightly moist. She was probably very sensitive and really loved Ella.

I took the album and went up to the children's rooms, where the new baby was presented to me. He had already been examined and approved by Dr. Pachkowski. He was five months old. I looked at him and scrutinized his appearance: blue eyes, a light layer of fair hair on his head, and a round face.

I held him and felt terrible. I couldn't hug or kiss him from the heart. I didn't feel I belonged to him. Maybe I was expecting a child that looked like Ella. There was no resemblance between the two, not in color, the size of the body, or in the glance. No, this child wasn't mine, wasn't right.

I didn't know what to say, I was embarrassed. Ilya looked at me and seemed to understand. He took the baby, handed him to the caregiver and said I had no obligation. Perhaps he'd encountered situations like this, where there was no connection. I didn't dare ask him. I asked to go to the hotel, saying that I was tired from the flight. He nodded and accompanied me.

In my room that night, I was restless. At a certain point, I called the association in Israel to talk to someone, to get advice. I had so many questions. Was I doing the right thing? Should I return the following day and try and feel something different. What should I do? What kind of a person was I?

"Hi, Katya. It's Tali." I knew Katya from the Adoption Association and I shared my feelings with her.

"You don't have to take him," she said decisively. "Return to Israel and we'll find another way. But since you are already in Russia, go and visit him tomorrow and the next day. See how you feel and decide. Who knows, maybe you'll get used to him."

I so badly needed to hear that.

I managed to calm down. Maybe one doesn't need to fall in love with a child at first sight, maybe one just needs to get used to him. And I'm under no obligation, there is no reason for me to feel uncomfortable.

The following day I returned to Orphanage No. 10. Ira met me and, signing with her hands, asked about the album. At first I didn't understand what she meant, but a moment later I realized and responded partly through pantomime, "Ah, sorry, I forgot it at the hotel."

She appeared disappointed. I shrugged and went to meet the baby. I suddenly felt nervous with butterflies in my belly. Entering the babies' room, I went over to him and picked him up. He smiled at me. I smiled back. I held him close to my body, stroked his head and kissed him.

Something about his smell and response to me suddenly began to waken in me certain feelings of closeness, even the start of a sense of belonging. I started to feel, yes, this is my baby, he will be my son. Briefly, I asked myself if this is what I was really feeling, but the longer I spent with him, the stronger the feeling grew. When visiting hour was over, it was hard to get up and leave.

I waited for the next day, I already wanted to see him again. I kept trying to recall his face, the feelings I'd had. I was confused, wondered if I hadn't made it all up, if I wasn't feeling like that out of discomfort or because of the circumstances. But doubt didn't manage to gnaw at me too much because I was overwhelmed by a sweet longing and the need to see him again.

On the last morning before my flight back to Israel, I remembered to bring Ira the album, but couldn't find her. I went directly to the babies' room, picked up my son from his playpen and held him. Ilya, who was with me, breathed a sigh of relief. His eyes seemed to light up. I hugged the baby, trying not to squash him, and looked at the clock. I wanted to make use of every moment.

At the end of the visiting hour, I put him back in the playpen and suddenly felt like running away with him. I closed the door slowly and left with Ilya. I felt a mixture of sadness and joy.

That evening, when I boarded the plane to Israel, I could still feel the baby on my body but, most of all, I began to feel the beginning of a sense of longing. When would he be mine? I tried to do the math in my head with my eyes closed, as the plane took off.

32

Tali

For the next trip to Russia, I was provided with the required translated papers and documents signed by a notary and apostille. These documents are intended for countries that are signatories to the Hague Convention in relation to child protection. Ella stayed with Rinat. This arrangement had worked well on the previous occasion and this time, Ella very happily agreed.

I traveled again to St. Petersburg, this time via Moscow. I placed the papers, critical for the continuation of the adoption process, in my carry-on, which came with me on the plane so they wouldn't be crumpled and would be near me at all times. The overhead compartment was full and a polite flight attendant found an empty compartment for me at the front of the plane, about ten rows ahead of me.

When the plane landed in Moscow, I had to hurry to make the plane to St. Petersburg. Those sitting in front were the first to disembark, and when I reached the compartment where I'd placed my blue carry-on, I found it empty. I felt as if I was about to have a heart attack.

I waited until all the passengers had disembarked and, together with the flight attendant, searched all the compartments. They were all empty. I broke out in a cold sweat. I didn't know what to do. The plane staff told me that I'd put my carry-on above a Russian woman who had drunk a great deal and she'd probably taken my carry-on by mistake.

I ran toward the exit in the direction of passport control, apologizing to every Israeli and Russian I passed on the way.

Someone shouted after me half-jokingly, "Haste is of the devil."

I paused. Maybe he was right. Was it perhaps a sign I wasn't supposed to adopt this baby?

I ran, jumping over the suitcases of other people, but nothing helped – "the drunk woman" had disappeared. I failed to catch her. She'd already left the passengers' hall. I was left in a tiny room with the El Al staff and asked them to call the staff in London, my niece's husband, who could explain how important it was and persuade them to help me. In the meantime, I contacted Yevgeni and explained what had happened.

"Wait." He sounded calm.

But I couldn't calm down at all. I stayed in the room with the staff. I didn't know what to do. Should I return to Israel? Should I fly without the papers to St. Petersburg? After all, I couldn't continue the adoption process without them.

I wanted to bury my head in the table with despair when, suddenly, I noticed a young woman running toward us with a carry-on, a blue one like mine.

She stopped and explained in Russian to the staff that when she reached the taxi waiting for her with her husband, she went to put the carry-on in the trunk and then discovered her carry-on, which her husband had put in a few minutes before. She apologized.

I felt the blood flow once more through my veins. I'd already believed there was no chance this would happen. And I knew, together with the staff, that this was indeed my carry-on, they smiled coolly and I went on my way. If the loss of the carry-on was a sign that maybe I shouldn't adopt, what did it mean when it was found?

I left the large airport. Moscow in December was white and cold, set in all its glory. The walk to the plane was freezing cold and over thin layers of ice. As we waited for the plane to leave, I talked to a pleasant Israeli. I understood he lived on a *Moshav*, a collective farm not far from my kibbutz and he frequently traveled to Russia to help guide agricultural workers in rural areas. We were the only Israelis on the plane to St. Petersburg.

We landed in the evening. Yevgeni was waiting for me at the airport and took me to the hotel, this time to the elegant Hotel Astoria. A friend had arranged a discount for him. The entrance was decorated for Christmas. In the center of the foyer stood a fir tree hung with shining gold and red balls the size of tennis balls. Underneath it were brightly colored gift boxes. Next to the reception desk was a large table covered with a gold tablecloth with chocolate figurines some thirty or forty centimeters high – Santa Klaus with a red jacket, white beard, and red hat. Nearby was a small dolls' house made of sugar, a fir tree, and a cake that resembled a roll filled with dry fruit. I banished the memories of that terrible encounter with the businessman, to prevent it from interfering with my excitement and joy.

Opposite the hotel was a church with an enormous, gold dome that was beautiful both inside and out. The following day, I had time for a visit before going to the orphanage. I loved churches and wherever I go in the world I never forego a visit: the high ceiling and extraordinary decorations, the singing of the choir, the dimness and candlelight – all these made me feel a sense of perfect detachment from the external world and an entry into another one.

After the visit to the church, I set off for the orphanage. The trees had dropped their leaves and a layer of ice covered the ground and the River Neva. After greeting the staff, I hurried up to the second floor.

I found my baby inside a large playpen together with at least seven other babies. This seemed to be the daily activity of these babies – from bed to playpen and back again. Opposite, stood a wood cupboard with glass doors that were locked. It was filled to the brim with amazing toys, probably brought from all over the world by adoptive parents. They were well-preserved as precious treasure for display only. I remembered it well from Ella's time.

I went over to my baby and immediately gathered him up. Two weeks had gone by since I'd last seen him and he'd grown a little. He was still very different from Ella externally but his face was already familiar to me and, unlike the last time – I immediately felt a spark of connection between us.

He was wearing warm clothes and a hat that covered his ears and hair. The caregivers allowed me to take him down to the playroom on the ground floor. I called it the "gym" because of the style of toys there: large plastic balls, ladders on the walls, a walker, a slide, and padded "tunnels" to crawl inside.

The room hadn't changed at all since Ella had played there, two and a half years before. On the carpet, I showed him pictures of Ella and told him about her and how much fun they'd have together. I wanted to call him by name to attract his attention, realizing at that moment that I wanted to call him Daniel or Jonathan.

Since there were no other adoptive parents there, the caregivers let me feed my baby and stay with him without any limit whatsoever. In between, Ira invited me to her room on the ground floor. She brought another cup, boiled water and made us tea. She seemed like a simple woman, and her face was a good one. She didn't smile a lot but I sensed she liked me. Before I finished my tea, she took the baby from me and played with him.

A few minutes later, she returned him to me and, from her gestures, I realized she wanted to see Ella's photographs, even though she'd seen them two weeks before. This time I'd arranged them in a light green album of soft plastic, a single photograph on each page. It was unbelievable to watch her go from one photograph to another, kissing each of them, without missing a single one. She smiled a little and even wept.

How sensitive she is, I thought to myself.

I glanced briefly into the corridor and saw the head of the kitchen carrying a huge slab of meat that revealed parts of the cow. They cut up this slab and ground it up to make soup for the children. I remembered Luna, the head of the kitchen. We'd made friends without language during the period I'd adopted Ella, and I was particularly grateful to her for filling a bottle with porridge for the flight to Israel.

The caregivers used to take the meals to the children's rooms from the stainless steel counter that separated the corridor and the kitchen. I approached and glanced inside the kitchen. On the wood shelves were tins of imported powdered milk, I think from Holland. The letters were rather small. I was relieved to see that the children were given good food. Naturally, they continued to cook the apples for the four o'clock meal until there was no longer any nutritional value left. I remembered the method in the army: first we ate almost rotten tomatoes and then the fresh ones. I thought they probably cooked apples that were about to go bad.

On my way out, I briefly considered leaving the album with Ira, but she at once pushed it into my hand with embarrassment, as if apologizing for her behavior. I took it and parted from her with a handshake.

From the orphanage I went with Ilya straight to the City Adoption Center, where I was asked among other things to fill out the baby's name on one of the documents. Again I deliberated between Daniel and Jonathan, liking both of them. Finally, I decided – Daniel.

In the course of the visit, Ilya and Yevgeni spoke to me about a quick adoption, at the age of six months. I heard the representatives of the Israeli Association mention a delay. They gave no details but after a few days, when I was back in Israel, I understood that Daniel's biological mother was a single parent of thirty-seven, who also had a seventeen-year-old daughter at a boarding school. Although she wasn't yet eighteen and had no legal standing, the judges of St. Petersburg insisted on finding her and having her sign her approval of the adoption. Since this was my second adoption, the members of the Israeli Association were more open with me, hinting that the judge was an anti-Semite who would send people back and forth endlessly with strange requests before allowing the adoption of children to Israel.

Thus, I learned that the whole business was based on personal connections. For example, if the representative of the association had a relative who worked in the city with someone whose relative was a secretary at the courthouse – through her, one could get to the judge. It was forbidden to go directly to the judge, and all these gestures by acquaintances and relatives were rewarded with money or perks. The more connections there were of this kind, the shorter the processes.

At the beginning of January, about two or three weeks after I'd returned, Yevgeni updated me by telephone that Daniel's sister had been found in a boarding school in Russia and had signed the necessary document.

"Do you want to go to Russia now for the court case?" He surprised me.

I was in the middle of a national campaign for the promotion of organ transplants and had a feeling that a trip now would not be well received by the Minister of Health. "Would it be possible at the end of January?" I asked,

"Yes, of course,"

I didn't feel bad about a delay of two or three weeks. I didn't experience the hysterical expectation I did before my return with Ella. Then, I'd come home every day to an empty house, whereas now, waiting for me at the daycare gate, was a happy little girl who jumped into my arms and we'd go home together.

At the beginning of February, I received a summons to court for March 2002. I was disappointed because I'd thought to delay the adoption process by two weeks, not two months. Days passed and I was starting to feel uneasy. Since the sister from the boarding school had signed, I'd been ill several times. Sinusitis or bronchitis. Something connected to the respiratory system. That very morning, I got a very bad headache and discomfort in my neck, together with a fever and dizziness.

I immediately called my family doctor. She wasn't sure what was happening and asked for blood tests. I was sent to the hospital. A string of neurologists came and went. Among other things I was asked to walk with my hands stretched in front of me, with small steps, heel beside toe. I thought I carried it out rather well.

The symptoms weren't severe. The stiffness of my neck wasn't that significant either and didn't require a lumbar puncture to rule out meningitis. I hoped to be released but the results of the blood tests weren't good and they decided to hospitalize me.

I was given a room on my own and I arranged with my aunt to pick up Ella from daycare and bring her to me that afternoon. I was so happy to see her and promised her that I was all right. Late that evening, the director of the ward herself arrived to examine me; again the test I'd done at noon, walking with my arms stretched out before me, and a neck examination. My headache was still very bad, but to my joy, she concluded that it was viral meningitis and, if there wasn't any change the next day, I'd be released to my home with a referral for the headache.

That's what happened and after my release I was very relieved. However, two weeks later I had an attack of breathlessness. What was happening with my immune system? I wondered. I was terrified I wouldn't be able to fly to the court case in Russia. I was even afraid I had leukemia. Again, I felt the scarf tightening around my neck.

I was afraid I was dying. My family doctor gave me medication for breathlessness and it passed within four days.

"It's all from stress," she said to calm me, but I didn't really calm down.

When the first almond blossoms emerged, we went to Eshtaol Forest; we were six families, six little girls from Russia. We spread out a mat and a tablecloth where we set out picnic treats. Full of energy, the girls played on the play structures.

These joint get togethers seemed to serve not only the girls but also our needs as parents. We exchanged information on raising the girls, and there seemed to be a subtle competition among us – who invested more, who bought more. I could only boast about the artistic gymnastics class Ella had recently joined.

In the middle of our conversation, we suddenly heard a shriek. Lilach had slipped on a stone. The other girls stood around laughing. Only Ella went to her, brushed the sand off her pants and said, "Never mind. I'll give you a kiss and it will go away."

Toward the end of the get together, I had a conversation about life with Lilach's mother, who was a social worker.

"It's important to continue these get togethers, to stabilize and reinforce the girls' relationships, create an affiliation group for adoptees," she said.

I nodded, adding, "Yes, being adopted should be legitimate, talked about and normalized, so they learn they aren't alone with regard to adoption and that it isn't uncommon to be adopted."

We laughed, suddenly grasping that we sounded as serious as if we were at a therapeutic staff meeting, although we believed what we were saying.

The court case was set for the morning of March 6th. Two days before that I picked up Ella from daycare on the way to the airport. While I was organizing bags in the car, Malka the daycare worker who had just taken a break, ran out to us. She wished us luck and kissed and hugged Ella until she was harnessed into the car seat in the back.

We were standing next to the driver's door when I said worriedly, "I hope the rockets fired on Sderot yesterday won't harm us."

She nodded. "I hope so too."

On the plane, Ella seemed excited, everything was new to her. She stood on her seat, examining all the people in front and behind us with curiosity. Once I'd sat her down and fixed the belt, she put her face to the round window and looked out. After takeoff, the kind flight attendants brought her paper and crayons and I read her stories.

We landed that night in St. Petersburg, Ella wore a large down-filled jacket and fell asleep on the luggage cart. I took a taxi straight to Hotel Astoria.

The following morning, we went down to the dining room. I took a box of cornflakes I'd brought from Israel out of my bag and poured milk into a bowl. Ella put two teaspoons in her mouth and at once got up to examine other people's tables, came back for two more teaspoons and up she got again. This time she gazed at the waiters and the buffet, and I kept my eye on her all the time. In the meantime, I finished drinking my coffee and eating a small croissant and we got ready to leave.

The burst of excitement and flurry continued even when we got to the foyer in appropriate clothing. Ilya arrived to take us to Orphanage No. 10. Outside it was cold and snowing. For a moment, I felt as if we were in a spy movie taking place in the days of the Cold War.

When we arrived, we went into the playroom where Ella met her brother. I was overjoyed at their meeting and photographed it. The two lay on a special rug on their bellies while Ella tried to amuse him and he handed her tiny dolls.

Suddenly, Ira came in, surprised, murmured a few indistinct words and immediately joined us on the carpet. She began to talk to Ella in Russian and her face momentarily lit up. After ten minutes, I took out the bags of instant coffee I'd brought and within two minutes the cups were set down on a nearby stool and we drank the wonderful beverage.

Ira blew kisses into the air, then crossed herself and prayed, eyes raised. Apart from the coffee, I also offered her raisins. She was glad and shared half with Ella.

After twenty minutes, Ella went back to play with Daniel and tried to give him a raisin.

"He's too small," I said.

Later on, she helped me feed him porridge from the bottle Ira brought.

At the end of the visit, Ira gave Ella a big hug and through Ilya, wished us good luck in court the next day. From the orphanage, we drove with Ilya to a playground especially for conditions of snow. I was already imagining the cakes I'd buy the next day, after the court case, for the traditional farewell to the orphanage.

At the playground, I asked him about Ira, and he told me she was a widow with a son and a ten – or eleven-year-old grandson, he didn't remember precisely.

While I was freezing cold, Ella merely increased her cries of joy, going from one apparatus to another with Ilya's help. I could barely take my hands out of my pockets to photograph her. I waited for her to tire. I so appreciated Ilya's efforts. He really didn't have to, it wasn't his job.

At the meal after the playground, I spoiled him until he blushed with embarrassment.

The next morning, we went down to breakfast and found everything decorated with hundreds of red roses. "They're in honor of International Women's Day, in two days' time," an English speaker explained to me at the entrance to the dining room.

To my surprise, I met Ricki in the dining room, an Israeli whose eldest daughter also came from Orphanage No. 10 and who was a year younger than Ella. She, too, was on her way to adopt another child. Ricky had arrived in the city the day before for the first meeting with her second daughter.

When we arrived at the courthouse, Ella waited in the car with Ilya. After her enjoyment in the playground, she had no problem parting from me and remaining with Ilya.

I went into the courtroom with Yevgeni. At the table sat the large judge in her black gown and, beside her, was Valentina.

Naturally I didn't understand a word but when it was all over, after merely a few minutes, it turned out that the adoption was disqualified!

"What? Why?" I asked Yevgeni.

He was also surprised. Something was wrong and he said he'd make a few calls to find out. Stunned, we left the courtroom.

After a few nerve-wracking minutes of uncertainty, during which he talked on the phone, Yevgeni explained to me that since there was currently a state of war in Israel, the judge chose to disqualify the adoption. "She's afraid the Russian toddler will be killed."

"War?" I was astounded. "What war? How could he be killed?"

He tried to soothe me, indicating that this was by no means the end of the story, but I couldn't relax. I felt like I was choking again. "What will we do now, Yevgeni?"

"I will call the association in Israel now and the people in the city adoption system and then we'll talk. In the meantime, Ilya will take you and Ella back to the hotel."

On my way to the car, Yevgeni added, "Now I understand why the judge called me last night and asked me not to bring flowers."

"What? What are you talking about?"

"You must understand that Russia is not like Israel, Women's Day is considered a holiday. Women receive gifts from family, work, and friends."

"I don't understand, what does that have to do with it?"

"She knew yesterday she wasn't going to approve the adoption. She'd already planned the ruling."

I was crushed when I arrived at the hotel and wondered what to do, and if there was anything I could do. In the hotel foyer that evening, we played creative games that I'd brought with me. The sense of distress that seared my throat turned into tears.

Ella took on the role of explaining, approaching all those sitting in the foyer and telling them in Hebrew, "Do you know why my mother is crying? Because they didn't give Daniel to us."

Before the flight, Yevgeni had time to update me about the possibility of appealing to the Supreme Court in Russia within thirty days from the date of the court case. He didn't expand and said we'd talk about it. I thanked him and, utterly exhausted, went to bed.

The next day we took a taxi to the airport, and there, while going through all the stages until the plane, I wondered whether I'd return to Russia. For a moment I had the horrifying thought that maybe this was my last visit there.

33

Tali

The day after we landed, I tried to find someone who understood this field. It was complicated. Quite a few people tried to persuade me not to appeal to the Supreme Court. I thought about Ricky. If I lose this case, she'll lose her daughter. And then, not only would my Daniel not be adopted, but neither would her daughter.

We'd stayed in touch since that hurried breakfast, and she never said a word to me about the appeal. I greatly appreciated that. Association people themselves were divided: if the Supreme Court in Moscow turned down the appeal, it would be a tough blow to ongoing Israeli adoptions from Russia.

With all the telephone calls and meetings, it turned out that Lilya, head of the association, was herself in the final stages of adopting her second child. Although this was in another city, another district, and I'd already learned that each district had its own regulations, it was clear that disqualifying Daniel's adoption would also nullify the adoption of her son, who was supposed to come to Israel in June.

I spoke to a senior Israeli lawyer I knew, sat opposite him and still couldn't understand. He tried to persuade me to drop the idea of the Russian Supreme Court. Personally, he explained, he couldn't help me there because he wasn't familiar with the ins and outs of Russian law, especially not in the field of adoption.

He asked, "Why do you need all this? Adopt another child from somewhere else. What relationship could you have created with a baby you met three times?"

I didn't have an answer, but was nonetheless disappointed by his reaction. I expected him to try and help, to be a friend. Maybe he felt that professionally it was the right step, and maybe by trying to prevent me from being disappointed, he was expressing the friendship between us.

He managed to undermine me a little and after the meeting I wondered whether I was right. Were three visits and a few photographs reason enough to upset the applecart? Could I fall in love with another child as quickly?

In the meantime, I focused on my work. One day, I was approached by an organization established by an ultra-Orthodox Jew that provided information and counseling services regarding family, parenting, and death. Following repeated requests from the association to the Ministry of Religious Affairs regarding the burial place of fetuses who died while still in the womb, they were referred to me at the mothers' request, saying that maybe I could discover the burial place.

"Why me?" I asked.

"The Ministry of Religious Affairs said that you know and are familiar with the *Hevra Kadisha*, who prepare the dead for a Jewish burial and have contacts there and could probably find out."

I wasn't sure that this was exactly what the people from the organization had been told, but they skillfully managed to challenge me. It was true that I was in constant contact with the Hevra Kadisha in order to take care of the burial of organ donors who "weren't Jewish" and in special cases, but this was a long way from finding a burial place.

The CEO of the Ministry of Health allowed me to take on the task and even asked me to regulate related procedures. The ministry's legal counsel expressed the opinion that I had no chance of success with the *Hevra Kadisha*. His words were even more of a challenge for me and I went for it.

Before anything else, I wanted to understand the mothers' wishes and needs. I compiled a questionnaire, contacted the Tapuz website, the forum of mothers who had suffered pregnancy loss. I introduced myself and, to my surprise, they responded and were willing to cooperate and answer the questions. The answers taught me about the connection between a mother and a fetus that dies before it is born; about the memory that persists, sometimes for years after the event.

Something else that caught my attention was the name each mother gave herself on the site: cookie's mother, peanut's mother, etc., each mother and the name she gave the fetus during pregnancy.

I began to comprehend the connection between a mother and the fruit of her womb, even if she hadn't enjoyed the accepted maternal experiences with it. I was persuaded that even a mother who has lost her fetus during pregnancy and never seen or held it, never exchanged a smile with it, will forever be its mother, will forever mourn it. Actually, I realized, this was also the case with my Daniel. Mine!

I also realized that just as parents don't give up on their dead children, there is no chance I'll give up on my living child. The deeper I went into the task, the stronger I became, trusting myself that Daniel was indeed my child. The love I felt for him was real.

I decided to fight. I was determined to do battle.

Two battles, in fact.

The *Hevra Kadisha* examined the graphs of the research findings and willingly sat with me to find a solution. Despite the doubts, new regulations were formulated within a few months.

During that period, I managed several times to talk privately with Katya from the association. I tried to encourage her to tell me what was happening in the association.

"It must stay between us," she requested.

"Of course," I promised.

"We had a staff meeting on the subject, and Lilya said that if you appeal, there is no way the association will help you. If we go against the Russian authorities, they will make problems for us afterwards, when this difficult period passes."

I realized I could expect no help from them. I felt lost, and the language barrier made it difficult for me to act. None of my Russian friends had any ideas whatsoever on the subject. What else could I do?

Distraught, I set up an unofficial forum to bring Daniel to Israel. Friends with connections or long-term public standing mobilized to act independently to help me.

Supporters were also joined by Professor Nurit Feldman, my thesis supervisor and Head of the Health Communication Department at Tel Aviv University. She brought her colleague, Professor Charles Salmon, who was attending a peers' training program in Israel. Salmon immediately volunteered to help and wrote a moving letter.

I received a letter from my niece, Gaia, in London, in which she invited me to visit in the following fashion: "We can allocate you about three spacious rooms in the house including a bathroom and everything necessary to raise children. I'd be very happy to host you in my home and help with the children."

Despite all the support, I needed something else.

I began looking for Russian translators and a notary in order to send official requests to the adoption authorities in Russia. I didn't really know where to send them or to whom. In Israel, Passover was approaching and, at holiday sales, I bought perfumes and nail polish for the next trip to Russia, gifts for the women on the orphanage staff, whenever we should meet.

At the same time, relatives suggested I appeal to Rabbi Berel Lazar, Chief Rabbi of Russia, who was close to President Vladimir Putin.

Since Baal Ha Tanya, who founded Chabad, in my appeal to him, I emphasized my family origins. I also sent him a detailed letter with the help of his office staff in Russia.

We celebrated Passover night with friends in Tel Aviv. In the middle, telephones suddenly started ringing. The hostess's brother, a senior editor of the "Yediot Acharonot" newspaper, received messages on his beeper. We turned on the television. A terrorist attack at the Park Hotel in Natanya. Nineteen people dead and one hundred sixty wounded. Another terrorist attack after many months of unquiet, blood and victims, and the pictures were no doubt shown all over the world, including Russia. I returned home sad and dejected. The next day I had to deal with organ donations from two of the dead.

After another terrorist attack, the government decided to launch Operation Defensive Shield. If until that moment it could be argued that Israel was not at war, now there was no doubt. I suddenly felt things closing in on me.

A week later, knowing that the deadline for filing an appeal was about to expire, I again called Katya at the association.

"You got in before me, I was just about to call," she said.

Despite the good energy in her voice, I guessed she was about to say that in light of the terrorist attacks, it would be better to give up the appeal and think about other options.

"We had a meeting this morning," she said. "You won't believe it, Lilya is so angry about the situation, she's decided to fight now in favor of the adoptions and your Daniel. She also said something else, that if we have to choose a mother to lead this struggle, then you are the one, because you are determined and don't give up. She didn't say a word about the risk to her son she is supposed to adopt and bring to Israel before the summer."

It was hard to breathe. I didn't expect this. I thanked Katya and so wanted to call the head of the association, but feared to spoil things. Suddenly, the possibility that Daniel would be here at home, with me, seemed realistic and concrete again.

The appeal was filed on time, but Operation Defensive Shield continued, escalated, and there were casualties. And if this wasn't enough, the Russian lawyer hired by the association had a stroke. What does it mean? I wondered. How is he? At the same time, the terrible pictures of the operation were transmitted all over the world.

When I looked at them I was unable to feel optimistic, but there was still a small flicker of hope. I threw off the bad thoughts. In my mind, I pictured the bad judgement of the court and made it smaller and smaller, until it disappeared. I did the same with the pictures of the terrorist attacks, a method I learned in meditation, and I replaced the bad thoughts with action. A lot of action – mothering Ella, the Israel Transplant Center, and preparing for the appeal on May 6th.

My friend, Ya'alah Lipshitz, organized an emergency meeting at her home for close friends who had connections in order to plan our actions. The plan was to approach senior people and ask them to write letters to the Russian court. We came up with names and contacts, among them CEO of the Ministry of Foreign Affairs, Avi Gil; Foreign Minister, Shimon Peres, and Shimon Hefetz, military secretary to the president, to whom, it later turned out, most of the achievements could be attributed.

I appealed to all these people, requesting: "There is a chance to change the court's decision – letters from government and public authorities stating that Israel is not in a state of war," and the message needs to be: "That daily routine in Israel goes on as usual." I ended by saying that letters received by the court secretary in St. Petersburg would bring about a new discussion of the file and a changed decision.

In an attached document, I prepared the writers a formula with points and strengths in their fields likely to help in court with regard to Israel's state of "war" at the time.

Zvi Bar, mayor of the city, wrote that life in in the city was active; cafes, cinemas and theaters were open with bustling streets both day and night.

In her letter, the Minister of Education, Limor Livnat, noted that children in Ramat Gan go regularly to daycare and school and that there were no changes in their education.

I managed to obtain letters from MK Avshalom Vilan, Minister of Welfare, Shlomo Beniszri and other ministers. Even the prime minister at the time, Arik Sharon, signed a letter.

Several weeks before the court case, I noticed a small article in one of the newspapers: "Rabbi Berel Lazar is coming to Israel for a series of meetings." I thought it worthwhile to reinforce telephone conversations I'd already had with him and his staff in Russia by meeting with him in person.

I arrived at the hotel in Jerusalem where a conference was being held in his honor and managed to catch him as he left the stage. He was about thirty-eight at the time and moved quickly. It was difficult to penetrate the circle of aides surrounding him.

I didn't give up. Appropriately dressed – in a long dark skirt to my ankles and a particularly modest white blouse – I managed to introduce myself and hand him an envelope in which were the details and my request. I hoped he'd help me.

During those weeks, when I was busy collecting letters to help in court and bring Daniel to Israel, I was under a cloud of social pressure. Fifty-five adoptive families and fifty-five children in Russian orphanages waiting to be adopted were depending on my ruling. Nothing was said explicitly, but it was felt and to an extent it was true. The results of the court case could have potentially hurt other parents, many parents and many children. Nonetheless, I didn't feel like I was putting myself before them. It had nothing to do with me. It had to do with Daniel, even if he was only an infant.

Nevertheless, I still felt responsibility toward the other babies and their parents and, finally, at the end of April, I sent an urgent letter to Avi Gil, asking him to organize a letter from the Russian consul in Israel to the Russian Foreign Ministry. I described the situation to him, ending with: "I am, nonetheless, appealing to you, Mr. Avi Gil, because this subject is far more than my own personal case. Tomorrow, the door might close in other places, which would have implications for Israel's foreign relations with Russia. I would be grateful for your intervention in this issue. The appeal to the Supreme Court is in a week, but because of the holiday we have barely three or four days."

The appeal in the Supreme Court was finally set for May 30th. On the advice of the association, I prepared a large poster with a map of Israel, where it was easy to see the location of Ramat Gan and the distance from Sderot, where the rockets were falling.

Although the terrorist attacks added to the atmosphere against Israel, the text disqualifying the adoption related specifically to rocket fire on Sderot. In addition, I enlarged a photograph of Ella playing with Daniel at the orphanage. We were told it was important for the judges. In Russia, I learned, the perception is different. In Israel, a single parent, who wants to adopt a second child, immediately raises eyebrows and evokes questions like "how will she manage?" In Russia, a mother who adopts a second child is considered fitter than someone who hasn't adopted and for this reason I was advised to bring Ella to the courthouse.

We were accompanied by Lilya, head of the association, her husband, and their daughter, Yana, who was a year older than Ella and had also been adopted from Orphanage No. 10.

The entire team was waiting for us at the airport in Moscow: Yevgeni,

Ilya, and Vadim. Nobody considered missing the event, knowing that the eyes of fifty-five parents waiting to adopt were trained on us, praying that we'd succeed. We were all excited and nervous.

I don't remember which hotel we stayed at in Moscow, or what I ate for breakfast, if at all, but the Supreme Court? That's another story. Inside the large building, we went up to the second floor that seemed very high up indeed. With us came Lilya, who was supposed to translate from Russian into Hebrew and the opposite, and Ilya. We sat in a large foyer and waited to be called.

In the corner near the stairs sat the local lawyer hired by the association. He appeared pleasant and smiling and I could see no significant trace of his stroke. Ella showed him her enlarged, framed photograph with Daniel, and he responded by stroking her head and smiling. I photographed them.

We waited for a long time. We didn't know if our court case behind the big wood doors had already started. We had no idea what was going on inside or how things were being handled, and we were all tense.

After an hour I lost all sense of time, but suddenly the door opened and our lawyer was called in. After him, I was called and they allowed Lilya in to translate. We took Ella inside for a second, so they could see her. Afterwards, she remained outside with Ilya.

The courtroom looked like a theater hall. Instead of a stage three large female judges in black gowns sat at a long table. Lilya and I stood at a distance, at an elevated angle and we felt as if we were in a gallery. How distant and alien could a situation be? I asked myself.

The judges wasted no time and immediately started with personal questions, about my work, about where I lived, and about my education. Then they asked about Ella and the daycare. Not a word was said about politics or security. Afterwards, we left the courtroom and were asked to wait again.

Lilya remained with the lawyer, and I left the building and went to a garden where Ilya, Ella, Lilya's husband, and their daughter were waiting. We all waited tensely for the results. The girls played and passed the time. A long time. I was distraught and didn't know if the drawn-out time meant good or bad news. To take my mind off, I organized a game of hide and seek with the girls, they hid and I looked for them. I needed to run and use up energy.

At a certain point, Lilya joined us, the lawyer remained in the building to wait for the ruling. We jumped on her for the tiniest hints and crumbs of information. She told us that in addition to all the documents we'd gathered and had translated into Russian, the lawyer had approached a large number of travel agents in Russia and had confirmation that there were no security alerts regarding flights to Israel. But there was still no answer.

We continued to wait.

After a while, Lilya returned to the courthouse to wait with the lawyer. Within minutes both of them came down to us. Lilya took me aside and explained that the lawyer's move had been brilliant because the judge in St. Petersburg, who had disqualified the adoption in March, had based her judgement on an email from the Ministry of Foreign Affairs that described rocket fire on Israel, but without accompanying instructions. That is, the judge who had disqualified the adoption had acted on her own initiative and not on instructions or government directives.

"And the ruling, what did they say?" I asked Lilya impatiently.

"Our appeal was successful!" she answered, her eyes shining.

I hugged her, feeling the flow of adrenaline burst into my veins and overflow. Filled with energy, I released her and asked, "So what now, are we going to pick up Daniel?"

"We aren't done yet and it's impossible to take Daniel. We have to go back to St. Petersburg for another court case."

I went to thank the lawyer for his work and he explained that after the Supreme Court, the local court has to take the same line. I was still afraid. Who knows what could happen in Israel with terrorist attacks and lack of security.

Despite my concern, I chose to be glad about the good news and held onto the thought that the St. Petersburg court had to act in accordance with the Supreme Court ruling. I realized there was no point in dragging Ella to St. Petersburg to visit Daniel, even so, the trip with all its experiences was a significant departure from her routine, and I preferred to return home at once. In any case, I told myself, "I'll be going again in about two weeks, for the last time, in order to bring Daniel to Israel at long last."

The next day, before the flight home, the sun suddenly broke out in the center of the sky and it was warm and pleasant. Ella was wearing her red velvet dress she got from my niece in London and we decided to erase the joyful and exhausting previous day with a visit to Red Square.

Back in Israel, I continued to check every week regarding the summons. I realized very quickly that my assumption of two weeks was very optimistic, and the ruling had not yet been transferred from Moscow to St. Petersburg. I cynically asked if they'd sent the letter by donkey.

June arrived, thirty days before the court ruling arrived in St. Petersburg. Again a wait. A closer reading of the ruling revealed that a new assessment of the situation in Israel was required. This was a blow below the belt, after all, we'd won our appeal.

I had to approach the people from the Ministry of Foreign Affairs again, as well as the people from Rabbi Lazar's office, and the intervention appeared to bear fruit: thankfully, a summons to appear in court again on October 25th, arrived. I felt it was a long time and decided I had to visit Daniel again.

I flew in July. The moment I arrived, I went straight to the orphanage, full of longing.

I found a child who had grown. His blond hair had grown and he played a lot near me. It worried me that he didn't respond when I held out my arms to pick him up – a movement that wasn't familiar to him and he didn't know what it meant. Strange, with Ella it had been the opposite. True, he'd been in the orphanage for a year, but was it possible that this period of time had such an impact? On the other hand, he was good at putting colorful rings on a stick and building a castle. He then put tiny plastic mobile cups inside medium and then larger ones. Fine motor skills would not be a problem for him, I assessed.

At some point he was called to lunch. Next to him sat Adi, another infant intended for adoption by Israelis, Ricky's daughter in fact. She was pretty with brown hair and blue eyes. I photographed them at the dinner table.

After eating we went down to the playroom and Daniel was absorbed in an extraordinary game hung on the wall at the height of a sitting child. I couldn't understand how come it hadn't yet become a commercial asset. It was a large rectangular board with taps, switches, and handles of varying kinds.

Daniel pressed, screwed, turned, and endlessly enjoyed it. It was hard to distract him. The game had everything, but I couldn't hold back and toward the end of the visit I pulled him to me for a hug. I had to, I hadn't seen him for so long. He certainly couldn't remember me.

Suddenly, Daniel wriggled out of my embrace and crawled toward the ladder. Another twenty seconds and the child was standing on his own two feet. I was in seventh heaven with happiness. I photographed him from all angles. I'd seen him standing for the first time, apparently. I'd missed most of the "first time" events in his life:

turning over from his back onto his belly and the opposite, his first smile, first tooth.

This was the lot of adoptive parents – I knew it.

Later on I met up with many of the caregivers I already knew well. They were all glad to see me and everyone had heard about the court case. I treated them to butter cookies. This time, they didn't limit my visit time and even Valentina honored us with her presence and played with Daniel on the bench outside.

They still didn't let me put him on the ground or sand to crawl a little, feel other textures. Honestly, I'd already learned my lesson with Ella, when they punished me and wouldn't let me take her outside after I allowed her to touch the ground, feel the earth.

All this time, Ira never left me alone. We became friends. Every break she had, she'd come to us, play with Daniel and ask to see Ella's photograph album again and again. And she wasn't the only one, all the caregivers took an interest and looked with pleasure at the album. And then, I got it – Daniel was one year old.

I had to celebrate!

The next day, on the way to the orphanage, Ilya and I stopped at a cake shop and Ilya pointed out the cakes the caregivers and Valentina particularly liked. I remembered cakes with a lot of cream. I bought several cakes like that and when I arrived at the orphanage, I put them in the kitchen.

With Ilya's help, I asked them to cut slices of each cake and arrange them on three plates: one for Valentina, one for Daniel's group of caregivers, and another plate for the group of caregivers who had looked after Ella. Ira joined Daniel's group with me.

The caregivers sang "*S dnyom rozhdeniya tebya!*" And I taught them the Hebrew version.

Despite all the happiness, there was one difficult moment in Daniel's bedroom, a large room with empty white walls and fifteen empty cribs. Daniel was in this room alone. Was this how he had to fall asleep? On his own? The sight of him sleeping alone in a room full of empty cribs didn't leave me, not that evening and not for the rest of my visit. In fact, it didn't leave me for many years.

34

Ira

That evening I felt confused. Although it was a pleasant surprise to see the nurse from Israel, why didn't they tell me in advance about her visit? My heart almost stopped when I saw her. How could Valentina not tell me? I needed to prepare.

At first, I was in seventh heaven from the surprise, particularly when I saw Ella's album, but I immediately felt distress afterwards, as if I'd fallen from a high tower. Suddenly, the pictures really saddened me. The longing, the distance, the knowledge that we'd never meet again.

And all this happened because of me.

Why had I done this to Lena? I suddenly caught myself in horror. Who knows what would have happened if Sveta had stayed with us? Lena might have overcome the addiction to drugs and alcohol; perhaps for her baby's sake, she'd have made more effort?

But I didn't really have an answer. After all, she didn't take care of Misha. True, he was already eleven years old, but even at that age, a child needs a mother.

Sometimes he'd be his mother's mother: make food, clean a little, give her tea, remind her it was their turn for the shower. If I didn't take him every weekend, and on two other days go to them to cook and clean more thoroughly – who knows what would have happened to him.

So maybe I did have an answer: it wouldn't have worked. Even if Lena could get herself together and function, she'd only manage for a brief time, and then fall again. I was so distressed by my Misha's fate. I only wish I could have taken him to live with us, but with Yuri there was no change, not with his heart or his mood. I wanted to save Misha and enable him a normal life with functioning parents, but I failed.

At least I hoped I'd saved our Sveta, and that her life in Israel would be a good one. I saw how nicely she was dressed in the photographs, how she played with cats and dogs, and went walking in nature. I saw her laughing, happy.

I suddenly remembered that a month ago Misha called to say he thought Mama was going mad, that she'd bought a little cake and lit three candles, quietly singing, "Happy birthday to you," and it wasn't his birthday. For a moment, I also thought she might be going mad, but then I realized: it was June 15th, Sveta's birthday. Lena was celebrating her birthday! Thoughts confuse me.

Only more vodka calmed me down, a little.

35

Tali

When I returned to Israel, there were already signs of security tension at the exit from the airport. A lot of soldiers and police everywhere. On the radio and television were reports of single acts of terror. I was afraid that by the end of October, the date of the new court case, Russia would have already imposed restrictions on travel to Israel. We were four families soon to adopt. We stayed in touch daily. We collected information, checked, asked.

Each one found an uncle or a friend with some information, who supported, helped, and approached people of influence. We only had one request – not to forbid adoptions to Israel. In the meantime, I wrote another letter to Shimon Peres. Among other things, I wrote him that since March we'd encountered considerable obstacles, claiming that Israel was in a state of war and the country could not provide protection for an adopted child, and for this reason all court cases in St. Petersburg for Israelis were denied.

I went on to describe the difficulties simply and clearly, noting that at this moment, the St. Petersburg court is waiting for new instructions from the Russian Ministry of Education. These will be determined at an inter-Ministerial meeting to be held on August 9th, along with a decision whether or not to continue approving adoptions to Israel, despite the security situation.

I ended by saying that if Israel is barred from adopting from Russia, tens, even hundreds of Israeli families won't be able to realize their dream to adopt a child: "We have no doubt that in Israel, at present, despite painful events, we have all the conditions for a normal life and the education of our children. It has been suggested that you could even prevent the meeting from taking place in Russia next month by means of a document from the local Ministry of Education that would allow relations with Israelis to continue as in the past. Due to your reputation and the appreciation you have won all over the world, you are the only one who can save us."

I had the impression that the letter reached the right hands, because that same day I was asked to resend the letter, changing the font from twelve to fourteen, for Peres' convenience. And indeed, within two days, a reply came from the Minister of Foreign Affairs office. It stated merely that there had been a personal intervention through Igor Ivanov, the Russian Minister of Foreign Affairs.

Once again, I was in a state of tension and alertness, monitoring the daily news to make sure no further security event had taken place that could end all hope. It was almost impossible for me to sit and do nothing. I felt a strong need to do something but didn't know what else was possible.

In the meantime, I invested my time in Ella and her talents. She tried an artistic gym class at the neighborhood school, adored the teacher and left the class in Givatyim, which she'd begun when she was two and a half. She was the smallest and youngest in the new class. She had difficulty throwing sticks and ropes into the air, but Ludmila, the teacher, loved her from the very first day and forgave her. She was more successful with balls and hoops.

Two months later, I arrived at the Beit Russel performance hall for the annual class performance. Ella was practicing in the dressing room and wearing a special dance costume. Ludmila had pulled her long hair back and twisted it on top of her head. The girls looked festive and excited. The hall was filled with parents and family.

I filmed it all on video. Ella stood on the left at the back. In front, of course, were the older more talented girls. I think Ella was too young to pay attention to the meaning of her position. The performance was rather long, and she probably didn't remember it from beginning to end.

At some point, one of the girls stumbled and fell. The audience was on its feet, but the music continued. Some of the dancers continued a few more seconds, but most stopped dancing and crowded round their friend who was sitting on the floor. For some reason, I continued filming.

Suddenly, in the corner of the lens I saw my Ella. She made her way through the others who had stopped, found an empty place at the front of the stage and continued to dance, alone. A thought occurred to me: why hadn't she gone to help the girl who'd fallen. She didn't want to, maybe she wasn't focused on what was going on? Was she perhaps disconnected?

I wasn't sure whether her movements were part of the original performance or whether she was making them up. She seemed to be floating, seeing nobody but herself, moving with a hoop and, when it fell – she went on to a stick with a red ribbon on the end that was lying at the side of the stage. It fell from her hand as she waved it the second time and she began to do a series of cartwheels.

The audience realized that she was no longer doing the original dance and because of the situation and her young age, spectators began to whistle and clap louder. At this stage, tears in my eyes, I put the camera down on the seat, stood with everyone else and clapped.

I was moved by the gesture of the audience and, perhaps, by Ella's initiative – identifying a gap and filling it. However, I had doubts about the confidence she demonstrated. Was she really confident or was it a kind of unconscious, dissociative, autistic behavior over which she had no control. Fragments of concern filled me, which were mixed with joy when Ella rushed into my arms.

I didn't stop thinking about and planning the trip in October for a moment. I hoped this trip would see me bringing Daniel home once and for all. I knew that during my maternity leave, I wouldn't be able to disconnect completely from work, so I wrote to the chairperson of the Emunah Movement, the national, religious women's movement, with an unusual request – to put Daniel into daycare intermittently.

I wrote that my adopted son, Daniel, would arrive in Israel in about two weeks after which I'd be on maternity leave as usual. "Because of the special role I fill, as director of the National Transplant Center, I will only have to be on standby for emergencies. This would be several hours of work from time to time when necessary. Since this is a child who has already experienced disappointment in adults; caregivers who leave, no experience of a personal, maternal relationship. I am thinking of sparing him meeting and becoming attached to another person – a nanny – for a short period of time.

"I appeal to you to allow me to bring Daniel for several hours at a time, to the Emunah daycare in Ramat Gan, Ramat Amidar, which is run by Ms. Carmela Malach. I will pay for these hours according to the fee you determine."

Toward the end of October, I was once again in cold St. Petersburg, the day before the third court case. In the suitcase were clothes for Daniel and toys for the journey. As far as the third court case was concerned, I understood that the judge was obligated to hand down a different ruling from her previous one in March, that is, to approve the adoption.

In court, I stood quietly next to Yevgeni. I was questioned for about an hour and a half, in depth, about security in Israel.

The evening before my flight to Russia, about fifty armed Chechen terrorists broke into the Dubrovka Theater and took eight hundred and fifty people hostage. Some of the terrorists carried explosives and demanded that the Russian Federation acknowledge the Freedom Movement, remove its forces from Chechnya and end the second Chechen war.

"How can she ask so many questions about security in Israel when at this very moment the lives of hundreds of hostages in the theater depend on terrorists?" I said to Yevgeni. He shrugged and didn't answer.

At the end of the court case, we waited outside. If everything goes well, we joked, the gates will open, the "iron curtain" will be removed and the new Russian emigration will begin. But the judge apparently wanted to prove she also had something to say, not only the Supreme Court. Although she was forced to approve the adoption, she put a spoke in the wheel.

"Approval will only take effect in ten days' time," she stated, without any logical explanation.

On one hand I was happy, on the other, I didn't really know what to do. Fly home to Israel and return? Remain in St. Petersburg? I actually didn't have much choice. I went back to the orphanage, hugged and kissed Daniel and promised him that this would be our last parting, that these would be the last nights he'd have to fall asleep alone without a caressing hand. I returned to Israel with the clothes and toys I'd brought for him.

On November 4th, I was again in St. Petersburg. The city was already beginning its decorations for Christmas; tiny lights on trees; stores with fir trees, and wrapped gifts intended to tempt customers. On the way to the hotel, Yevgeni showed me the casino and prestigious cafes.

Most of the residents had no money to spend. They worked hard, and when they returned home, made do with bread and sausage, cabbage salad with mayonnaise, and most of them had a glass of vodka to warm their body and soul.

The following day, bearing the required documents, I flew with Yevgeni to the embassy in Moscow in order to arrange the visa. To document the event, I photographed the embassy building with the Israeli flag flying on its roof. Not two minutes passed before security men approached me. It was a sensitive time and they were generally anxious. In the end, I was able to take one quick photograph. I hoped it wouldn't come out blurred and the building and the flag would be clear.

When I returned to St. Petersburg, I became impatient. I didn't feel like seeing the city or buying anything. I only wanted to return home with Daniel. On the first evening, I went to bed early, promising myself that this would be my last time in the city.

The next day I went with Ilya to the orphanage and on the way we stopped to buy cakes for the staff. I took my time parting from the staff who had accompanied us through the process. I was a little afraid to feel free, as if our troubles were behind us, because several possible hurdles still lay before us – leaving Russia, the flight to Israel, and absorption by the Ministry of the Interior.

Ira the doctor didn't leave me for a moment. We both seemed to realize we wouldn't meet again, and she seemed to want to say something to me, but was tense and couldn't explain herself. As a parting gift, I gave her a gold chain with a heart encrusted with zircon stones, which I bought in Israel and almost forgot to bring with all the excitement. She immediately began to cry.

After a moment she again asked to see Ella's photograph album, which was always in my bag and, opening it emotionally, she paged through, kissing each picture.

Finally, Daniel parted from his favorite toy, a small dog on a long string, he'd managed to pull the length of the corridor. The toy was restored to the toy cabinet that was locked.

I held Daniel in my arms and the feeling was as natural as if it had always been like that. But I had no place for joy. I was busy organizing: carrying bags, porridge, a place for passports that was accessible and, primarily, I was tense and impatient. I only wanted one thing – to get away from there. To get through passport control, and to receive the final permission to leave Russia. Together.

That very day we boarded a direct flight from St. Petersburg to Israel, without a stopover in Moscow. Everything was easier. With us on the flight were the toddler Hila, her mother, and her aunt. The plane was almost empty, and Daniel enjoyed the meal table, which we turned into a play surface, and he pushed a little car along it. He quickly became tired and fell asleep on a bed I made up on the two seats next to me. Before landing, I changed his winter clothing for summer clothes.

We landed in the afternoon straight into absorption issues at the Ministry of the Interior. Ella, with bangs and her red dress, ran toward us in the passenger hall, followed by my brother, sister-in-law, and her daughters. What a party.

Later, I was informed that Ella had told the daycare that her brother was arriving that day, and had taken a pair of scissors and managed to cut her hair into bangs. "We knew it was a special day for her and we didn't get angry with her," said the daycare worker the next day.

After we got home and the guests had left, I tried to put Daniel to bed. The other adoptive parents always said, even before I brought Ella home, that the children fall asleep without any help, without a story, or water, or a hug. They fall asleep quickly and sleep quietly until morning.

Putting Ella to bed had gone quite well, but she'd wake up to eight times a night. I thought Daniel might sleep peacefully until morning. After changing his diaper and dressing him in his pajamas, I put him in the crib that had been Ella's, placed next to her bed. I kissed him and said "good night." I darkened the room, apart from a little night light, and left.

Within two minutes, I heard a noise coming from the children's room. I went in at once and found Daniel standing and holding onto the railing. He was crying and repeatedly throwing himself forwards and backwards. Despite my initial shock, instinct made me go to him and hug him.

With one hand I stroked his head, hugging him with my other arm. He stopped rather quickly throwing his body backwards and forwards, resting in my embrace until he calmed down. After a moment, I helped him lie down, continuing to stroke him until his eyes closed.

I was upset. I knew from stories I'd heard that in the orphanages toddlers would repeatedly throw themselves forwards and backwards, while holding onto the crib railing, making themselves cry until they tired and fell asleep. Despite the joy of Daniel's homecoming at long last, after an exhausting journey, I was filled with sadness and sorrow for the nights he'd experienced in the orphanage. For his painful loneliness. Every baby in the world deserves a parent who is present and hugs him. I realized that part of this behavior he'd had time to acquire because of his age – he was already a year and four months, in terms of adoption this was a lot.

If only he'd come to Israel in March, as planned, after the first court case, when he was a baby, he'd have been spared this terrible falling asleep experience.

I vowed to myself and promised him that the rest of his nights until he went into the army would not be like that.

From Daniel's first day in Israel, he clung to me and, unlike Ella, didn't respond to any family member or passerby who held out their arms, offered a smile, or reached out. He was attached to me alone, and after a few days he began to trust me and lay his head on my shoulder.

Luckily for him, he left Russia just before he was supposed to move into a room with older children because of his age. Adi, who was adopted around the same time, and was born three months before him, moved into the older group, which included meals at a table and feeding themselves.

I photographed her at the end of October. She sat at a long table, with small chairs on both sides. There were children on either side of her, some bigger than she was. The moment the caregiver put down the plate of food – the same for each child – the older children grabbed the food off the plates of the little ones. The little ones apparently learned the laws of survival, hitting the older children and grabbing back, biting and leaving marks like watches.

When Adi arrived in Israel, the signs of the orphanage and the older children's room were apparent. She ate constantly. Whenever she saw food, no matter what kind or texture and no matter where – at home, at a café, or a restaurant – she'd grab it, and she'd grab food from other people's plates as well. She was so lovely that everyone was enchanted by her. But her mother would glance at me. We both knew that a food disorder was part of the syndrome.

In the middle of the maternity leave, which was combined with work, I managed to organize a daily routine for us all and even found time to thank the score of dear people who had helped me in this operation. I formulated a skeleton letter of thanks and added suitable, personal words for each one and the role they played. I added the first photograph of the three of us at home with a chocolate cake and sweets.

At first, it was apparent that Daniel wasn't accustomed to a lot of attention. Ella took care of him, making him laugh and singing to him. His temperament was calmer, and he surrendered and responded with love and chuckles.

In the mornings, after accompanying Ella to daycare, we used the time to go to parks. I took off Daniel's shoes and encouraged him to walk barefoot on the ground and on the sand in the area of the play structures.

He examined the ground, dipped his hands into the earth and sand and even put it in his mouth. We moved onto the path. He seemed to enjoy the changes. He sat down and touched. Someone walked by with his dog. He agreed to my request to stop. I took Daniel's hand and taught him to stroke the dog. The dog licked him. He was surprised, but unafraid and continued to stroke him.

After a fairly long walk, we reached a café. I sat him down in a highchair, tied a napkin around his neck and he seemed happy to gaze at passersby. I ordered breakfast and offered him a teaspoon of scrambled egg, then tuna with white cheese and herbs. After the cheese he made a face and spat it all out. At the end, I spoiled him with a fruit shake and ice-cream.

The highchair he sat in at the café was rather like his chair at the orphanage when he was in the group of six – to eight-month-old children, regardless of their development or whether they were able to sit on their own or showed signs of so doing. I assumed that most were still unable to support their upper body when sitting. The caregivers developed an effective system to feed them in as short a time as possible.

A soup or porridge bowl was held to the mouth of the toddler and immediately emptied into the mouth, as well as some on the neck and below. Astonishingly, the children seemed to have gotten used to it and didn't resist. Maybe because the food was tasty or maybe because they were hungry.

That evening, Ella asked me to watch a video with her. "A video for little ones," she stressed. "I want to teach Daniel to sing."

She sat him down beside her on the children's sofa and turned his head toward the television. "Hands up, on your head…"she sang, gesturing with her hands and he looked confused and didn't know where to look – at her or at the television.

At this stage, I felt the task had been completed. Both my children home, happy, and singing. I sank into the armchair and streams of happiness gradually overwhelmed me, from my head to my toes, which felt full and swollen. I didn't know if this was from exhaustion or gratitude for all the goodness in my life.

36

Tali

One afternoon, we made our way to the nearest mall to buy Daniel his first pair of shoes. His blond hair had grown and he captivated everybody. For a moment, I felt uncomfortable about Ella because of all the attention given him.

In the children's shoe store, two young sales ladies helped us. Daniel sat on the counter and women took off his shoes, measured his feet, and put shoes on him.

One of the sales ladies helping us blurted out a question. "Tell me, is his father Russian?"

"Yes," I murmured.

I immediately paid and left.

I didn't understand why she'd asked me. After all, I'm of Russian descent, with green eyes and blond hair. Didn't I look Russian enough for her? And what business was it of hers?

At home, Ella embarrassed me, "We don't have a father, so why you did you say in the store that his father is Russian?"

I quickly handed her the drink she'd requested and turned to the sink to prepare Daniel's drink. Drinking eagerly, she wanted to open the package of hair bands I'd bought her. I got out of it thankfully and comforted myself – she was small and we hadn't yet reached a time for explanations.

In time, Daniel developed technical skills, he built tall castles with blocks, built and knocked them down, and he also liked photographs of animals, and a story before bed. He knew and remembered the names of birds, including those nobody knew. I quickly bought a subscription for the safari.

Unlike other children his age who would go from cage to cage, Daniel insisted on visiting all the animals at the safari, and standing next to each cage, I'd read the name of the animal. He would stand close to the wire, and astoundingly, the animals would approach him. They weren't afraid of him. And for some reason, he wasn't afraid of them. When I unintentionally attempted to bypass an animal cage on the side, he'd scrunch up his face and get mad at me.

When he'd been in Israel eight months, we received an invitation to meet with Foreign Minister Peres, who wanted to see the baby he'd worked hard to bring from Russia. It was the CEO Avi Gil who arranged the meeting with the help of his personal assistant, Efrat Duvdevani.

The meeting took place one Friday morning. I dressed the children in their best clothes and we drove to the Tel Aviv office. We went through all the security checks and entered. Peres was sitting in an armchair, in front of a low wood table. I was embarrassed. I didn't know what to do or say. But Peres made it easy for us and began to talk to Ella. At his request, she performed somersaults at the side of the room. Then he offered her coca cola and, in the meantime, the others passed Daniel from one to the other. Near the end of the visit, we left a memento – a large framed poster I'd prepared with photographs of little Daniel's life story up until he came to Israel, with the words: "To Mr. Shimon Peres, in gratitude for making it possible for us to be a family."

The first picture: the orphanage with its green, iron gate. The second picture: Daniel as a baby alone in a bed in the room at the orphanage. The third picture: Ella playing with Daniel at the orphanage.

Fourth picture: The court disqualifies the adoption because of the threat to children's lives in Israel. Fifth picture: Ella and I at Ben Gurion Airport, returning empty-handed. Other pictures: May 30th, Moscow, the Supreme Court; Ella with the local advocate. The last, irreversible opportunity to change the ruling and get Daniel. Despite the Supreme Court victory, Israel was still perceived to be a dangerous country and Daniel wasn't released; Fall 2002, Foreign Minister Peres' personal intervention with the Russian Foreign Minister; Daniel on the plane on the way to Israel; the family united; Tali, Ella, and Daniel in Ramat Gan. And the final picture: Daniel playing in the daycare in the summer of 2003.

Before leaving, we were photographed with Peres: Efrat took the photograph and Avi stood to one side, trying hard not to appear excited.

One day in summer, we drove to see Dana and Yoram, friends from Raanana, adoptive parents I met at one of the parents' workshops. Ella loved their son, Nir, and they were old friends. Exactly two days before, the family had returned from the Ukraine, where they'd gone to adopt a girl, a sister for Nir.

Ella was really excited before the visit. In her hand, she held the gift we'd brought for Nir in honor of his new sister, a racing car with remote control. In the cradle lay a tiny baby girl wrapped in a white blanket embroidered in pink. Her hair and face were slightly dark. Something in her expression was strange, as if she'd only just come out of her mother's womb and was still crumpled from the effort of the birth.

Ella glanced at the baby and immediately went off to play with Nir. Dana spent time telling us about the experiences, "When we reached Odessa, they took us into the orphanage, to wait in a room that looked like a waiting room for parents. Anatoly, the local mediator who accompanied us, explained that the director would come in soon with an album of photographs from which to choose our daughter."

"Are you telling me you chose from a photograph, didn't they let you see with your own eyes?" I was astonished.

"They showed us pictures of children who had blood tests and were approved by a doctor."

"You're very lucky to have been given a six-month-old daughter. It is very rare. And she's very lucky too."

I thought about Ella and Daniel, who had to wait long months in the orphanage, without a caressing hand or a mother, who was alert to every sound even before the crying started. My heart contracted.

Two weeks later, Dana asked to meet with me alone. "I can't explain it, but something isn't right with the child," she said. "They referred me to the children's hospital where they took blood tests. I have some of them, I want you to help me understand what they say."

I examined the results and saw very high liver enzymes as well as a positive test for Hepatitis C. The child seemed to be suffering from a liver infection. But how could she have become infected? The disease passes through the blood. I remembered the transmission among dialysis patients, but that made sense, because with dialysis the blood is taken from the body into the machine, and many patients use the same machine. There was also the possibility that the poor baby had gotten the disease from her biological mother in the womb. The mother may have used drugs intravenously, transmitting the disease via improperly used needles.

Dana looked at me and said, "Well, tell me, what do you see?"

I didn't have the authority to tell her things like that, so I answered, "There's a rise in liver enzymes but I'm not familiar with pediatric disease. Tomorrow morning you should go to the hospital."

She did as I suggested and the next day told me that not only did the child have Hepatitis C but she'd also contracted AIDS from her mother.

"What do I do?" she asked. "I'm really afraid, particularly for Nir."

I was also worried. Ella was a good friend of Nir's and they always played together. I tried to hide my fears and was rather pressured by her expectations of me, as if I was the director of the public health department in the Ministry of Health, someone who knew everything and could guide her.

"I'll make a few calls," I told her.

I made several calls, checking things and making enquiries. The hospital gave some guidance but they weren't all that experienced with AIDS in such young children. We had many questions: how would it affect her development and general health? Was there treatment for that age group? Later, other questions arose: how did it happen, after all, she was examined and tested before she came to Israel, and a pediatrician from Israel, a specialist in child development, had examined her. Could there have been some mistake with the blood tests?

Dana made me swear to keep it all a secret.

"Naturally," I promised.

There was nobody to blame, in fact, nobody to get angry with. It was also hard to be angry with the doctor, who hadn't explained about the risk of taking such a small child. We always knew that the younger the adopted child, the less he or she would suffer physically and emotionally. We also knew that some diseases were discovered at a later age, but we mostly repressed this information.

How hard it is when there is nobody to blame.

But with regard to Dana and Yoram, it seems they took out their anger on the doctor. They began to grieve over the situation, constantly asking: why did it happen to us? What have we done wrong? What did she do to deserve this? She's barely begun her life, and how will we raise her like this? How will it affect Nir? Are we, in fact, able to raise her? Can we return her? We've already signed the adoption papers. We're her parents.

In simpler words – they were lost. Completely lost.

I couldn't imagine what I'd do in their place. I couldn't find even the tiniest piece of advice to give them. I don't think I'd have considered returning her, even if it was possible. My pity and compassion were endless but raising a child out of pity is not the right way, not for the parent or the child.

Fortunately, I wasn't faced with this question.

As a nurse, I knew a person's blood that was infected by the virus could penetrate someone through a sore or scratch on the skin or through saliva. So, for me, their questions regarding Nir raised the issue of Ella being infected and, as the days passed, I stopped visiting them.

Dana also stopped calling me. I was somewhat angry with myself for abandoning a friend in trouble. On the other hand, I wasn't sure she wanted a connection with me. I had the feeling she had imposed isolation on herself and distance from her surroundings.

A few weeks later, I began to hear rumors here and there that the baby had been transferred to the Ministry of Welfare children's home. I didn't even know there was an institution for situations like these, I was sure there was adoption or foster homes. From the rumors, I understood that her parents had been advised by Rabbis, although they were secular, and helped by welfare personnel.

I was curious about whether they visited her at the institution or whether they'd completely given her up. I was afraid of the answer I might receive.

After a while, Dana and Yoram moved to another city. They didn't refer to the subject again and I didn't ask, but was certain they hadn't forgotten for a second.

37

Ella

When Nir's parents went to bring his sister, they were given an album of babies' photographs and they pointed at the one they wanted for themselves. They brought her to Israel when she was really tiny. When the baby got to Israel, I brought Nir a gift, a car with remote control. Later, Dana called my mother to help her with blood tests from the hospital. We went to visit them again. Nir and I played with blocks. After Mama looked at the tests she didn't say anything but I saw in her face that something was wrong.

After that, we didn't visit them for a long time.

When I asked Mama if we could visit Nir and his baby sister, she said that the baby was very ill and they'd sent her to hospital and that we'd go some other time.

But we never did.

When Mama went to Russia to take care of everything to do with Daniel, I stayed with Rinat and Shmuel. I was three, bigger than their son, Niv. I was used to his being blond with white skin while his parents were brown-skinned with black hair.

Mama suggested that their next child should be blond too, so Niv wouldn't feel different. When we went for a walk, I saw that people asked them questions about Niv, if he was adopted. Nobody ever asked my mother if I was adopted. I wasn't blond, I had honey-colored hair. But once when we went to buy Daniel shoes, the saleslady said to Mama, "His father must be Russian."

I think Mama got upset.

When I grew up, we joked about it. When people in the street would say, "You look so alike," we'd look at each other and nod. Later on, when the people were far away, we'd roar with laughter.

I wasn't told how my friend Niv came to Israel. I came before him. I was older than he was. I knew that Mama had met his parents in Peterburg, and it was there they discovered that we lived on the same street in Ramat Gan. But he didn't come from my children's home.

Whenever I asked Mama, she said she'd tell me another time.

After a long time, Niv went with his parents to Russia and they brought back his sister. She was very pretty. Her hair was blond, like Niv, and she had blue eyes, like his. Niv told me he'd been with his parents in the courthouse and they'd seen the woman who gave birth to his sister.

That's great. Now they know if his sister looks like her mother.

Mama told me that none of the people who brought children from Peterburg saw the birth mother. It's not fair. Why did they see her in one place but not in another? How will I know who I look like? Only a long time later did I understand from Mama that it depended on the judge.

38

Tali

All primary school students and parents were invited to the school for Family Day. We were divided into groups of children from all classes, the same age in every classroom. I didn't know the teacher who facilitated the event.

She began with a poem she read in praise of Papa. Ella moved restlessly on her chair. I had no idea if this was because of the words of the poem or because the effect of the Ritalin was fading. When the poem was over, I left the classroom to find the school counselor.

Only two months previously, when Ella was due to start school, I'd had a meeting with her. I explained the issue of adoption in relation to Family Day, Independence Day, mother and father, and in general.

"You're bursting in through an open door," she responded with a smile. "It's our way. We're a professional staff and always behave with sensitivity."

I was relieved and understood I could rely on them.

That evening, when I found her, I was irritated. "What was that poem about fathers? Did you hear it? I saw you. How could they do that? Educators. How insensitive can you be?"

She looked down. "Yes, I heard. I don't know… I told them."

"That's your response? Is that how you take responsibility?"

Ella had followed me out and heard some of the conversation.

She stood beside me. Holding out my hand, I said, "Come on, we're going home."

At home, Ella remembered she had homework for Family Day – write down on one page all the members of your family including grandparents and where they live. The children barely knew how to write, clearly this task was for the parents.

We stuck a picture of the family in the center of the page, Ella drew a line from each head with a ruler and I wrote down the name, the relationship and where they lived. An easy task. There were only three of us at home, and apart from us there was grandma on kibbutz, an uncle and an aunt – my brother and sister.

The task was complete.

The next day I accompanied Ella to school with the homework in a transparent sheet protector, took Daniel to daycare, and went to the office.

At noon, the school director called to say that Ella was very upset and unwilling to talk. I trusted the director who had known Ella since daycare. She agreed to let me talk to her.

"Mama, come and get me right now!"

I'd never heard Ella speak like this. I left the office immediately. The minute I arrived, Ella ran into my arms.

She sounded very upset. "I want to go home now!"

I realized she didn't want to talk on school premises and we went home. We had an hour before going to pick up Daniel from daycare. When we got inside, Ella began to pour it out, "Today, the replacement teacher did a lesson on Family Day. I didn't hold up my hand but she called me to the board. I thought it was something good. And then she said to the whole class, 'Do you know that Ella is adopted?'

"She said more, but I didn't hear. I looked down. My face felt hot. And then I left the classroom. I felt everyone was looking at me and talking behind my back. During the break as well. Why did she say that? It's my secret. Only the children who came from my daycare knew."

I thought I was going mad, what nerve! What was that teacher thinking? "She has no idea of who she was up against," I said furiously to myself, but stopping the anger and frustration; at that moment I only wanted to calm Ella.

I held her tight. "You won't ever let anyone hurt you or tell your secrets. And only you will decide about yourself." And after I caught myself, I added, "And I will decide about you… until the army."

I wasn't sure she understood the nuances, but I knew she understood the intonation and the message. To make sure, I stressed, "Most important of all, my Ella, always tell me everything and together we'll decide what to do. And don't give up and don't give in because you are a winner."

Encouraged, she smiled. "And when I have a hard time I'll come to cry at home. With you."

"Of course, sweetheart, naturally." I felt a tear on my cheek. "Come, darling, let's wash our faces and go get Daniel from daycare. I'll talk to the school later on." A moment later I added confidently, "Don't worry, that teacher will never teach you again."

39

Ella

I liked first grade. The school was really near our home and Mama walked me to school every morning. I had different colored shirts with the school badge on each one and every day I chose a different color, red or pale blue or white or black. I wore any pants I liked. It was nice having children I knew from kindergarten in my class. And there were some new children as well. I didn't know the teacher but she was nice.

We started learning to read and write. They said that we'd learn until *Hanukkah*, the Jewish festival of lights, and whoever managed by Hanukkah would go on. Whoever found it hard, they'd change the method of reading. Because I was taking Ritalin, they didn't have to change the method for me.

Homework was hard for me and I had a private teacher who came every Monday. I liked her and did everything she said. I knew it was important to Mama. She wanted me to be a good student and do my homework. She said we don't save money on learning and culture and because of this she always let us choose as many activities as we wanted. Other children were told they could only have one or two.

We also went to lots of plays and movies, from the age of two. And I really wanted to do what Mama asked. Sometimes, when I felt like making her mad, I wouldn't do stuff, like not take a shower and get angry, until we really had a fight.

Once I even walked out the door I was so angry. I got to the stairs, I wasn't allowed to take the elevator alone, and I yelled, "I'm leaving home, and you aren't my mother anyway!"

Mama said in a teacher's voice, "You aren't going anywhere, this is your home. And I am your mother."

I remember going quietly back inside, to the bathroom. I liked hearing that this was my home, even when I really wanted to make Mama mad and not shower.

Every year on *Tu B'Shvat*, Jewish Earth and Tree Day, all the families that had adopted children from our children's home in Russia drove to a forest near Jerusalem, to see the almond trees. I liked walking there, because there were play structures in the forest and we'd play with our friends. Among all the "Russian" friends, Noga was my best friend.

Every time we went on a trip, Noga and I were together. We weren't alike – I had brown hair and Noga was blond and blue-eyed. Noga and I liked to jump and fool around, and we didn't stop even when all our friends got tired and sat down to eat.

That evening, after the teacher had embarrassed me and told everybody that I was adopted, I asked Mama why I was different from the others, and she said it was because I was special, because I was a gift-child. Then we read the story *"Sigal's Flower"* – about the adoption of a girl called Sigal and whose real name was Lihi, which in English means "she is mine." Her parents gave her that name because they meant to say that she was theirs.

The very next day Mama made sure that teacher never came into my class again, but it didn't help. I felt the girls in the class looked at me strangely. Even the girls who were my friends in kindergarten. It was because they wanted to please the queen of the class and be her friend.

In the breaks I wanted to play football with the boys. I was small but I was really fast, even with the Ritalin. I left the girls from my class, I decided I didn't care about them. I didn't like them anymore. I was accepted because I was good at sports, and also because I performed artistic gymnastics.

Mama would leave work to run with me to rhythmic gymnastics and Hapoel Tel Aviv, an israeli sports club. She'd work with her papers and telephone until the activity was over. Work, work, all the time. I loved Ludmila the teacher from Russia. She was so pretty with long, honey-colored hair like mine. Sometimes she braided it. And she would draw a black line on her eyelids, like a fairy.

Everyone who came from Russia and knew I was born there, loved me. I had a lot of friends, a lot. But I only told Noga secrets and things from my heart, like what the teacher said to me then.

40

Tali

One Friday in June, we were on our way to the kibbutz to spend the weekend with my brother and sister-in-law. Their daughter was working in the local zoo and Daniel, who was now three, joined her enthusiastically to see the monkeys and the great turtle, and to feed the chicks and rabbits, as he'd done on his previous visit there.

I went with Ella for a walk through the fields and the fish ponds. We passed the banana plantation and avocado orchard and a beautiful landscape opened up before us in the afternoon light on one side the fish ponds, and on the other, rising up beyond the fields, were the Gilead Mountains. Ella noticed fish on the sloping sides of the pool, where there wasn't any water.

I explained that fish can only live in water and the ones outside were already dead. And indeed, the wind brought the smell of dead fish, which wasn't very pleasant to say the least. We stood in the opposite direction of the wind and I took the opportunity to teach Ella about the life of fish and why they were grown in artificial ponds.

Before returning to the kibbutz, we played at throwing stones in the open area. We checked to see how far each stone got. And then, out of nowhere, Ella surprised me and blurted out, "My Mama stank of fish."

I didn't know how to respond. I didn't want to deny her words and block what she had to say on the subject. On the other hand, I didn't want to encourage her to think negatively about her birth mother. Finally, I came up with a psychological sentence, "Are you thinking about her like that because we just went past the fish ponds?"

"My mother stank of fish," she repeated and that was all.

I left it. In my heart I very much wanted to know why she thought so. How were the fish and their smell connected with her mother? And was the bad smell she attributed to her birth mother related to rejection?

Maybe she guessed that her mother had rejected her and so she was rejecting in turn.

I felt helpless.

The bedtime ceremony with Daniel continued for a long time. He was already three years old and I still couldn't leave the room before he'd fallen asleep. If I left for a moment to go to the toilet or answer the telephone, he'd stand up in bed and start crying. Each time, I had to start the bedtime ceremony and falling asleep all over again. Each time, I was careful to not wake Ella, because she slept lightly.

I'd heard about children who were afraid at night or who were spoiled and wanted their parents close by, not letting them leave the room until they'd fallen asleep. I deliberated what to do. Maybe Daniel still had some issue with parting in relation to the orphanage? And if so, what was I supposed to do?

I decided to talk to a psychologist. Efrat, my sister, recommended a well-known educational psychologist who specialized in treating adoptive families.

So one morning, I arrived at Dr. Nava Ronen's clinic. An antique-looking carpet in Bordeaux-blue with a white design covered the floor. In the middle of the room was a low wood table on one side of a wine-colored, velvety sofa.

I sat down on it. Dr. Ronen sat opposite me on a chair that appeared to be antique. I admired her special clothes and wooden beads around her neck. I felt safe, everything was so special and the atmosphere was pleasant.

I told her what was going on at home and she taught me that Daniel saw me as a regulatory, soothing figure and that he was afraid to fall asleep in case I disappeared.

"Going to sleep," she explained. "Is like constantly parting all over again."

"So what do you advise me to do?" I asked.

"Stay with him until he falls asleep. It's a long process. Until he develops confidence in you."

I understood the message, but still didn't know what to do at night when he woke and came to my bed.

"When he wakes up from a bad dream, he can't self-soothe on the basis of the memory that you exist for him. He needs something real, he must be sure that you exist and so he comes to your bed," she explained.

On the ensuing nights, I continued to wait with Daniel until he fell asleep, and if he came to my bed I let him stay with me. In a sense, it was a relief, and I decided to continue my sessions with Dr. Ronen. There was something about her that I liked, I felt every moment with her had value for myself and for the children.

41

Ella

I was surprised when Noga once told me that her parents in Russia were a king and queen who lived in a magnificent palace, and when she grew up she'd go to them. If this was true, then she was a princess. But how did she know all that? Mama always told me she knew nothing about my parents in Russia.

I didn't talk to Noga about this anymore because it didn't feel good to hear that her parents were rich and lived in a palace, while I knew nothing about mine.

And did my mother really stink of fish?

In third grade, I remember twin sisters coming to school. They had blond hair and came from Russia. Their mother was amazing, with blond hair and blue eyes and she always wore heels and short, mini dresses, sometimes with fishnet tights. The whole school would look at her when she brought the twins in the morning and picked them up in the afternoon. Everyone talked about how she dressed, that she looked like a prostitute. I thought she was beautiful. And then the queen of the class remembered that I also came from Russia and told the children in class to shout "Russian" at me, or "elephant ears." There were some really bad children who would shout "Russian whore" at me!

I'd run away from the playground to the classroom and sit quietly on the side, waiting for it to end, pretending I was reading something, but actually I disconnected. Didn't feel. Didn't hear. But Mama knew about this and went to talk to the principal. She told me that many emigrants came from Russia and the Russian girls were beautiful, and this was why they teased me. Mama said that anyone who teased me like that was jealous of my beauty, and that they had no self-confidence so they tried to behave as if they were strong and I was weak. She also said that the children enjoyed seeing me get angry and hurt and that I had to behave as if I didn't care and then it would stop.

Mama also said she herself came from Russia, because her father, the grandfather I didn't know, was born in Russia, in Kiev, and so was his grandfather and great-grandfather and great great grandfather. So they could laugh at her too. It helped a little that I wasn't alone, that Mama was with me.

"Be strong outside, at home you can break down," she told me, and I told Noga that too. Apart from that, Mama promised to arrange surgery for my ears so they wouldn't stick out. I didn't understand how the children saw because my hair always covered my ears. Maybe they saw during artistic gymnastic classes or ballet.

One day I had the surgery in the hospital. For two weeks afterwards I wore a special stretch band that slightly pressed against the place instead of a bandage, and after that I wore it only at night for two weeks. Mama said the doctor had done a good job.

It really did come out well.

Apart from that, my brother also had problems at school. When I was in fourth grade and Daniel in first grade, he came home one day with a cardboard flower in a pot. There was a note on which was written: "I'm Mama and Papa's flower." Mama was shocked. She told Daniel it was lovely, but afterwards I heard her speaking angrily on the phone to the teacher.

"How can you do something like that?" asked mama. "How did you think children who have no father would feel?

And Yonit's father died two months ago."

Mama always took care of us as well as other children so nobody would get hurt. Maybe Mama was hurt too because we had no father. We didn't talk about it at home. Once, when Daniel was in daycare and the children asked him where his father was, he said his father was dead. He didn't invent it. He thought that Mama's friend Udi who died, was his father. He might have made it up so he'd have something to say to his friends in daycare. And maybe he understood it that way because Udi's parents – Debby and Moolie – behaved as if they were our grandparents.

In fourth grade, I was sick for the first time and didn't go to school. I was at home for three days. I felt fine but I had a fever. Mama was glad I was sick because, finally, she could take days off from work and be with me at home, just the two of us.

Every day she read me stories and played games with me. And she also explained that maybe in Russia we caught things from a lot of children in the children's home and so our immune system was strong, which was why we didn't catch every virus once we got to Israel.

I didn't really understand because every time Mama came to visit us at the children's home in Russia, we were healthy. And it was also always warm there, they heated a lot in winter. From the stories about her trips to visit us, I remember she always told us how she'd arrive with a large coat and scarf and underneath a thin shirt, so she wouldn't be too hot.

So how could our immune system be strong if it was always warm and we weren't taken outside, and we weren't so sick?

I didn't understand, but one thing I did understand – it's important to know about illnesses in the family we knew nothing about. Every time we went to a doctor who didn't know us, the eye doctor or the dentist, he'd ask about family illnesses.

"What, don't you know?"

"What, didn't they tell you?"

They were always surprised. What was there to be surprised about?

Mama, who was very careful about health, would nag me and Daniel because we didn't know about our family genetics, and we needed to take care of our health, so there was only healthy food in our home. When Daniel would gobble down candies, she'd get mad. "You're finishing off your natural production of insulin. If you go on like that, you'll have diabetes by the age of forty."

When we'd ask for larger helpings of chips with a hamburger, she'd say, "You're filling your veins with fat. When you're adults, your arteries will be blocked and you'll have a heart attack."

The mothers of our Russian friends would laugh at Mama, who'd give us yogurt to drink on trips or vegetable and fruit sticks she'd prepared at home, while they gave their children Bamba and Kinder Eggs.

Mama said that sports were also important and the ballet class for which I was registered, was certainly perceived as sport.

42

Tali

In sixth grade, Ella was given a project on family roots to prepare. Cynically I said to myself that this was exactly what she needed, learning difficulties as well as her unknown family roots. I talked to my family. My brother took pity on her and sent the detailed project his daughter had done. At least half of it could be copied. And what did Ella think? She didn't bother with it. The task was too much for her before she even started.

At my next session with Dr. Ronen, I told her about the project and she, too, couldn't understand the school. "After all, they understand her disability, and there's no way she can take on a long project with her ADD," she told me. "You need to talk to the teacher and work out several short tasks with a beginning and an end. Not something ongoing."

"And what about the connection to her roots and adoption?" I asked.

"Don't do the traditional project. Take subjects that are connected with her name or areas she particularly enjoys, her hobbies."

Later, I sat down with Ella and encouraged her to think about what interested her and made her curious. She didn't volunteer many ideas.

"What do you think about going to see the Bat Sheva Company and getting to know the dancers?" I tried.

Ella got enthusiastic. "Really? Do you think they'll let me watch a company class?"

So the conversation flowed and we soon had a whole list of ideas. The prominent one was to interview a dancer, if possible someone from Russia, and we also thought of looking for a movie about the Bolshoi Ballet and other things. She infected me with her excitement, and I very quickly began to build a strategy for reaching an understanding with the school, who did approve it in the end.

From Wikipedia, we learned that the Bat Sheva Company was established in 1964 by Baroness Batsheva de Rothschild, and choreographer, Martha Graham. Through a personal acquaintance, we met the choreographer of the Bat Sheva Company in a small room adjacent to the company rehearsal studio. She was enthusiastic about Ella and the notion of the Bat Mitzvah project and answered all the questions on Ella's list. I recorded the entire conversation because Ella couldn't write fast enough and she was also nervous.

To her disappointment, the company had no Russian dancers at the time, they were all born in Israel. At the end of the interview, Ella received two gifts: two tickets to the next performance of the company two weeks later and a video of Bolshoi Ballet dances.

We spent the evening in front of the television. Ella frequently changed position from sitting to standing and back again. She always did this when she was excited.

Since the subject seemed important to her, I suggested we go online and learn a little about the history of the Russian Ballet. She wanted to know at what age the famous dancers had started to learn ballet, and if they learned in ballet classes, and she wanted to know about the well-known dancers.

Two weeks later, festively dressed, we arrived at the Suzanne Dellal Centre in Neve Tzedek. We were impressed by the audience, which included both young and old, many of whom seemed to be Russian immigrants.

Ella was hypnotized for the entire performance; she sat erect, her eyes almost bulging out of her head. I had never seen her sit so still before on a chair. During the encore she stood clapping until the last people had left the hall. She suddenly caught herself and was slightly embarrassed.

When we got outside, she jumped on me and gave me a huge kiss. "A dream, Mama, I was truly in a dream."

The following day, not to lose motivation, which ordinarily faded rather quickly, we sat down to learn the history of the Bolshoi. While collecting information, she suddenly amazed me by saying, "Mama, I want to open the adoption file."

For a second, I wasn't sure I'd heard correctly.

After collecting myself – after all, she was only twelve – I answered that by law children are only allowed to open the adoption file from the age of eighteen. She nodded and didn't ask anything more on the subject. But the sentence echoed in my mind. Why did she want to open the file? Who told her such a possibility existed.

With these questions and more about coping with adolescence, I came to Dr. Ronen, who said, "Ella seems to be flirting with her identity in terms of the adoption. The matter of the Russian ballet. Looking for a Russian dancer. She's curious, it's natural. And it's also age-appropriate." She continued to explain that at school they discuss adolescence, and hormonal development is already taking place. "Even the child of biological parents raises similar questions about his identity in relation to himself and those close to him."

She reassured me, but not entirely. Fear stole into my heart. I asked the other mothers in our group and it turned out that Noga and Lilach had also raised the issue, even with greater intensity than Ella. Reluctantly, I concluded that our situation was normal.

Two months after Ella's Bat Mitzvah, my mother, who was over ninety, was hospitalized with pneumonia. I managed the treatment by telephone. I made sure of an infusion of antibiotics and of course a room on her own. We siblings shared the shifts. I took the Sabbath. I left at six in the morning to get there in time to give her breakfast. She didn't look bad, had no fever, the infusion dripped at the proper rate, the sheets were clean.

"How are you, Mama?" I asked.

She nodded.

I'm going to get you breakfast," I said. She responded with a motion of her head that I didn't understand. Food was never her strong suit and when she got ill, even less so. Very little tasted good to her and it was impossible to force her to eat.

I returned with the tray of hospital food: a bowl of semolina porridge, a tablespoon of cottage cheese, half an egg, a few pieces of tomato and cucumber. I assumed that egg and porridge would be enough for energy and recovery. She needed protein.

But she didn't open her mouth. I raised my voice to be sure she'd heard me, "Mama, breakfast now. Come, eat the porridge. Help me, Mama. Open your mouth."

Her mouth opened a little. I looked into her eyes. Suddenly, I didn't see the familiar expression. There was something else there, something glassy. I didn't know what to do. Intuition told me to call my brother and sister, but I didn't think it was the end. I wasn't prepared. Two years previously, we all thought her life was ending, but she recovered.

Within half an hour, my brother and sister were in the ward. By the time they entered her room she didn't seem to be communicating at all. Her breathing became labored. The three of us were dismayed. They expected me, the professional sister, to lead things, to say something, call someone. But I did nothing. I sat and held her hand.

At a certain point, there was an exchange.

"Do you think this is the end?" asked my brother.

I didn't answer. He wasn't really asking. He knew. We all knew.

A quarter of an hour passed. Her breathing became heavier and heavier. After another quarter of an hour, it stopped. She looked beautiful and clean and groomed.

We kissed her. Each of us said parting words in our hearts. We were good at writing and speaking, but not so good at expressing feelings in situations like these. We weren't practiced. When Papa died suddenly in hospital, many years before, we weren't beside him. When I arrived, Mama hinted at me not to cry in front of everyone.

After a few minutes, I called Ella and Daniel and told them that Grandma's situation was severe and that I'd be home later. They were independent and knew how to manage. Afterwards, I changed my mind. It didn't seem right for them to be on their own in this situation. My niece from Ra'anana was on her way to them, to pick them up for lunch. I made her promise not to tell them anything. I said that I wanted and needed to tell them.

Two hours later, when we got home, I called them into one of the rooms. I hugged them and said in a slightly trembling voice, "Grandma was very ill—"

I hadn't finished the sentence when Daniel interrupted to say, "What, has Grandma died?"

"Yes, today. Not long after I arrived. I'm glad I had time to see her and that she saw me."

They asked what would happen now, and Ella said, "I'll remember her in my heart for the rest of my life."

Daniel and I said we would too and I told them that the funeral would be the following day and we'd all go to the kibbutz. After the Sabbath, when we told everyone, our religious uncle and aunt said the righteous die on the Sabbath. It was nice to hear.

Two hours before the funeral, Daniel wanted to go with me to put up notices on the kibbutz, directing people to the graveyard. A lot of people were supposed to be coming from outside the kibbutz: relatives and friends from work, among them donor coordinators, people who had received organs. I hated all the bustle around me. I wanted quiet. I was sad and didn't want to share my feelings with everyone. I felt most comfortable on the kibbutz. My family was there. My roots, my home. My father was also buried there.

Daniel wanted to go with me to the graveyard, which lay in a forest on a hill. I stopped him at the entrance, not wanting him to see the grave dug beside his grandfather's grave. His grandfather? He'd adopted his grandfather without knowing him at all. Got him in a package deal with me.

For a moment I lost focus and Daniel dropped my hand and ran forward right to the grave, which he examined. I gasped. I thought of joining him, but decided to wait for him to come back. I didn't wanted to look into the grave, into the abyss.

When we returned to my sister's home, where we gathered before the funeral, Ella informed me that she was staying to look after all the little grandchildren, who were very happy. Daniel insisted on coming to the funeral. I tried to persuade him to stay, but he resolutely refused.

At the graveyard, I couldn't determine where he'd stand, but I preferred him to stand away from the grave. He stuck to me from behind, holding my hand in his. I tried to hide the burial from him. Although Grandma was buried in a coffin, it still seemed too much to me. Afterwards, the three of us paid tribute to her, one after another, my sister, my brother, and myself.

"I was never without a book," I said. "I remember going with her as a young child to the hospital, to an out-patient clinic, where we waited for a doctor. She took a book from her bag, saying, 'We must always have a book on hand so we don't wait doing nothing.'"

My brother said the Kaddish, the Jewish prayer for the Dead, and we ended the ceremony by singing "*The Valley Song*," which Mama loved. The *Shiva*, the Jewish seven days of mourning, lasted two days because of *Rosh Hashanna*, the Jewish New Year, after which we returned to Ramat Gan.

Life returned to normal very quickly. I was invited to a meeting with Daniel's art therapist, who was about to give birth and wanted to have as many sessions as possible before the birth. "Since your mother died, the child has been heart sore," she suddenly told me.

"What?" It took me a moment to digest her words. Heart sore? What did she mean? I suddenly caught myself. What had I done? Why had I allowed him near the grave? "What do you mean?" I asked out loud.

She explained that in all their games, he crashes the cars into each other. He describes the injured.

I looked at her confused. I had the feeling that she herself didn't understand very much. After all, she was young and busy with the approaching birth and the changes in her life. I understood her, and with the feelings of a mother I realized I had to invest in more touch, hugs, and time together.

One evening, a month after my mother's death, Daniel came inside. He was supposed to be playing in the neighborhood playground. "Mama, I want a pet," he said.

"Really, Daniel? Who will take care of it? You see how I work. It isn't appropriate."

But he insisted, almost begged, "I'll take care of it. You won't have to. I promise."

"Let me think about it, okay?"

I thought he'd maybe give up but a week later, he came to me again. "Mama, I want a cat. We won't have to take it outside. Why won't you agree?"

My wall of resistance began to crack.

"Let's talk about it tomorrow, okay?"

"Promise?"

"Promise."

The next afternoon, hand in hand, we walked to the veterinary hospital. The waiting room was full of parents, children, and pets. Some had come for vaccinations or treatment, while others, like us, had come to adopt an animal. Daniel knew exactly what he wanted – the black cat with the white markings he'd found in the street the previous month and brought in for treatment and rehabilitation. I knew nothing about this.

Beside us on the bench, sat a mother and her daughter who was crying. She looked scared.

Daniel tugged at my hand, pulling me into the corner. His eyes filled with tears. "The girl with the skirt who's crying has taken my cat," he said.

Oh my goodness, I thought, that's all we need now. I felt helpless. I suddenly remembered what had happened at the airport in Moscow when I discovered that my carry-on with all of Daniel's adoption papers had vanished. I didn't know what to do there either, and so I did nothing, but after a while, things worked out.

I tried to take the same approach and do nothing. I took a deep breath and bent down until our heads were at the same height. "Don't worry, we'll find a solution," I whispered to him.

He seemed to trust me. I wished I trusted myself like that.

After half an hour of waiting in all the noise, it was our turn. The staff already knew Daniel, who often visited there. It turned out that since he'd brought in the cat, he'd gone there almost every day to visit it. They allowed him to stroke it and sometimes to feed it, and he'd put food in its bowl.

I said we wanted that cat, and Daniel added, "The one she took."

The doctor came out from behind the counter in the animal room and stood next to us. She hugged Daniel and whispered a secret to him. Suddenly he was beaming and hopping around.

"Mama, the girl was afraid of the cat and they didn't take him. He's ours!"

I suddenly felt so carefree and lighthearted.

After receiving instructions and before leaving, I was asked to leave my details and set up dates for a series of vaccinations and then the secretary asked, "What name have you chosen for the cat? I'll type it into his file."

I asked Daniel and he wasn't sure and looked at me, asking with his eyes. He knew that in relation to words he should ask me for help.

"What does he remind you of? Think for a moment."

He shrugged.

"Where did you find him? Why did you think to take him to the vet for rehabilitation?"

"He was alone. He had no food."

"Did you feel he was homeless?"

"Yes, he was homeless, I didn't see his mother. He had nobody to love him."

I believed I had a direction and continued, "Do you think he'll be happy with us?"

"Yes! Yes!" he responded confidently.

"So, actually, you want us to take him into our family?"

"Yes, Mama."

"Okay, if that's what you feel, maybe we'll call him Takein."

Daniel seemed impatient, wanting to take the cat home. I closed with the secretary that she type "Takein" for the time being.

After we took the cat and before we got home, I bought a litterbox for his toilet, a bag of food, and bowls for food and water.

Once we got home, Daniel organized a corner with a blanket and a cushion and the litterbox. He took a tray for food from the kitchen cabinet and on it he placed the red bowls we'd bought. He filled one with water and the other with food. There was no end to happiness and excitement.

The cat didn't take easily to hugs, but enjoyed games. Daniel would throw him an embroidery thread spool and the cat would go nuts.

Early the next morning, I found a white note under my door on which was written in pencil, with large letters in a child's handwriting, the word "thank you."

When I left my room I saw the cat sleeping in Daniel's bed, next to his head.

43

Ella

Two months after my Bat Mitzvah, we went to Noga's Bat Mitzvah. I'd never seen a party like that. It was at a hotel, out on the lawn. There were a lot of tables with white tablecloths and the chairs were covered in shiny cream material with a bowtie of the same material on the back. It was such a fancy place.

After we'd eaten and played, we were taken to sit opposite a stage built on the grass, it was like a play and there were huge lights on tall poles, like those for singers at a performance, and the light was very strong and colorful. At the side, there was the DJ's table and the ceremony was just like a fairytale.

Suddenly, special music started to play and Noga came on stage and performed a solo dance. Behind her was a large screen and a film that showed pictures of dancers moving. She had a pretty garland of flowers on her head, luckily it didn't fall off in the middle of her dance.

Then her parents went up on stage, hugged her and read blessings in her honor. They said all sorts of words like princess and queen and it was a bit weird. Then they screened pictures of her when she was small in Israel. They didn't talk about Russia or that she was adopted, as we did at my Bat Mitzvah.

Then someone, an employee perhaps, put a large Menorah on the stage and Noga lit it and read a blessing to her parents. Then there was music and dancing. And then Mama said we had to go home because we had school the next day.

On the way home, Daniel fell asleep and I said to Mama that I'd never seen a Bat Mitzvah like that.

"It reminded me more of a wedding," she replied.

"Maybe Noga's parents made her a princess party like that because she once said she was born to parents who were a king and queen," I said.

A few days later, when I met Noga, we decided we wanted to know about our real mother, our birth mother. What was she like? Tall or short? What color were her eyes? I wanted to know if my eyes were the same color as my mother or my father. Noga probably wanted to know if her mother really was a queen.

And maybe my mother was a fish seller.

When I talked to Mama about it, she told me that I can open my adoption file when I'm eighteen and this is how it is all over the world. It's like a law. I already knew that from Noga, because her parents told her.

So, in the meantime, I stopped thinking about it and continued to focus on school and ballet.

During my second year of middle school my hair was really long and I refused to cut it. My eye doctor said I could stop wearing glasses, that my eyes were fine. I was glad because the glasses were a punishment for me. I was sure that I was the ugliest in the class. Because of that nobody looked at me. Because of that I had fewer girlfriends. And I could never find them, which wasn't comfortable. The glasses didn't really help me see, they were for what the doctor called "plus," to train the eyes.

Later in the year, I was a little more accepted. Mama called this "class queen," but Mama didn't know anything. Class queen was for little girls. The older girls said "accepted." I was invited to parties. Every time I left the house, I was accompanied by several girls. I was no longer alone like in primary school.

I was only half a friend to them, I didn't tell them my secrets. Sometimes they'd get mad, because they would tell theirs and I'd be quiet. Because of this, I started inventing stories, so they'd leave me in peace. I invented stories about my parents in Russia, about how they were famous dancers who traveled all over the world.

They also wanted to know which boy I liked and who I hated. They sometimes asked me which boy I liked the best, which was instead of saying 'love.' I said I didn't like anyone, which was true. They didn't believe me, thought I was lying. They'd already marked the boy they liked best, and two girls couldn't like the same boy.

The most accepted girl won the handsomest boy in the class, the one after her got the next handsomest boy, and so on until the end of the list. I didn't like those boys, and I'd disconnect every time the girls nagged me about it.

Ever since second grade, when the teacher embarrassed me about the adoption and then with ballet, I knew how to disconnect so I wouldn't really care, as if I'd press an imaginary button and it would work. But however well I used it, there was still something there, some feeling that seemed to come out of the earth, like a weed that was very hard to pull out.

When I was little, Grandma would call me, "Ella, come and help me weed."

We'd go down to her garden and it was really hard to pull the weeds out of the ground. Grandma said they were stubborn weeds. And that's how I felt, I couldn't pull that stubborn feeling out of myself.

I suddenly got terribly jealous.

When my friend, Limor, from a parallel class who lived in our building, started meeting with Reut from my class, and even went with her to a movie, I could barely breathe. How could my friend betray me like that?

I called Limor, I was angry at her for betraying me, how could she go behind my back, leave me, to go out with another friend. I told her our friendship was over. That's what I did every time I discovered that a friend of mine went out with another friend. I wanted her to be loyal only to me.

Luckily, I had several half girlfriends like that, because I think some of the girls couldn't bear me any longer, but my disconnection from them helped me. When I disconnected, I didn't feel anything, as if I was just inside myself. That was best for me.

Only with Noga did I feel safe and not jealous. I really loved her, but only her.

Although I was more accepted than I used to be, I was happiest alone in my room at home. I liked looking at the silly pink wall in my room that we painted for my Bat Mitzvah. I'd sit on the gray beanbag Noga gave me and sink inward.

If I was in Russia, for instance, what kind of room would I have? Would I have my own room there too and would I be able to choose the colors? Would I have grandparents? Other siblings?

Mama taught me that when I didn't know what to decide or choose, it was best to draw a table of good and bad. I tried this with my family in Russia. I divided the page in two. On one side I wrote down one family and on the other side two families. I divided each part in two again – the right side for the good things and the left side for the bad. Under "two families" I wrote down good things, that I might have a father and more grandparents and I'd have a family that was only mine, without my brother. Under the bad things, I wrote that maybe the second family didn't want to know me at all, had maybe forgotten me. Maybe the mother in Russia was ashamed of falling pregnant with me.

Later on, I stopped making tables, it made me feel sad. I left it in the drawer of my gray desk.

I chose everything in my room. The walls were shades of pink, but all the furniture was gray. I loved my desk the most; it was actually a long shelf. On it was plenty of space to do my homework, which I didn't really do, and for my computer and most important of all – for my box of jewelry and make-up.

Apart from the gray beanbag, this was my favorite corner. I enjoyed putting on makeup.

Yesterday, for instance, I made myself up like my teacher, Yaeli, and I also made ringlets with Babyliss. I imagined myself putting on makeup, looking exactly like my imaginary sister from Russia and, like Noga, maybe a princess.

44

Tali

Over Passover, I set the date for Daniel's Bar Mitzvah in the middle of July. A few weeks later, the three boys from Gush Etzion were kidnapped and the entire country followed with concern. Eighteen days later, it turned out that they were murdered on the night they were kidnapped.

In response to IDF actions following the kidnapping, rockets were fired at Israel. The country took it for a week and then embarked on "Operation Protective Edge." Sirens were also heard in the center of Israel. It was rather frightening. Many people had panic attacks. Despite fear of sirens, we managed to celebrate the Bar Mitzvah as planned, but several guests didn't come, mainly those who lived in the south.

At the height of the Operation, I enlisted in an emergency unit. I felt at home there, because my work with transplants had accustomed me to a quick pace of work, resolving issues under pressure, and making decisions in times of uncertainty. The children were big and I felt a need to help.

During this time, Daniel began to say that he wouldn't enlist in the army. "I'm Russian, I don't have to be in the army," he said.

I was disconcerted. My son not enlist? My son not a fighter? Where had I gone wrong? Most of the men in the family were officers in Golani, one of them even attaining the rank of brigadier general. I took a deep breath, felt this sentence dancing in my belly, but I remained silent.

The children already knew that in times of military operations, the news on television took preference over any youth programs. This time, the numerous newscasts presented IDF attacks on Gaza as well as casualties on our side. Quite a few were killed and we worried about all the soldiers in the line of fire, particularly our cousins. Three family members were Golanchiks and fought in the battle of Shuja'iyya, during which Hamas soldiers hit an IDF armored troop vehicle and seven Golani soldiers were killed.

The news was hard and sad. Daniel escaped to his room.

I connected this with what his art therapist had said after my mother died, three years before – that he was heart sore. I began to think that maybe he was afraid. I went to his room and found him playing with Takein the cat.

At the end of the summer, Ella, now sixteen, began high school. This time I didn't volunteer to be on the parents' committee and nor did I intervene too much in disciplinary issues, but I was alert. All the time. I made sure the teachers were teaching properly, that they understood her learning disability. At the first parents' meeting the school principal made promises and praised his and the teachers' actions. I was already used to words like these.

A few weeks later, I was called in for a meeting with the principal and Yaeli, the class teacher. After two polite questions, the principal began with smiling authority, "There is something unclear about Ella's behavior. She hugs and kisses everyone. It looks somewhat seductive."

I didn't understand what the hell he was talking about.

Yaeli continued, "Look, the boys drool over her. You know she's good-looking. It seems a little too much at school."

I thought I was going to die and immediately reacted, "She has a boyfriend, there is nothing sexual about this. She's a very sociable girl. In our family, we hug and kiss when we meet."

We all repeated our comments and the conversation ended without decisions or conclusions. I was sure they would discuss her studies with me and I was annoyed when I left. They had set up a meeting with me in the middle of a work day, there was no parking at the school, and it was all for nonsense.

Impatiently, I returned to the office. Fortunately, a family agreed to donate organs, which immediately put me in another world with other rules. Stress of one kind instead of stress of another kind. This time, a toddler up north had drowned in a tub. There was no match for a liver transplant in Israel because of the small size of the body and rare blood type. I asked the parents if they agreed we offer the liver to a toddler in Europe.

"Yes, no question about it," responded the mother.

I was moved by her nobility. I didn't have much time to reflect because I had to contact the European transplant organization, who updated me on the country and medical center with the toddler who was a match for the liver. I then coordinated with the transplant team from Germany who would send their own representative to collect the cooler with the organ from the airport.

After the surgery to harvest the organs from the toddler, I waited at Ben Gurion Airport, and when the ambulance arrived from the north with the cooler, I conveyed it through security to a representative from Lufthansa and left.

It was already dark by the time I was on my way home, and while I was taking care of the final details of the transplant, I remembered the meeting at the school. I told Ella about the conversation and she got mad, made a few derogatory remarks and slammed the door of her room.

I suddenly regretted stopping the sessions with Dr. Ronen and thought the time had come to return to her. Believing there was no further reason to continue, I'd stopped the sessions, but agreed to return the moment I felt the need.

At home, I prepared supper, called my sister, Efrat, and told her about the meeting at the school.

"I don't think she's trying to tempt the boys. I think she wants to please them. It's characteristic of adopted children to be wanted and loved. It's something deep because of their experience of abandonment," said my sister, leaving me somewhat astonished.

"What? Where did you get that from? Since when did you become such an expert?"

"Look, it was part of the study program on education, and I didn't tell you. At the last advanced training, we had a whole day on the subject of abandonment and attachment among children whose parents abandoned them. Loss through death, and children whose parents didn't function or who neglected them, not only adopted children."

"Wait a moment, do you think that Ella is behaving like that because she wants to be loved?" I asked, wondering why my love wasn't enough and how much love she still needed.

Ultimately, my sister's words created order in my mind. I thanked her for the conversation and immediately returned to work issues, making sure with the hospital that kidney patients waiting for transplants the following morning were already on dialysis.

The following day I tried to find out more about the issue. On the internet, I found rather a lot of nonsense and some theories about the age of twelve to seventeen, at least. I didn't remember so many deliberations when I was that age. On kibbutz everything was so clear: what came first, afterwards, what we had to do. Even leisure time was structured.

I realized that seeking boundaries increased, that it was normal at that age, that getting mad at parents and teachers was normal, but I wondered about a sentence I read, according to which between twelve and eighteen or more: "They look for themselves." What did that mean? I wondered.

I asked around the adoptive mothers and it turned out that the same thing was happening with them also at the ages of twelve, thirteen, and even more derogatory words came out of their mouths than with Ella. I thought I was fortunate to have gained a few years because with Ella it only started at the age of sixteen. In addition, I suspected Ella was smoking. I could smell it on her. She denied it.

A few weeks later, Ella decided to organize a birthday party for Dima, her boyfriend. She filled the house with balloons, including a special one in the shape of a heart. Dima wasn't adopted, and although he was born in Israel, he spoke fluent Russian. His parents had a small apartment and so the youngsters spent more time at our place.

I was glad for her that she had a boyfriend and even happier that they spent most of their time at our place. I suggested to Ella that she go and see a gynecologist, a friend of mine, who prescribed birth control pills, and so I achieved a line of communication without secrets. They shut themselves up in her room and listened to particularly loud music. Ella would occasionally emerge and go into the kitchen, returning with a tray of snacks. She seemed happy.

And then the telephone rang.

Mellie, the new transplant coordinator from Kfar Saba, said agitatedly, "A six year-old was visiting friends and when he ran inside from the lawn, he didn't notice the glass door and ran full tilt into it. He broke the glass with his head and his neck was injured. He lost a lot of blood and they resuscitated him for a long time."

I understood that it had happened that afternoon. "They should stabilize him in intensive care, maybe they'll manage to save him," I said.

"I hope so. His brain CT looks really bad."

I continued hopefully, "With children we've seen it all. They have a better recovery capacity. What about the family?"

"I saw his mother from a distance. The father, I understand, doesn't live in Israel, and she has two other older children at home. He's the youngest. She seems to be surrounded by friends."

"So let's talk tomorrow morning, maybe the child's situation will improve."

"I hope so. I hope he'll improve. I could never think about those waiting for transplants at this stage."

But there was no improvement the next day. According to procedure, they carried out a test that indicated a lack of blood flow to the brain. These processes are so hard with children. I couldn't imagine how parents feel when they lose a child. I tried to think – if anything should happen to my child, how would I go on?

My doctorate dealt with parents adjusting to the loss of a child and I'd facilitated support groups for bereaved families, most of them parents, for more than a decade. Bereavement should have been familiar to me and easier to contain, but this was apparently so only with strangers.

I knew the new world the mother was about to join. I wanted to allow her one more day to assimilate the situation, part from him, and I asked that the Brain Death Committee be scheduled for the next morning. I made sure that a social worker spoke to the mother and siblings.

The committee was set for the following morning at eight o'clock, and the mother was summoned for nine o'clock. She left the place only at night to be with her other children. I hoped she'd prepared them. They probably understood the situation from her expression. No mask could hide such pain.

The staff understood that the father would not be returning to Israel. He hadn't been in contact for years. This information was significant because in this case there was probably no need for his agreement to organ donation when the time came to address it.

I arrived at the hospital at seven o'clock in the morning. Mellie the coordinator accompanied me. We waited in the doctors' room. I made sure not to approach the family before death was legally and formally determined.

At eight thirty in the morning the committee of doctors' convened and they determined unequivocally that the child was dead. I immediately counseled Mellie on how to invite the mother and advised her to ask if she wished to bring a friend.

In the meantime, the head of the department and I stayed in the doctors' room; I put glasses of water and tissues on the table. We planned how to give the bitter news. The doctor updated me that the mother understood the situation and that she was highly intelligent. He thought she worked in education.

On one hand, I thought, working in education could help her cope with the situation in terms of her living children, but on the other hand, there are times when no knowledge can help when it happens to you. Emotion overwhelms, and perhaps this is also good. In these situations, it's better to feel than to educate.

Mellie took time with the mother, who couldn't leave her son's bedside. Only after twenty minutes did she enter the doctors' room in gray clothing and dark glasses that hid her eyes. For a moment I lost my confidence, and my eyes, too, filled with tears.

Dear God, this can't be. I felt the floor shaking beneath my feet – in front of me stood Dr. Ronen.

I went to her, we embraced, and she whispered in my ear, "I'm donating, what did you think?" She didn't wait for the formal discussion with the doctor who would inform her that her child was dead. She already knew. I was embarrassed. I had never been in a situation like this. She tightened her embrace. She seemed to stand more firmly on the ground.

Dr. Ronen asked us to wait so she could bring her children in to say goodbye and turned to leave the room.

I remained silent while I texted the staff in the office about the consent to donate organs and asked them to send me the waiting list of children with blood type A.

I usually accompanied the parents when they told their children about the death, even joined them to help and support during the physical parting at the bedside. This time I was confused, so I walked one step behind her. I felt the pain more strongly.

I had to call the hospitals and inform the doctors about the donation so I went into another room and dealt with the allocation of organs to transplant recipients in privacy.

I informed the liver transplant team about the organ donation and the name of the child to receive the liver. I continued to the heart team. I hadn't found a child who was a suitable match in terms of the size of the body and blood type, and so I called cardiologists to find out if there was a child in the last stages of preparation before transplant who wasn't on the list. They went to find out. There certainly were children on dialysis who were waiting for kidneys, but it was necessary to wait a few hours until we knew if the tissues were a match and only then could I check to see if the first two on the list were a healthy match for the transplant.

In the meantime, I went to the Schneider Children's Medical Center in Petach Tikvah. I went with the transplant cardiologist to the ward to see the little girl he thought was a match for the heart.

She seemed small in relation to the size of the dead child's body, but her heart disease caused the heart to grow and there was a chance the heart was a match. More imaging tests were done immediately.

The mother, who was sitting beside her bed, looked alarmed. She hadn't thought it would happen so fast and she wasn't mentally prepared. She immediately called her husband, because both of them had to sign the form for surgery, and only afterwards could the child be registered for the transplant.

Time flew. Everyone was stressed, the tests were carried out swiftly, but the doctors' clinical discussions with regard to the size and match of the heart delayed us. Transplant doctors joined the cardiologists' committee. Another X-ray and more imaging, more measuring and assessments, and it was already four in the afternoon.

Only then did they decide to register the child for a heart transplant.

I scheduled an operating room to harvest the organs at Meir Hospital only after I managed to coordinate operating rooms in three other medical centers where the transplants were scheduled to take place. I still had to close final details of ambulances, taxis, and ice coolers.

In the meantime, I was informed that the funeral was set for the following day at noon.

I arrived half an hour before. I stood at a distance. I wasn't connected with the family or relatives. I heard the eulogies. I wept. I was very familiar with the burial of children but this time I felt cold and tingling throughout my body.

During the burial, I distanced myself even more. I didn't want to see. Or hear the sound of earth thrown into the grave. I managed to see the siblings bending over the grave and putting in the toys and games he loved.

"So you won't be bored," said his twelve-year-old sister during her eulogy.

I took deep breaths. I looked down at the ground and couldn't see anything for the flood of tears from my eyes. I stood there without a sense of time. Suddenly, I felt an embrace. I looked up. It was Dr. Ronen who was embracing me.

I didn't understand how she'd recognized me among the circle of mourners. I realized that everyone had already left and only the two of us remained. Wordlessly, I went with her to the grave. Mountains of flowers hid it, and only a small sign with the name and date indicated who was there.

Because of his mother's nobility, four children were saved that day.

Without a word, we walked away from the grave together, up to the exit from the graveyard. And without a word, we parted.

45

Ella

In high school, I stood out in the ballet class. We were about twelve girls and I had the most beautiful clothes that Mama brought me from France when she returned from a conference. In the package were three leotards and matching tights – purple, which was my favorite color, light pink, and white, and in a separate package were white flip flops.

I really dressed up for the end-of-year performance and the entertainment stages on Independence Day. I gathered up my hair in a tight bun on the top of my head, I used a black or blue pencil under my eyes and blush on my cheeks, and over the white leotard and tights I wore a pink tutu.

But it wasn't my clothes that made me stand out. The teacher was enthusiastic about me, saying I had the legs of a professional ballerina. At every lesson, when she complimented one of the girls, we'd clap, but when the teacher said, "Well done, Ella," or "That's exactly what I meant, look at Ella everyone, learn from her," there was a sudden silence.

Nobody clapped.

I was hurt to the depths of my soul. I was so upset. And that teacher, even though she really was excellent at ballet, was really weak in the face of those witches. She didn't say anything to them about how they were behaving. I didn't want her to say anything, which would have hurt me even more.

Today in class I performed pirouettes and managed to complete three whole turns. I felt I'd done it well and the teacher was enthusiastic.

"Wonderful, Ella!" she said, and this time too I waited for clapping, but there was none. I knew they were shunning me.

The week before, when the teacher said I had the legs of a dancer and everyone heard her, I saw it. They gathered in groups in a corner, looked at me and whispered together.

I could see them from all directions because the walls were covered with huge mirrors. I felt them gossiping about me. At first, my belly constricted, and my eyes filled with tears I could hardly hide and once I even said a Russian curse in my heart, but then all the disconnection that started in first grade came back and I went on with the lesson as usual.

Nobody noticed.

I didn't tell Mama. I didn't want to cause her pain too. Again I buried everything inside. I think I had a giant graveyard in my belly. In each grave was hidden something painful or hurtful I didn't want to remember. That graveyard was a good place to hide. The bad, painful, and unpleasant things were there, and I'd sit among the graves on an imaginary yellow bench and feel nothing.

But I was really hurt by the shunning of the girls and it cut into my flesh. I suddenly couldn't feel the pain, the only thing I knew how to do when I felt like that was to disconnect. In the background, I heard Tchaikovsky's *Swan Lake* and I started to float around the studio, from one corner to another, pirouetting diagonally. I didn't see the girls, felt nothing, just floated and floated on the tips of my toes, in my white leotard and tights. I looked like a swan.

I remembered some of the steps, some I improvised and I did endless pirouettes. When the music ended, I danced toward my bag, picked it up and left the studio. I escaped home and immediately shut myself in my room, my safe place.

I shocked myself that day.

When Mama took me to school the next morning, I suddenly felt I had no relationship with her, that she wasn't my mother. As if I didn't belong to her at all.

I said, "Thank you" when I got out of the car.

She said, "Have a good day," and went to work.

At the entrance to the school, I kissed everyone as usual, I had to be sure every day that everyone wanted me and liked me, unlike the dance lesson. I also tried to make an impression and when everyone came to school in sweatpants, I'd arrive in tight, Diesel jeans. That's how I felt protected. Luckily, the jeans were stretchy and soft and felt good on my body.

But I was still bothered by what I'd felt with Mama. Or, actually, by what I hadn't felt.

At each break, I escaped to the school hideout, to smoke and disconnect. I didn't even eat my sandwich. Since starting high school, I'd had enough of Ritalin, I wanted to eat on the break like everyone else, but I couldn't put a thing in my mouth.

Yaeli, my class teacher and language teacher, said she felt it hampered my studies. I also felt this. I couldn't sit still like the others. I sat on one side, then the other, and then I got up and moved around or changed my chair. And even when I sat down everything bothered me. Anyone who spoke a little loudly, felt to me as if they were shouting. I also heard all the buzz from the other classrooms.

After school, I again ran home and shut myself in my room, sitting on the beanbag and listening to Russian songs.

I wanted to know the city in which I was born. I opened my laptop and looked up St. Petersburg. This was how I learned about the

Hermitage Museum and the main road, Nevsky Prospect – I think mama mentioned this road. I learned about the Marinsky Theater, about the Winter Palace, and about the Church of the Savior on Spilled Blood.

I found plenty of amazing things in that city. I suddenly wanted to be there. I shared this with Daniel. He had excellent senses, he knew how to manage in new places, and after a few days he actually knew our city as well as our cousin Nirit who lived in Modi'in, knew Damascus without visiting, when she was in the army.

Dima was my new boyfriend. At first, we'd talk a bit in the center near the grocery store. Once he bought a can of XL and offered me a taste. I didn't really want to drink from where his mouth had been but felt uncomfortable saying no, so I drank a little. I really liked it.

Later, I went to ballet and felt it like a turbo in my body. After that, every day after school, we sat on the bench next to the grocery store and drank. I was always in a hurry, either I had a ballet class or I went to work in the hoodies store at the mall.

I only allowed Dima a tiny path to my heart. Once I invited him to our home because his parents' apartment was small and I had a room of my own. I was a little in love with him and did everything he wanted and asked. Afterwards, we went to drink XL.

On Friday and Saturday we always sat in the middle of the neighborhood, because that's what he wanted. He also wanted me to stop smoking. I went down to four cigarettes a day. I tried everything. As long as he stayed with me.

Yesterday, I heard Mama on the phone, talking to her sister about me.

I listened hard to what she was saying, "I don't think Ella has enough space in the relationship with her new boyfriend, she's making too much of an effort to do what he wants, to please him. Maybe she's afraid he'll leave her."

I didn't hear what Aunt Efrat said to her, but Mama said, "Yes, maybe it is fear of abandonment."

So I googled "fear of abandonment." I found lots of things. There was stuff written about children who are afraid of leaving their mother, afraid of staying alone in daycare, stuff like that. I didn't feel like reading any more. And I wasn't afraid that Mama would leave me. Or, perhaps I didn't understand?

I was in eleventh grade and things were bad, so bad. I didn't understand what was happening to me. Everything irritated me. At home I'd get mad at Mama or Daniel and slam the door. It drove Mama mad, but I noticed that she only commented that it was destroying the door frame and our apartment, but she didn't yell at me.

I preferred being alone, undisturbed. I'd had enough of school. I felt tired all the time, and even though I went to bed early, I could barely get up in the morning. Mama sometimes had to drag me out of bed and then I'd get even madder at her.

She kept asking what was wrong, why I was so angry. Sometimes I apologized.

After the Succoth holiday I'd play truant from ballet and school. I couldn't sit still in class. My grades weren't as good as they'd been, and the fact that I'd stopped taking Ritalin made it hard to focus. Sometimes I'd eat my sandwich and sometimes I'd give it to one of the boys.

After school, I'd shut myself in my room. Mama would sometimes make me come out to eat. I had no appetite. I asked her what she wanted from me. I just wanted her to leave me alone. My amazing, tight Diesel jeans I'd bought for Rosh Hashanna were starting to hang on me. I didn't notice.

"Hi, what's up? I looked for you at school," Dima called one day and asked with concern.

"Ah… I didn't feel well. I stayed home."

"So I'll come and see you after school."

I didn't want to say no. "I think tomorrow would be better."

I realized I didn't want to see him then either. I just wanted to disconnect. It was best. When I disconnected, I couldn't feel anything. But Mama didn't stop asking questions.

One morning, when she left early and didn't know if I'd gotten up for school, she called to check and asked loudly, "And what's going on at school? They warned me that they'd make a surprise home visit and send a truant officer, do you know what that is? It's an officer who can decide to transfer you to another educational facility. What's going on with you?"

I was silent.

"Can you imagine a truant officer coming to our house? *To our house*? Does that seem right to you?"

I sighed, not knowing what to say.

"Please get dressed now and go to school immediately!"

A moment later she added, "And how come you've given up ballet? What happened?"

I shrugged but she couldn't see.

"Okay, I'll go to school," I gave in. I didn't have the strength to listen to any more.

I could barely move myself. Exhausted, I got to the last class of the day. I stared at the teacher and left. I didn't want Dima to see me but he did.

"Hey, wait for me!" he called after me.

I stopped and waited. He saw by my face that I didn't feel well, and I think he really thought I was ill. And maybe I really was ill. I waited for him. We got on the bus together and got off at my house. In my room, he sat on the beanbag and I lay on the bed. Then he took out a cellophane package of three Ferrero Rocher. He knew it was my favorite chocolate.

I took one and couldn't put it all in my mouth.

We listened to old familiar songs in Russian, like *Kalinka* and *Katyusha*. I sometimes tried to sing Katyusha in Russian. I read that the melody was written by a Jew, and that it was about a girl whose boyfriend went to war.

Dima loved hearing these songs. I didn't tell him that I was actually trying to learn a little Russian and had to find my roots. I wasn't sure he'd understand me. Someone who'd been born to parents who had raised him, couldn't feel what I was feeling.

We listened to music and I felt I was sailing inside a subterranean tunnel. Then I came to a round surface, took off my sneakers and began to dance. I danced and imagined my parents, who were dancers. They were real professionals and did "*Romeo and Juliet*" and "*Giselle*." They were wonderful. I discovered that I looked like my mother and had her eyes and nose. I got my forehead from my father.

They invited me to dance with them. Papa wore earth-colored tights and a light orange shirt with an old-fashioned white collar. Mama wore thin white stockings and a pink lacy dress with another layer of white lace. We danced and Papa lifted me high and put me down into the splits, and Mama glowed and smiled at me and clapped. I felt as if my body was melting, that my whole body was filling up with something else, and then I heard Dima, "I'm going."

My tunnel turned black.

"See you," I said, trying to go back there, but I couldn't.

That evening, Mama came into my room.
"What do you want"? I asked.
"I want to know how you are."
"Okay."

"If you're okay, then you have to go to school. If you don't feel well, we'll go to a doctor. I'm with you."

"I don't have the strength anymore!" I started shouting. "I'm sick of that school. I don't have the strength. Just leave me alone!"

Fortunately, Mama got a call from work about transplants and she had to work.

She started talking in that serious tone of hers, while bringing me a plate of pasta and red sauce. Not bought from a jar, but a sauce she'd prepared with fried onion and tomatoes. I really liked it, but had no appetite. The chocolate Dima had brought me still hadn't made it past my throat.

I put my earphones back in and fell asleep. In the morning I woke in the clothes I'd worn the day before. Mama made me shower and, on the way to school in her car, she talked to me again about the truant officer. I didn't care. Let the officer come. I'd open the door. See what she had to say to me.

I entered that horrible school. During class I lowered my head and looked at the desk so no teacher would notice me, or call my name to answer a question. Because I'd stopped the Ritalin, I heard everything going on in the other classrooms. The flies too.

Everything bothered me.

My soul ached. It hurt me that I didn't know who I was, where I came from, or who I looked like.

I was sure I looked like both of them. Like my mother and my father. With my head on the table, I remembered that Daniel said he was beginning to learn about our city. I felt that this irritating brother of mine had grown up and was starting to understand me. That we were a real team. And that he really was a genius, as the diagnostician said. He knew everything. On all our trips, when we almost got lost, he always found the way.

Once, we went to the forest with the Russian group; the parents stayed behind to make the meal, and Mama took us walking a little far. When we wanted to return, Daniel got mad at her for taking us in the wrong direction. Mama insisted on the direction she wanted. Then it was late and she decided to listen to Daniel, who was only four. And he was right. I was sure he'd know the city well and teach me. And I'd teach him songs in Russian.

Sometimes, I hated him, but most of the time I loved him. He'd also irritate me, like Mama, like everyone. It wasn't his fault.

I sometimes felt as if I had a layer of pain under my skin that wanted to come out. It was all over my body, on my hands, and on my face as well. It stressed me. Suffocated me.

I wanted to leave my body and nobody could understand me.

Daniel also kept his distance from me sometimes. He was afraid of my reactions, afraid I'd get mad at him.

Mama didn't stop calling or texting to ask if I was all right. Sometimes I had no choice, and answered her. "I'm all right. Don't worry." So she'd leave me alone.

46

Tali

It was about five-thirty. Ella called and caught me at the office. "I was at the doctor to fill out the green form for the recruitment office and he asked me to go to the clinic to do an ECG because my pulse rate was thirty."

"My Ella, sweetheart, a pulse rate of thirty isn't possible. Maybe you didn't hear right." I wasn't at all worried, he probably said sixty.

"Doesn't matter, I'm on my way to Dima. Tomorrow, or whenever the clinic is open in the afternoon, I'll do the ECG."

An hour and a half later there was a call from the pediatrician. "I'm waiting for Ella with the ECG, the clinic is about to close. She had a pulse rate of thirty."

"Thirty? Are you sure?"

Before my pulse rate reached a hundred and thirty, I grabbed my bag and flew to the doctor to get a referral, because our clinic had already closed. I picked up Ella from Dima's home and he insisted on joining us. We started looking for a Clalit HMO medical center to do the ECG but the nearest center was closed.

I got three addresses of other centers in the area and flew to the nearest, on Jabotinsky Street in Bnei Brak. When we arrived, I sent Ella and Dima to open a medical file and looked for parking. We didn't have to wait long and when Ella's turn came, a technician carried out the test while I gazed at my daughter, who appeared completely healthy to me. What could this pulse rate be all about? I wondered. If only I knew her family background, maybe I'd understand. Maybe she'd inherited some syndrome.

The ECG film was very short. It was strange. The doctor looked at it and said everything was all right. I relaxed, but Ella's doctor didn't and referred us for a holter monitor.

We did the test the following day and were told we'd have the results within a week. Well, there was no reason to worry, after all the ECG was normal, but not even twenty-four hours passed before the telephone rang – come and get the answer. Not another word. I didn't understand if it was good or bad.

The results indicated thirty percent arrhythmias per minute. It took me a moment to understand what I was looking at. Where did this come from? I felt my chest constrict. The girl was feeling well and didn't complain. I didn't understand what was happening to her.

We were referred to Schneider Hospital. All the cardiologists, including the head of the ward, surrounded us, and I wasn't sure why. I wanted to hope it was because we knew each other from our work together in transplants, but suspected that something else was going on, something severe. Something they weren't telling me.

The tests revealed that there were indeed many arrhythmias, but they couldn't find the cause. A cardiologist I didn't know, an expert in the electrophysiology of the heart, examined the tests and imaging and asked, "What is known about arrhythmia in the family? Heredity? Mother? Father?"

I swallowed. "No. We don't know. Ella was adopted from Russia and we had no information."

Ella tried to help. "Mama, are you sure that even in a situation like this it isn't possible to examine my file in Russia?"

"Unfortunately not. Neither am I sure how it would affect your treatment now."

"It wouldn't affect it," said the doctor. "But it could help us to know the reason."

"I'll be eighteen next year," responded Ella enthusiastically. "And will be able to open my adoption file."

I felt a small twinge in my heart each time I heard this sentence.

The doctor nodded and made an appointment to see us a month later. In the meantime, he prescribed medication with a referral for portable ECG equipment, teaching me how to connect Ella to it twice a day.

We did it the following day, morning and evening, and her pulse rate reached fifty-five. The improvement somewhat reassured me, but the arrhythmias were so numerous, manual measurement became impossible.

Tense, I sank onto the sofa and closed my eyes. Recently, Ella had been irritable and insolent, constantly playing truant from school. I thought it was because of hormones and adolescence, but maybe she was actually ill? I was terrified.

A few weeks went by and we went to see the arrhythmia specialist. The holter indicated that the medication had done its work and the arrhythmia was significantly less.

"Go on with the medication and come back in six months," said the doctor confidently.

On the way home we laughed in relief and agreed that I'd allow her not to tell the school she could go back to exercise classes. "But on condition you try and eat more, promise?"

"Promise, Mama."

47

Ella

What were these pains in my soul?

At four in the morning, I opened my laptop and checked to see if other people were feeling what I was feeling at that moment. I couldn't find any. I googled "pain in the soul." What I found there was quite scary. I closed the laptop and then opened it again.

I searched for how pain develops in the soul. I found something interesting: if there was something in my life that I didn't ask for and didn't want, it could cause a block and suffering of the soul, and if this considerably hampers regular life, it increasingly hurts the soul. And if we do nothing about it, and we receive more blows, it hurts more.

I understood that if, in fact, I didn't ask to be given up for adoption and didn't know why my mother couldn't raise me, then perhaps this is why I have a mental block. And if this is so, then how can I release the block? I didn't know. And maybe my pain isn't connected to adoption, because I didn't ask for Mama or Daniel.

My head began to hurt badly. Really badly. I felt as if my skin wanted to peel away from my body, face, and hands, as if something underneath was pushing it off. I didn't know what to do. I was confused. It was quiet and suddenly I was afraid. Don't know why.

I closed my eyes and tried to fall asleep. Not sure I succeeded.

At six o'clock in the morning, Mama woke me for school.

"Leave me alone… can't."

She saw I was exhausted, but still tried to wake me up two more times. The second time, she came up close, drew back the blanket from my face, looked at me and said, "Okay, I'll let the school know you're not well."

She left the room. I heard her shouting in the passage and then the door slammed.

I didn't know if Daniel had woken up or was still asleep or whether he'd already left.

At eleven o'clock I got up to go to the toilet and went back to bed. I wanted to go on sleeping and couldn't. I didn't feel well. I was in pain. I couldn't find a comfortable place for my body in bed. Everything in my head was spinning. As if my thoughts were racing, and my belly was cramping.

Suddenly, I felt as if I was high up on a ferris wheel that wasn't moving and I couldn't get off it. And then I was on the frightening spins of the anaconda. After the spins, I got out of bed and, from the shelf above my head, I took the gray stone Daniel had brought me from his last trip. It had a sharp end.

I didn't hesitate or think; I began to move it across my skin. Back and forth. To hurt. I saw scratches. That was good, the scratches. I made a space for my soul to breathe. Release the suffocation. Release itself from the skin. Calm down.

I moved to the other arm. I quickly rubbed and scratched. Back and forth. Without stopping. It didn't hurt. I couldn't feel anything. I tried to do it hard, until finally it hurt, and then I calmed down.

I felt the air returning to me once again. I took a deep breath. I felt my lungs swelling with air. Two balloons. And quiet. It was good to feel quiet.

Then I saw blood. A lot of blood. On my shirt. On the jeans I'd fallen asleep in, everything was bloody. I was afraid. I was just feeling good and quiet, and now there was stress again. And pain. What should I do with the blood? I took a lot of toilet paper and put it on my arms. I cried. I thought the bleeding had stopped.

I called Mama, I wanted her to come quickly. When she answered, I couldn't talk, I just cried.

"I don't know," I started to stammer and cry.

"Okay, I'm on my way."

"Come quickly."

Until she arrived, I sat with my back to the wall. I breathed. Tried to feel. The spinning in my head passed. I was calmer. Better. The blood had really stopped.

After a while, Mama came in. She wasn't alarmed by the blood, she was a nurse, but she was alarmed by me. She came to me at once, throwing her bag on the floor. She looked at my arms and said, "Oy." A second later she was on the bed beside me. Stroking my head and face. Holding me tight.

"Oh, my girl. You are in so much pain, how did I not see it. How come I didn't think. I am so sorry." She wept but lay next to me and I calmed down, wasn't afraid anymore.

Then she helped me up and we washed our faces.

"Come on, let's get you changed and we'll go sit in the living room."

She put a large glass of water on the table. I drank it all and asked for more. I was so thirsty. I hadn't drank properly in two days. I felt as if there were cracks in my tongue it was so dry.

Mama made her usual drink, Turkish coffee with milk.

We were silent for a long time, and then she said, "I think we should see a psychologist, it could help."

I agreed. I'm not sure I had a choice, but maybe I also wanted to.

48

Tali

I wanted to find a good psychologist for Ella, and didn't have anyone to call for advice, apart from Dr. Ronen, but since her tragedy and the visit during the Shiva, I hadn't dared call her. I didn't want to put pressure on her. I didn't know if she was working again. Nonetheless, I took a deep breath and called her.

She was glad to hear my voice and, within half an hour, returned to me with the name of a suitable psychologist. We immediately set up a meeting for both of us for that Monday. In the meantime, I informed the ballet teacher and the school that Ella was ill at home and that I was at home with her. I cancelled the support group I was supposed to facilitate at Soroka. I asked Ella what to tell Daniel.

"Everything," she said.

"What's everything?"

"Mama, I had an out-of-body experience. Do you know what that is?"

I was surprised. I had never heard of it.

Ella opened her heart to me.

"For a long time, I've felt that something in my body is trying to get out. Like a layer suffocating under my skin and wanting to get out and breathe. Out of my arms and legs and face and back. From my whole body. And there wasn't anywhere for me to be, I was suffering and it hurt. I wasn't in the mood for anything. Nothing interested me.

"It isn't only now, Mama, it's been happening for a long time. And the disconnections helped me. Didn't you see that I was disconnecting sometimes? Those disconnections helped me to rest from the pain and the pressure. As if I entered a cave that was quiet and I could rest, and when things were a little pleasanter, I connected again.

"Once, I even disconnected and felt a stream or river at the end of a tunnel and I swam up to a dance stage. There were two dancers there, I thought they were my mother and father from Russia. I really looked like them. I danced ballet with them. It was fun. And maybe it was a dream.

"Yesterday I was in a lot of pain and I was sick of it, I thought that if I scratched my skin the pressure underneath would be released. It would have places to leave the skin, leave into the air. Outside my body."

I listened to her and wasn't sure how much I understood, but about one thing I was certain – my girl needed help. After her confession, I made us something to eat and we indulged ourselves on the sofa in front of the television with a terrible series that Ella chose. I'd explained to her a million times that at work I constantly encountered people's personal tragedies and at home all I wanted was family dramas. Despite this, I gave in and allowed her to decide what to watch.

At some point Daniel came home. I'd asked him not to invite friends that day. He opened the door, threw his bag in the middle of the living room and asked, "What's happened?" But he didn't wait for an answer. The moment he saw our faces, he sat down in the armchair opposite.

Ella stopped the TV show and began to tell her brother bits of what she'd done and felt. His face grew grave and sad. He approached her and asked to see her arms up close. Ella consented and he looked a little alarmed.

Suddenly, he bent down over her arms and kissed both, next to the scratches. "So they won't hurt anymore. Don't be sad, Ella. I'll help you with anything you want."

Tears filled my eyes. I immediately hugged him. "You're a gift of a child," I whispered to him.

He freed himself from my hug, went to change his clothes, make himself a sandwich then left to play basketball.

In the meantime, Ella changed channels to a British movie "*Secrets and Deception,*" that we'd already seen.

"Are you sure? Today of all days?" I asked.

She was sure.

During the movie, Ella stopped it twice. The first time was when the adoption authorities in England warned the young adoptee that she'd have a hard time finding her biological mother, and the second time was after she'd found her. The biological mother told her she'd gotten pregnant when she was fifteen and her father made her give birth and then give the baby girl up for adoption.

I wasn't sure I was doing the right thing, but was tempted to ask Ella about these two points.

She responded, crying, "Mama, it's a relief, the movie and the crying. The movie shows that someone who makes an effort to look will find in the end. I know you'll help me and go with me to Russia to look."

"Of course," I promised, evading what was evoked in me regarding the preoccupation with opening the file and the journey to Russia. Was I afraid?

"I'll be eighteen soon. We need to prepare. But what do we do? Do we go to the adoption offices in Israel or in Russia?"

I didn't actually know, but promised her that by her birthday we'd know everything. "You know you can rely on me," I added. "Just remember that I have no intention of taking any step before you and the psychologist decide together what and when would be the best thing for you."

"Maybe I shouldn't be certain that my parents are ballet dancers," she said with a certain acceptance.

"Maybe not." I sighed.

A few days later, when I met with Dr. Ronen, she didn't appear surprised and explained that self-harm that isn't life threatening usually takes place in order to feel physical pain and release emotional pain.

"And how else can emotional pain be released?" I asked worriedly.

"There are ways, and she'll go through it with her psychologist."

I thought a while and went on, "Ella has started asking about the adoption again. Why? And how is it connected with the abandonment addressed on every adoption website?"

"The old attachment theories were written at a time when the focus was only how the 'child regarded the parent.' At the moment of birth, the fetus knows how to recognize the mother as a nameless experience, and modern theory refers to the fact that just as a child communicates with the parent, the parent communicates with the child. There is reciprocity. If the relationship is one-sided, disappointment follows."

I wasn't sure I completely understood what she was saying.

"With adoption, there is an expectation of mutual compensation. The adoptive parent attains attachment with the adopted child from a place of vulnerability, with the unconscious expectation that the child will compensate him or her."

"The parent's vulnerability?" I didn't understand what vulnerability the adoptive parent could have.

Dr. Ronen patiently explained, "Narcissistic vulnerability is the vulnerability of adoptive parents who cannot have a child of their own, with their genes. A child that will resemble them."

"Weird, during the whole period of treatments in order to get pregnant that was the only thing I wanted, a child of my own, but from the moment I decided to adopt, it passed."

This vulnerability remains even if you aren't aware of it," stated Dr. Ronen.

"When I see how calmly Ella accepts things that I would have been irritated or pressured by, I tell myself that it's actually fortunate that she wasn't born with my genes," I said.

"It happened this week, for instance, when I was late for work and didn't have time to prepare her cooked food. She said, 'Never mind, Mama, it's okay. I'll manage.' In her place, I'd have blamed me."

"Narcissistic vulnerability still exists. You have your own ways of coping with it. Think about how you cope with painful things."

After the session with Dr. Ronen, I went on to Haifa, to facilitate my support group in the north. On the way, I switched off the car radio and thought about the conversation with her. I still hadn't calmed down from the issue of narcissistic vulnerability. I recalled encounters with friends and relatives when each one would boast about his or her successful children.

I knew it wouldn't happen to me and felt just a tiny twinge of jealousy. When Iris' mother talked about her getting a hundred for every exam, I remembered the thirty that Ella got the year before for arithmetic and changed the subject. At ballet she excelled, until recently. When I was asked about it, at the grocer or by girlfriends', I told them that she was taking a break. And, naturally, I didn't forget that my neighbor Amnon's son, was already playing basketball for Hapoel Ramat Gan, whereas my Daniel had trouble practicing. I couldn't boast about grades or achievements; only about the compassion my children felt for vulnerable people and animals, but other parents didn't boast about this. It didn't count.

And despite this, I didn't grieve over what my children didn't have. I was just angry with myself for perhaps not doing enough. Maybe

I worked too many hours? How come I didn't see what Ella was going through in her internal world? And how do I actually cope with painful things?

In Haifa, at the session, we sat in a circle. I took a deep breath and, with Dr. Ronen's words echoing in my mind, I began, "Today, we will deal with how we relate to the pain of loss and how we live with it."

Group members spoke, shared, asked, and expanded, while I documented everything. Almost two hours went by and, toward the end, as usual, I concluded, "You referred to pain as a part of you that never goes away, as being immeasurable. Many of you mentioned that what happened was fate and so there is nothing and nobody with whom to be angry. There is also the belief that a guiding hand maintains balance. You also said it isn't right to ask why it happened to me. We heard from those who said they wanted to feel the pain, those who don't want the pain to disappear.

"Others described a lot of activity and volunteering so as not to sink, to distract them, and to create meaning. You mentioned friends as a source of support. Several of you commented that belief provides a framework and a way to go on and hold onto life, in addition to the relief of laughter. You said that reading a book or watching a movie are ways of disconnecting from the pain by entering the story of others."

Before I left, I didn't hold back and took two cookies from the refreshment table near the wall. I got into the car, unable then, too, to listen to the radio, only to quiet, the echoing quiet of my thoughts. How do I actually cope with painful things?

49

Ella

I told the psychologist that I didn't feel. That I didn't love anyone. Not my friends or my brother or my mother. Even at family events I no longer hug or kiss my uncles, aunts, or cousins.

"Describe situations or times when you did feel," she asked.

"There aren't many. I remember that during the last summer vacation I was afraid when Dima went overseas with his friends without me. I couldn't bear his leaving me. It was very hard for me, I gave in and cut contact with him."

"Why did you cut the contact? What were you feeling?"

"I couldn't bear his leaving me, so I left him."

"Tell me, what do you feel when you're left?"

"I can't think about it. It's so painful that sometimes it's even hard for me to breathe and I feel my heart beat. And then I disconnect."

I began to move from side to side, unable to find ease though the chair was really comfortable.

"When I cut contact, it's like disconnecting from what I'm feeling and then I don't feel the pain."

Her questions became oppressive. I glanced at the clock. There was still a long time left. My head started hurting. I drank a little water.

Even so, I felt she was on my side, that I could trust her.

"And do you always do this to avoid pain?"

"Do what?"

"Can you describe your pain a little? What exactly do you feel?"

I sighed, drank a little more water, my mouth was still dry. I looked at her and said, "I don't know. I get scared and immediately leave, cut the contact. It was like that with my friends. I'm very jealous. Once a friend of mine suddenly became friends with another friend so I cut the contact with both of them. I felt it was a betrayal, that they were betraying me."

"Do you see the connection between cutting contact and cutting your arms?"

"I don't know, I didn't think about it like that."

"Is it possible that cutting contact and cutting your arms is your way of not suffering pain?"

"Maybe. I don't know. Yes, could be. Can I have some more water?"

I was tired when I got home, but calmer. Mama was supposed to return that evening. Until Daniel came home I decided to search Mama's room, mainly her filing cabinet. There were a lot of files and nylon covers with documents.

My heart suddenly started beating fast. I was afraid something had gone wrong with my heart rate, but I felt all right. I found a folder with "Ella" written on it. Inside were envelopes. I opened the one marked "Russia," and everything fell out onto the floor. I began searching among the papers and didn't know what I was looking for, but I had a feeling that I'd find something important, something significant.

I found the flight ticket that Mama kept from her journey to Russia, letters to the prime minister, the minister of Foreign Affairs, the mayor, and all the telegrams and blessings we received when I arrived in Israel. There was an envelope with my tests and a lot of photographs.

I suddenly heard Daniel entering the house. He came into the room and asked what I was doing.

"Does Mama know? She'll kill you when she comes back and sees all this mess."

"Leave me alone, okay?"

He went into the shower. A few minutes later, he came out with a towel around himself and asked again, "What are you looking for? I can help you."

"I'm looking for my birth certificate, but don't tell Mama."

"You could have said so before, it isn't here. You know I'm a real sleuth. It's in the closet in Mama's workroom, on top."

Looking at him I wanted to squash him with love.

"Okay. You'll help me to get into the closet. And I'll collect what I spread out on the floor. And if you're nice to me I'll wipe up the drops of water you've left all over the house."

He nodded.

It felt like we were a team and I was so glad he was my brother. He climbed up the ladder and then slid half his body onto the highest shelf of the closet on the window side, and pulled out a brown folder with a black elastic tie closure. I opened it at once. Inside were documents in nylon sleeves. Everything was in Russian.

I immediately called Dima. "I need you to come, urgently!"

"What's wrong?"

"Nothing, I just need you to come quickly."

He arrived after a few minutes, and I gave him a document from the folder that looked like a certificate with dates.

"It says that it's a birth certificate and there's a name in Russian that I can't make out," he said. "There's also a birth date and that's it."

"Thank you," I said, disappointed.

"What were you expecting to find?" he asked.

I shrugged.

At my next session with the psychologist I told her about it. She didn't understand why I didn't ask Mama directly where my birth certificate was.

"I think I was afraid she wouldn't understand."

"What was she supposed to understand?"

"That I'm not betraying her. That I don't want to hurt her."

"I hear that you have special feelings for your mother. What does this say about what you told me, that you don't feel anything?"

I took a sip of water and said, "I don't really know how to explain it. I thought about what we discussed last time. I told you that if it seems to me that my friends are betraying me, I cut the contact. And then... if I betray Mama, maybe she'll cut contact with me? I'm afraid to think about it. I can't think about it."

There was silence for a few moments and then she said, "I notice that you are preoccupied with two similar concepts: leaving and disconnecting. If I understand correctly, you tell yourself that in order not to be left or betrayed, you are the first to leave or cut contact."

"Yes, that's true."

"So, is it possible that your leaving or cutting contact are actually your need for control, after being a 'victim' of your biological mother's abandonment?"

"Maybe. I really haven't thought about it like that."

"You're afraid your mother will leave you?"

"Don't know."

"Describe your relationship with her, okay?"

I took another sip of water and sighed. "I get mad at her, irritated with her and slam the door... I don't have the patience to listen to her. And I don't hug her. And don't tell her I love her. When I was little, I'd tell her I was leaving home and she couldn't tell me what to do because she wasn't my mother."

"And with everything you've now told me, she hasn't left you or cut contact with you. Can you think why not?"

"Because she doesn't have a choice?"

"I think she's simply not afraid you'll leave her."

"But there are children whose mother left them."

"What do you mean?"

"You know… like what happened to me… my real mother didn't raise me, she put me in a children's home."

"That's another subject, we'll talk about it next time. In the meantime, try and think of things you're afraid to tell your mother and what would happen if you did tell her, okay? We'll see each other next week."

That night, as I lay in bed, I thought about this conversation and that maybe I should tell Mama that I went through her things. I was still scared. Didn't know why exactly. I was afraid of the world. Afraid that gravity would suddenly stop and there'd be an end and death and graves.

Like yesterday when I traveled by bus and remained last. The driver thought there was no-one left on the bus and turned off the light. I was so afraid. It was really unpleasant. I quickly went to him and said weakly, "Excuse me…" He didn't hear me because my voice came out really weak. I couldn't speak, my voice vanished.

I was trembling with fear. In the end, he was really nice and took me home on the bus.

I arrived completely white and Mama immediately realized I wasn't all right. She asked what was wrong, and I told her I was okay.

She didn't ask, just announced that regardless of the psychologist, she'd take me to a psychiatrist for a diagnosis. I didn't say anything, went into my room and lay on the bed.

I didn't have the energy to talk to a psychiatrist, but I did manage to tell him that I'd tried to hurt myself and that when things are hard for me, I disconnect.

"I'll give you a prescription for Cipralex that will help you with your mood. But you will only feel the impact in three weeks' time, so please make sure you take it every day and that you're patient."

I nodded.

"And of course, continue with the psychologist and come to me in a month's time for a check-up. Okay?"

I nodded again.

But even now I felt those feelings returning. I was afraid. Afraid to be alone in the world and to die. Afraid to board a bus, be with people, of someone sitting next to me, and afraid the bus wouldn't stop. And I was afraid that I'd suddenly not manage to breathe as happened before, when something was trying to escape from under my skin. Afraid I wouldn't be able to fall asleep. And I was afraid I'd manage to fall asleep.

50

Tali

"It's important to understand that Ella and Daniel have two sides. The side that is lacking because they didn't receive love, warmth, touch, and stimuli from birth. But we mustn't focus only on what is lacking. Because during their first years of life, even if it wasn't right from the beginning, they received plenty of love and attention from you. You related to their needs and difficulties."

I was distraught. I wanted to understand Ella's needs and where I failed. I sat listening to Dr. Ronen, who continued, "You need to take into account what they also received. From you, they received a caring figure, which means you were sensitive to their needs and provided stability and consistency."

"I heard a lecture about research on the brain, consciousness, and how the brain correlates. They spoke about the plastic brain. That children who have experienced violence, or natural tragedies, or deprivation, manage later in life, developing positively due to interactions with a good carer. And they said that even when an adopted child experiences trauma, not necessarily physical, he or she can develop well with a beneficial parent. I do understand all that, so I find it even harder to understand what happened with Ella."

Dr. Ronen responded, "That's true, but there are other things. The issue of identity is very central. Children from four until six 'dress up,' changing identity each time. A policeman, a fireman, a queen, and a princess. At the ages of eleven, twelve, the hormones begin, the child's identity breaks down and a process of consolidating the identity of the adolescent begins. Here, too, there are 'disguises,' but they're different. Ella was a 'good girl' with friends and successful at ballet. She later changed her disguise to that of the 'bad girl,' who slams doors and is angry and insolent."

The issue of identity was somewhat familiar to me. "It's clear to me that with adopted children identity takes a different direction." I said. "I've visited websites about adopted children. They've written so much about themselves, who do I resemble, to whom do I belong, all I want is to resemble someone."

Dr. Ronen clarified, "And it's important to remember that there is also the DNA they received from their biological parents. Congenital neurological structure is also important in relation to regulating learning disabilities and attention in this context. In addition, we lack information about Ella's family history."

"But why did she do what she did?" I asked. "Why did she hurt herself?"

"Clearly it was the result of emotional pain, and it's good that she's in therapy with a psychologist now," answered Dr. Ronen confidently.

I was silent for a few moments before saying, "I keep thinking about things that happened and about things that Ella said. I'm trying to find a clue. For instance, Daniel told me that she listens to a lot of Russian songs through her ear phones and that she asked him to help her learn about St. Petersburg."

Dr. Ronen didn't appear surprised. "That's getting closer to her origins in a way," she said. "The more preoccupied with it she is, the closer she gets to her mother, so to speak."

I thought she glanced at the clock, but we still had time for our session and I used it to say that it was similar to what happens in the processes of loss. "In my bereaved family groups, I hear them say that talking about who they've lost helps them keep him or her alive in their memory and brings them closer."

She nodded. "They are certainly similar processes. In that process there is more than one process. For you and for Ella and for Daniel individually."

I sipped the rest of the water and felt oppressed. "It's hard to hear that in relation to my loss," I said. "Although I understood it after the last session with you. But the children's loss saddens and hurts me more. What else lies on their shoulders? Maybe I'm only just beginning to understand what Ella has been through."

Time was up. I was left feeling uncomfortable, maybe I hadn't been sensitive enough in raising the issue of loss before Dr. Ronen, after the loss of her son.

51

Ella

"How was your week?" the psychologist greeted me. She was wearing jeans, a tight blouse, and a long jacket. Even her black curls were always the same. Always the same length, she never seemed to cut her hair. I liked going to her. I liked talking to her. I looked forward to the weekly session.

I shrugged.

"Is there anything in particular you want to talk about?"

I knew in advance what I wanted to talk about and immediately poured it all out, "I talked to Mama when she came back from work. I told her I wanted to see my birth certificate. She asked me to wait a few minutes, she said she had to take a shower first and that in the meantime I should go get the ladder. While she had her back to me, I admitted that I'd already seen it."

The psychologist stopped me and asked, "And what did you feel?"

"At first, I felt my body constrict and my heart started beating faster but when she asked me to bring the ladder, I felt my heart beats slow down and my body relaxed. I think I realized that Mama wasn't mad and that it didn't anger her."

"And that she won't leave you," added the psychologist.

I nodded.

"Last time we said we'd talk about your biological mother, remember?"

"Yes. I really want to know why she left me. Mama also says she doesn't know. I used to be certain that my parents were ballet dancers and that's why I was a dancer. But I'm no longer certain."

I told her that I'd read online what children wrote after opening their adoption file. "I'm rather afraid. They wrote that their mother was drunk and their father a drug addict. I'm afraid of discovering that my parents are also like that."

"You don't have to look for them if you're afraid."

"I want to, I'm afraid, but I want to."

I reminded her of my fantasy when I was little and thought they were rich and traveled the world and wore beautiful clothes. But I didn't tell her that I also once imagined that my mother sold fish or something like that. Then we talked about disconnections. She asked if they still appeared. I said they did, that they help me to not feel.

"And what is so terrible about feeling?"

I didn't know what to say, but she didn't give up. I told her about the cave again.

"Do you feel safer there?"

I nodded.

"Are you running away from something?"

"I don't know. Maybe."

"Try and think about what things make you feel good."

"That I'm loved. Knowing for certain that I'm loved."

"And what needs to happen for you to believe that you are loved?"

"Look, I know Mama loves me, but it isn't enough. I myself don't understand what's missing. It's as if there's a black hole in my life. Half I know, it's Mama, Daniel, and my life in Israel, and there's a black part where I don't know what's happening or if there is love there too. Maybe it does have to do with adoption… the first ten months of my life, when I was in the children's home… I don't know. Maybe it remains black because I don't know what went on there.

And if everything is black I don't feel safe, like what happened with the driver who switched off the lights in the bus."

"What you're actually saying is that for you the black hole is connected with a situation in which you are afraid, one in which you aren't safe. This has logic to it, because a black hole can really be frightening. But how is this fear connected with love?"

"I think that when I'm afraid I feel insecure. And for me, security has to do with love. It's a kind of triangle."

She seemed satisfied, her eyes shone for a moment, and she leaned forward and said, "I feel you are allowing yourself to dig deep inside yourself and find connections with love, and this is very significant."

Time was up.

For my eighteenth birthday, instead of a gift, I said I wanted to go to St. Petersburg and open my adoption file. Mama already knew that's what I'd ask for. I was very excited and also curious to see the city. I frequently imagined the moment I'd open the file. I wanted to see if I had any other siblings.

Maybe my biological mother had given birth to other children. Maybe they'd never heard about me. She might have been ashamed to tell them they had another sister. She might not even have remembered that she gave birth to me, or maybe she didn't want to remember because she already had another family.

When Mama came into my bedroom, about a month before, I demanded, "So when are you booking the tickets to Russia?"

"Ella, it doesn't work like that. First, we have to submit a request to open the file, and only when we are summoned for a particular date, can we go. But obviously we will do everything possible before you enlist."

I understood and asked her to call them.

"Yes, tomorrow morning, I'll call the association to ask what we have to do."

As she left the room, I put on my ear phones to listen to Halo. I loved that Korean boys' band. I felt uncomfortable with Mama, maybe it hurt her, but I knew that no matter what I found in Russia, I would never leave Mama.

52

Tali

Before the journey, I met with Ella's psychologist. She asked me my impression of Ella lately. I answered honestly that she seemed relatively better, even six months after finishing with the Cipralex and the sleeping pills. I added that she more or less consistently attended school, was less irritable, but that she still wasn't happy.

She agreed with me and mentioned that Ella was trying to touch on painful issues, trying to explore things with herself, and that this was a process that would take time. I asked her to explain what she meant.

"She tends to connect security, fear, and love. She frequently explores the boundaries of love."

"What?" I was astonished. "Isn't she sure of my love for her?"

The psychologist reassured me, saying that she believed that Ella was sure of my love, but that it wasn't enough for her, that she was looking for more love and security.

I didn't understand where this need was coming from. In a home that provides love and a sense of security, children grow up with self-confidence, mental resources, and the ability to give back. I wondered which of us would raise the issue of the journey.

Dr. Ronen suggested we postpone the journey until after the army. She claimed that we couldn't anticipate Ella's mental state upon returning and said I should be there to support her, which wouldn't be possible because she'll only get leave every two weeks.

But, as expected, Ella didn't give up. I promised I'd talk to Vadim in Russia; he'd helped other adoptees, which comforted me with regard to accepted regulations. It turned out that the application to the court had to be written in Russian, and only then would they determine the date for opening the file.

"Has Ella ever mentioned the term 'black hole?'" Her psychologist roused me from my musings.

I shrugged.

She cleared her throat and continued, "It's a term that for her represents something incomplete, something she is lacking. She has your love and a warm home, but it has nothing to do with this."

"So what does it have to do with? The adoption?"

"I'm not sure," she answered slowly and hesitantly. "It might be connected and it's possible that Ella is projecting it onto the adoption. That she pins her difficulties on the adoption. We have actually started exploring this in recent sessions."

I asked for an example and also wanted to know where this exploration was leading.

"She's starting to be very assertive in her desire to find out what happened during the first ten months of her life. I see this as very positive in that she is recruiting emotional strength for a task that is important to her. It's a significant start for her, to believe in herself and go after the goals she sets. It's an important milestone for her as she builds and reinforces her self-confidence."

I wasn't sure if what mattered was that she was building her self-confidence or that she wanted to explore her past.

"Both paths are inherently important," answered the psychologist. "They can be independent and they can connect in such a way that one is an unconscious means of achieving the other in terms of the internal processes she is going through."

I was glad to hear that Ella was starting to reinforce her self-confidence, but still couldn't work out the psychologist's opinion regarding exploring her past and what I could and should do. "Do you think it would be right for her to open her file now? In four months' time she's supposed to enlist."

"I understand the question, but I'm not sure I have an answer. It isn't a simple decision to make. In the coming sessions, we'll see how she progresses in terms of her confidence and emotional resilience."

I left the meeting knowing a little more, but not enough, when it suddenly occurred to me to relieve Ella of army service and suggest she do National Service at a hospital. I tried to look at the idea from all sides, wondering how she'd react, the pros and cons of it, and then the telephone rang and jerked me out of my musings. On the line was the transplant coordinator from Safed. I was immediately sucked into the organization and coordination of transplant surgery.

53

Ella

We boarded the plane. I was in a strange mood. Mama told me about Vadim and that he'd promised to help us get to court, but that we should come without expectations. What did he mean? I suddenly became afraid and put on my ear phones.

When we landed, I was so stressed I wasn't interested in how the city looked, nothing, all I wanted was to reach the hotel and talk to Vadim. He was waiting for us in the lobby and it was only when I saw him that I felt reassured. We drove to the courthouse together, a huge building. The walls were painted a dark brown up to the height of the first floor and then the whole building was light marble.

The entrance was grand with four enormous, round, brown columns. We went through a security check and then up in an elevator to the third floor. We walked until we came to a small room with a wooden door with a closed, glass window. It was only when I was inside that I discovered it was one-way glass and while I could see who was outside the room, they couldn't see me. I began to be enthusiastic about the beauty and elegance of the place and was on a high because it was suddenly becoming real.

In the room, behind a counter, stood an elderly official with a black blunt haircut. She handed Vadim a sheet of paper so we could prepare the letter, then we entered another room with small tables, where several people were already sitting. Vadim sat down and I leaned against the wall.

It was as quiet as a library in there. We started writing the letter; I wrote it in Hebrew and Vadim translated it into Russian.

It stated: "I, Ella Chaikin, was born in St. Petersburg on the 15 June, 1998, to a woman called…" Vadim copied from the birth certificate I had, the one mama kept in the closet, and ended with: "I wish to open my adoption file."

When finished we handed in the letter at the counter and went down to the entrance floor, where Mama was waiting for us. Later, Vadim called me to go with him to a room, where I stood beside him while he finished talking and laughing with some official.

On our way out, he said that they'd call to tell us the date and it could take several weeks. That was why he'd talked to the official, to make friends with her.

We had tickets for a week and were due to return to Israel on Wednesday. Mama said it was an opportunity to see the city, but suddenly we didn't quite know what to do.

We saw by the clock on the wall that it was already almost four o'clock and we hadn't eaten since the small meal on the plane, so Vadim's idea of going to eat was ideal. He asked Mama what restaurant and she asked for Russian food, but somewhere I'd also have something to eat, something like a hamburger or shashlik.

He nodded and we went into a restaurant not far from the courthouse. I wasn't hungry. I let him order whatever he wished for me. A few minutes later a plate with four blintzes filled with sweetened cheese appeared on the table as well as four small bowls, one with cherry jam, one with strawberry jam, one with a thick brown sauce that reminded me of dulce de leche, and the last – Vadim said he ordered especially for me – a faded vanilla sauce or something that resembled it. I put a finger in the bowl, to taste.

His telephone rang. He answered and immediately smiled. He ended the conversation and said, "They've set the court date for this Monday."

I looked at him in astonishment, then suddenly felt so hungry, I gobbled down two whole blintzes. It was so delicious.

We went to the Children's Home. We passed through a lot of tiny streets, it all looked like another neighborhood, a poor neighborhood. I was so excited and imagined I would soon see the place where I was first raised. I'd see the director and the care-givers I'd seen in the album.

I was curious to discover if they remembered me. I thought maybe the care-givers were old and there would be new ones who wouldn't be interested in my arrival. I wanted to see the babies' room and my crib.

After a while, Vadim stopped the car. On the outside I saw a lot of tall weeds, papers, and dirt scattered around, considerable garbage that hadn't been collected. There were a lot of cracks in the sidewalk. In front of us was a curved wall.

We approached the green gate. At the entrance was a guard in a hut with an open door. He was old and wore blue clothes. A belt held up his pants and he smelled disgustingly of alcohol. He began to argue with Vadim in Russian.

"He says we can't go in, that the place is closed," Vadim said and looked annoyed.

"What does he mean closed?" I asked.

"The place was closed down five years ago."

I begged, "Please, please tell him who I am and ask him to let me have a peek. Just me."

Vadim gestured for us to get into the car, and then I found the courage to say, "No! I haven't come all this way from Israel to find that the home I grew up in is closed." I refused to give up.

Vadim sighed and made the request. The guard refused but in the end, allowed me alone to take a look through the window of his hut. Mama was next to me. We gazed at the building that seemed broken down. The windows were closed and across the door was an X-shaped barrier made of wood.

I realized we really wouldn't be able to go inside. The weeds were even taller there. I could see that the broken down building had once been u-shaped, as if there were three connected buildings. I heard sniffing behind me and looked at Mama, who was standing behind me. I didn't understand why she was crying.

She pointed with her finger and told me that my baby room was on the right side and that all the babies were on this side on three floors and that the entrance in front of us was the main entrance; management was on the left side, while on the other side was the kitchen and, in the middle, a staircase led up to the baby rooms. In the middle section were the rooms of older children aged one and a half to about three or four.

After wiping her eyes with a tissue, she told me about the director, Valentina, how in her room and in the corridor were photographs of children sent by parents from all over the world. She'd already told me about this, and about Luna from the kitchen who had given her porridge for me when we flew to Israel, and about Klara, who gave me physiotherapy and bubble baths, and about the doctor, Irena, who'd talk to her in Russian and mama would answer in Hebrew and with hand gestures, until Yevgeni or Vadim or Ilya would arrive.

I'd already heard all these stories a hundred times.

On the way back, Mama began to call Israel to tell all the mothers in our Russian group how hard it was to see that the Children's Home was closed. I was so annoyed with her: how could she not realize that this was my journey and she couldn't take it from me.

We'd discussed this at home when we decided that Daniel wouldn't come with us. Has she already forgotten?

But I calmed down on the way and was even a little alarmed by myself. It occurred to me that in a few days' time they might tell me my birth mother had asked not to see me. As if, again, she didn't want me. I felt that if this happened, it would crush me.

Later, we drove to a beautiful palace, I don't remember the name. On Saturday and Sunday we wandered around on foot, visiting the Hermitage Museum and the Mariinsky Theater.

I did the adding in my head and concluded that my biological mother must be more or less around forty and every time I saw someone around that age in the street, I checked to see if she resembled me. The girls there dressed beautifully and had high, teased out hairstyles I'd only seen in movies.

None of them really looked like me.

When Mama asked me if I wanted a hamburger or a pizza for lunch, I snapped at her that I didn't want to eat, and we continued our walk through the city. I was enthusiastic every time I realized something. When we bought ice-cream I knew to say "malinka" to the vendor, which means tiny, and afterwards I told him "spasibo," which means thank you, and he smiled widely at me. Maybe he saw I was Russian.

It was important to Mama that we visit all the special places in the city and we continued from one famous site to the next. Luckily there were no tickets for the ballet because I was exhausted. Al I wanted was for Monday to come.

When the day came, we got up really early, drank a coffee and I had a bite of the croissant and that's it. We hurried to meet Vadim at the courthouse. When we arrived at the security check, we discovered that the passports weren't in the bag. Infuriating. We ran back to the hotel, not caring if people in the street were looking at us. We took a taxi back to the courthouse so we wouldn't be late.

Vadim led us through the entrance on the right side of the building, we went through the security check and continued through a glass corridor to an empty space. Crossing it we took the elevator at the end up two floors. As on Thursday, we again walked along a narrow corridor, one person at a time and, at the end, along another corridor full of rooms.

We entered the first room, which was actually a long room divided in two, with transparent walls. Two officials received us and allowed entry only to those who were in court for my adoption, that is, Mama and me because I'd submitted the request. Just as well Daniel didn't come. They wouldn't have allowed him inside.

The officials took us into an inner room, where there was a table and chairs. On the table was the file.

I gazed at the file I'd talked about so much, built and planned around, fantasized about. It was yellow and looked like any cardboard file. I recognized a number, which looked like a serial number with a diagonal line on the right and the digits 99.

Mama guessed it was the year the court allowed the adoption.

I gazed at the yellow file and thought how simple it looked, like any office file, but in this file was the key to my entire life, the key that would give me the answers to everything I'd been seeking.

And, perhaps, as the psychologist had said, I needed to prepare for a situation in which I wouldn't find everything. Maybe my parents weren't really ballet dancers. I suddenly realized that in a few minutes I'd know everything, that the dream would become real. For a moment, I thought that maybe I didn't really want to know.

I was so afraid.

Vadim entered and sat down. He picked up the file and read what was written on the cover: the name Tali Chaikin and the date of the court case. He opened the file and took out a sheet of paper. It was a hand-written letter in blue ink. On the upper right hand side were the details of the biological mother, her date of birth, and address.

The letter began on the left side of the paper: "I, Lena Morosov, give up my child who was born on June 15, 1998. I waive all my parental rights and consent to the adoption of my child by any family. I pledge not to make any complaints to the adoptive family. The implications of the waiver have been explained to me and I am writing this of my own free will."

Underneath, on the right hand side, were many signatures.

My heart was beating fast, fortunately I'd taken the heart rate medication that morning. I was terrified of seeing her photograph, and asked Vadim to turn over the file, but there was no photograph, just the sheet of paper and that was it. I photographed the file cover with my iPhone. I couldn't believe I was photographing the letter my biological mother had written.

I nodded thanks to the officials and we left.

We sat down in a nearby café and I asked Vadim to read the letter again. I was stressed. I felt cold although it was summer. I called my friend Noga and told her what had happened, and when I said the word "waive" I felt like I was suffocating.

Noga encouraged me to meet her. We had her address, it was in the file. I thanked her and called Dima, updated him and he also said that if I was already in Russia, it would be a pity not to meet her, because that's why I'd traveled there. Honestly, during those moments, I didn't really know why I'd taken the trip. Did I really want to meet her? I suddenly felt it was too much for me that I couldn't. I wanted to return to the hotel.

Mama hugged me and said we'd do whatever I decided.

The moment we reached the hotel I got into bed. Mama suggested we go out for dinner that evening, but I didn't feel like it. Then she suggested she look for a hamburger or pizza and bring it to the room. I agreed. I don't remember the rest of the evening or if in the end I ate the pizza, because at some point I fell asleep and woke up the next morning.

I disconnected but it wasn't my usual disconnection. I simply became sad and didn't want to do anything. I didn't even get up to brush my teeth. The next day we flew home. I felt unable to listen to any more. Unable to listen to why she'd given me up, or what had caused her to give me up, or how she could have written that letter waiving her rights.

Back in Israel, I still felt that sadness, and all I wanted was to stay in bed.

I think I didn't leave it for at least a few weeks, apart from visits to the psychologist.

I was suddenly afraid to stay home alone. I didn't even get up to make coffee and I didn't walk around the house. I was paralyzed.

In the morning, when Mama went to work, I'd go to sleep. When she came home in the evening, or at night – I'd wake up. Fortunately, Daniel didn't always go to school, so there was someone at home.

"You're saying that you don't want to be alone. Can you try and explain exactly what you're feeling?" the psychologist asked at our first session after we returned from Russia.

I trembled slightly. "Yes, I'm afraid. I'm stressed, I torment myself internally with thoughts."

"What thoughts?"

"Why I'm not continuing to look for her, things like that."

"Do you want to look for her?"

"I'm not sure anymore."

She sighed, looked at me for a moment and said that she understood I'd returned without looking because I acted according to what I was sensing.

I said that was true, but it was also what made me disconnect. Unable to move at home and reluctant to be alone, and on the other hand, I feel stressed and afraid.

"What stress? The stress of looking for her?"

"Yes, because I always said I wanted to complete what was lacking. And I didn't really."

"You completed part of it because that's what you could contain. I respect your decision to act according to what you were sensing. You were right not to continue if you felt you couldn't."

I drank a little water and tried to organize my thoughts. I told her I was curious in the beginning about looking for her, but now that I know her address and that maybe she wasn't a dancer or rich…

"Now what?" she asked.

"Now it's as if I have to move on. I can move on already."

"The question is whether you want to and are ready to move on."

"I do, a little, and I'm afraid. I thought opening the file would help me. If I knew more about what happened and got closer to my biological mother, it would help me with the disconnections. That it would reassure me."

The psychologist asked if I felt stressed.

"Stressed from within, to have a place for my soul. And not to hurt myself again."

"And now that you are a little closer to your biological mother, what did it do to you?"

I said half angrily, "She gave me up. Do you understand?" I trembled and my eyes filled with tears.

Getting up, I heard her say, "We'll devote our next session to that, if you wish."

I went home, to bed. A few days later, I returned to her and she, at once, reminded me of the words "gave me up."

"She gave me up," I said. "She didn't want me, rejected me. Maybe she didn't like me. It's hurtful. Insulting. Humiliating. Everything."

"Ella, in our previous sessions we discussed leaving and the pain caused you when you're left or when you're afraid of being left, when you disconnect. Now you aren't mentioning the disconnections when you refer to being given up. Is it possible that you are allowing yourself to feel?"

I didn't know what to reply.

"Is it possible that for all the pain with regard to the words "giving up," you have calmed down a little because you have started to look for her?"

"It's possible," I answered. "But I'm no longer sure I want to know the truth. It might hurt even more."

"That's a good enough reason to consider if it's worth going to find her."

After we were silent a while, she asked if we could think of other reasons a woman who has just given birth might write a letter giving up her child.

I raised the possibility that she didn't have any money, that she was very young, that she might not have had a suitable place to live in and raise me, and she may not have had any family.

And then I added, angrily, "But why give up the baby? I'll never give up my baby."

"We don't really know what happened. I don't think she gave you up. She apparently had life challenges because of which she couldn't raise you."

"What? Are you telling me that she may have done it for my own good, because she wanted me to have a better life?"

"I think more than that, I think that your seeking, even if you've had enough at this stage of your life, before the army, has done you some good. You have allowed yourself to approach the area of your adoption in your soul. An area from which, until today, you've disconnected whenever you've approached it."

The session was almost over.

Before going, I said to her, "Her name is Lena, that mother's name is Lena."

54

Ella

Even before my release from the army, I began to think about what would happen afterwards. In the last week, I began to feel pressured about being without a plan, so in the last two days of my release leave, I visited several malls and found work in a prestigious shoe store. It was rather nice there and I also began a makeup course.

I enjoyed putting on makeup and hiding behind the masks I found for myself. Makeup for a wedding, old fashioned makeup, and light, daily makeup. The main thing was that I first rubbed on a thick layer of makeup. To hide.

The course was hard for me. The girls talked loudly, disturbing my concentration and I began to disconnect again.

I returned to my cave where I felt good. Fortunately, nobody noticed because the teacher who walked among the girls, checking and helping always went to the loudest ones and left me in peace.

After a few months, I asked Mama for Vadim's number and called him to tell him I was coming to Russia in May and asked his help in finding my biological mother. I didn't have the courage to travel alone and planned to go with Mama. Daniel had a new girlfriend and he was really happy for us to leave the house.

In May, we landed in St. Petersburg. Vadim said he had a few more things to check for us and sent a friend to pick us up from the airport. He only arrived at the hotel that afternoon. We sat in the foyer and he told us that my mother had died the previous year but that I had a brother, Misha, whose life had been very difficult, that he wasn't in a good place, was an alcoholic, unemployed, and not easily available.

Vadim had managed to track him down and said that Misha was excited to hear that his sister was looking for him. He knew he had a sister from something his mother once let slip.

I needed a little air to process all that new information. So, my mother, Lena, had died and I had an alcoholic brother. Surprisingly, I felt all right. All at once, the fear fell away.

"I've arranged a surprise for you," said Vadim.

"That's why I was late."

"What surprise?" we asked in unison.

"This evening, Misha will come to the hotel and we will go out for coffee together."

I looked at him and, at first, I didn't believe him.

"He'll tell the person at reception and she'll call and connect us, and then we'll go down to the foyer. I've already told reception that if someone comes, to call you in your room."

My heart beat fast. I looked at Mama. She also seemed excited. To pass the time, I took a long shower and spent half an hour on my makeup. My hand shook as I put on eyeliner.

At seven thirty, as I was getting dressed, Vadim's assistant called to say that Misha was drunk. I couldn't believe it. How could he miss an opportunity to meet his sister? I realized that there would be no meeting. I sat on the bed and looked out the window.

But suddenly, at ten to eight, the phone rang again. It was reception. Afterwards, a man spoke to me in Russian and I tried to understand what he wanted and if it was Misha. At a certain point, I put the phone down and ran downstairs to reception as fast as possible. I saw a man of about sixty, well dressed, with a large gold ring on his finger. It wasn't Misha. Reception had made a mistake.

After a few moments, Mama joined me and we decided to go out to eat. We found an Israeli restaurant called "*Bekitzer*" that served hummus, falafel, and several other familiar dishes.

I ate without much appetite and we then returned to the hotel. My soul felt heavy. I thought that if I'd looked for my mother three years ago, I'd have met her. I had so many questions for her. Even if I'd gone two years ago, I'd have met her. But maybe it was better this way.

55

Ella

The next morning, we drove with Vadim to look for my brother. We didn't know where he was or in what condition. We drove for almost half an hour. It turned out he was living in the same apartment he'd lived in with his mother since he was born. He didn't answer the phone. We knocked on the door. No answer. We knocked on the window and a woman said he lived in the next entrance.

We knocked on number 64, and my heart was almost jumping out of my chest. The door was suddenly opened by an elderly woman with white hair gathered up on her head. She wore a white dress like a nightgown or pajama, and when she spoke we saw she had a gold tooth. She said that Misha only got home at night and that she rented a room from him. We asked if we could come in but she refused.

"You shouldn't meet Misha either," she added.

We decided to leave and return later on.

When we went back later, we saw someone outside with a black coat, jeans, sneakers, and a military-looking hat. As he approached us, I knew it was him. I got out of the car and approached him. He also knew. He immediately hugged me. He smelled of alcohol but I didn't care.

He hugged my mother as well. We were in shock. It was quiet. Nobody talked. We stood there, not knowing what to do. And then he took his mother's death certificate out of his pocket. He asked if we wanted to go to the grave. We assented.

At the entrance to the graveyard we were asked if the government or the family had buried her, and Misha said the family. They asked if she'd been cremated or buried in a coffin, because then they'd know how to tell us where she was. Misha said she'd been buried in a coffin, and they let us in and gave us the name of the plot and the row.

At a hut at the entrance, I bought twelve pink roses, ten from me and two from Misha. The graveyard was huge and full of graves with a lot of grass and headstones like boards stuck in the ground. Some of them had sunk, maybe because of the weeds that were growing there. Everything was green and seemed rather well kept. I think I saw a gardener wandering around.

At a certain point we reached her grave. There was a jar of plastic flowers there. Maybe someone did come to visit. We stood in front of the grave. I quietly asked to be there alone. I had tears in my eyes. I choked. I felt cold inside.

I said, to myself or out loud, "I'm sorry we're meeting like this. I didn't expect this to happen, to meet like this. And I hope you're all right up there. I'm not angry with you and I even want to thank you for what you did. That you gave me up for adoption. I only ask that you take care of Misha. His life is hard."

I felt really strange and thought that maybe my mother shouldn't have gone through this experience with me. It was absurd for me to be standing in front of the grave of the woman who'd given birth to me, while my mother was standing there, behind me. I was sure my mother was afraid I'd want to stay in Russia. She told me that on every birthday, she'd think about her, about what she was feeling.

Next to the grave was another old grave and there was a jar of the same kind, with the same plastic flowers. There was also a photograph on the headstone of that grave. Misha said it was his grandmother.

Mama approached the grave and photographed the picture on the headstone.

We then went with Misha to a café. I showed him a photograph of myself in uniform and he said he'd read about the Israeli army, that he knew we had a good army. I felt he was proud of me. He said he'd only learned he had a sister when he was thirteen, his mother had blurted it out when she was drunk.

And then, out of his pocket, he took a photograph of himself as a baby together with his parents. He told us that his mother's name was Lena – which we already knew – and that his father's name was Yuri. In the photograph, he looked really sweet. He said that I got my height from mother and my face and hair color from father, and that I also looked like Grandma Ira, father's mother.

Before we parted, he said that Mama Lena had done me a huge favor by putting me up for adoption. That if I'd stayed with them, I wouldn't have had a childhood. Only drugs and alcohol. He added that father died when he was fourteen and then Grandma had taken him in.

"He died young from heart disease, like his father, Slava, who died before I was born. And about five years ago, Grandma also died. She was already weak and tired. And she also drank alcohol. It was strange, because drink may have killed her, but it also held her together. It was looking for drink that got her up in the morning."

He was very moved while telling how much he'd loved his grandmother, she was the best woman he'd ever met. She always helped and supported him. She was the only person he could ever rely on.

We parted then and set a time to meet the next day in a park.

On the way to the hotel, I bought a notebook from a shabby little street store and sat down to write. I tried not to miss a single thing that had happened. Mama also seemed very moved.

Later on, we went down to the foyer for a glass of wine, and I suggested to Mama that maybe we have vodka this time, in honor of my parents and grandmother who had died. In their memory. I didn't believe I'd fall asleep after a day like that, but the vodka did its job.

The next morning we met Misha in the park. He arrived in the same clothes as the day before, but without the smell of alcohol. He'd also invited a friend who spoke English and could help with translation. She didn't look drunk. And her clothes looked ordinary and pretty. She already knew about us from Misha, and about our visit to the graveyard.

We walked around a bit and took photographs. His friend told us that yesterday, Misha had told his friends about his sister from Israel and boasted about her serving in the army. Before we parted, I gave Misha a watch as a gift. He said he didn't wear watches but because this was special he'd wear it. Then I gave him an album of photographs of me from infancy, with the whole extended family in Israel.

And then came the moment of parting. I saw in his eyes how sad he was. I hugged him. And he also hugged me. And then we let go and went our separate ways.

56

Tali

I kept my distance while Ella spoke at the graveside. I saw she'd come prepared. She wanted privacy and I stood at a distance. When she was done and approached Misha, I myself approached the grave and spoke to Lena. I told her that she was brave to let Ella go. That I can imagine how hard it was to sign that waiver. That I always remembered her even without knowing her.

I also said that she'd always had a place in our home, even without words, and that on every one of Ella's birthdays, I thought about her, tried to imagine what she was feeling and thinking at the time, and I tried to give Ella everything I knew about and could and that I'd continue to do so. I told her that she was now twenty-one and had finished military service, that she was goodhearted, sensitive, beloved, and that I was grateful to her for signing the waiver. With all my heart. With all my heart.

And then I went to the grandmother's grave. I looked hard at the photograph on the headstone. I wasn't sure. I took a tissue and began to clean it to see better. It wasn't dirt. The picture was blurred, maybe because of the moist conditions and local weather. I took my glasses out of my bag and suddenly I seemed to be looking at Ira from the orphanage.

I went back to Misha and with Vadim's help, I asked him his grandmother's name.

"Ira," he said.

I suddenly felt like I couldn't breathe.

"She died after they closed down her place of work. She was a doctor at the orphanage."

It was enough for me.

"Mama, are you all right?" Ella asked.

"Yes, of course," I answered.

57

Ella

Mama remained in the car for a while to take an urgent call related to work and suggested I go up to the apartment. I looked at that courageous woman, picked up one suitcase and walked toward my home. Something inside me felt different. I think for the first time I felt that this was my place, this was where I needed to be.

Daniel was waiting for me, the door wide open. He had a new, military haircut and his arms were held out for a hug. "Hey, sis, what's up? What did you bring me?"

"What you asked for, but don't you touch it before enlisting. Daniel, you will only open this special whiskey at your enlistment party. Promise?"

"Promise, promise. Tell me what it was like for you."

"Okay."

"Well, no evasions. You must have been disappointed at missing your mother the last time."

"Why? Because she'd died?"

"Yes, of course, that's why you went, to see her, didn't you?"

"I'm not sure. I wasn't disappointed that she was dead. Maybe it's better for me this way."

"Are you serious?"

"Completely serious."

I went inside. The familiar scent of the house was pleasant. I put down my suitcase and sat on the sofa. My whole body was relaxed. My brother asked where Mama was, if I'd forgotten her in Russia. I told him and sent him to bring me something to drink.

"Well, come on."

"Really, come on?" I continued from where we'd left off. "You don't understand, but I received almost all the answers to what I wanted to know."

"Relax, sis, why all the secrets?"

"Okay, then… I met my brother, I saw we weren't alike. And he showed me a photograph of my father and mother and told me who I looked like."

"So, that whole trip was for a photograph?"

"Oof… the photograph too, yes. It was important to me. Who my parents were. What they looked like."

"Okay, don't kill me, I was only asking."

"Ah, and something else that was important. I know where arrhythmias come from. From my father and grandfather."

"Diabetes as well?"

"I don't think so. Why?"

"So you can eat as many candies as you want. Remember what Mama used to say to us all the time?"

"Of course I remember. 'Stop eating so many candies. We don't know whether your parents had diabetes.'"

"So I don't need to watch over you anymore?"

"Excuse me?"

"You know… when you were hurting yourself—"

"Maniac! How do you know about that?"

"You told me, what, have you forgotten already?"

"I feel that all of that is behind me."

"Now you know the names of your parents, you know what they look like, you've met your brother, and went to the house he grew up in, where you would have lived if you'd stayed there. So lucky you didn't."

"Hey, you're a psychologist all of a sudden? But it's true. My mother in Russia did a very brave thing when she gave me up for adoption."

"Naturally, otherwise you wouldn't have been my sister."

"Yes, it takes courage to adopt. Was our mother brave?"

"I think both mothers were brave."

"Oho, we have a philosopher here."

"Well, I'm an expert now. Shall we go looking for your mother now?"

"Absolutely not, I'm quite happy with my identity. I'm only looking to enlist now."

"What does that have to do with the army?"

"Everything. I'll be a fighter. I have to prove to the judge who tore into Mama in the Supreme Court. The one who said she wouldn't send a Russian baby to die in Israel's wars."

"Good luck, bro, you show that judge."

"Give me the whiskey first."

Mama came in with her suitcase just as Daniel sat down next to me. She closed the door and put down the suitcase next to the one I'd brought in.

Without a word she sank into the sofa between the two of us, one hand on my shoulder, the other on Daniel's shoulder, and closed her eyes.

ACKNOWLEDGEMENTS

Ira

I wrote two characterizations and erased them before I got to you. Kirill Grozovsky, a friend and colleague, my first guide, who corrected me in relation to the spirit of the time, from when you were a medical student, through checking each stage of your progress. His mother, once a doctor in Moscow, reinforced and added. Dr. Yevgeni Berkov, Director of Internal Medicine C at the Sharon Hospital, detailed and completed the structure of the medical school, its student program and your specializing in pediatric neurology.

Julia Gur-Arieh, herself an adoptive mother, and founder of the adoption agency "Taf," taught me the secrets of adoption through local Russian eyes and, together with her mother, helped me put together and connect the story to the regime, procedures, and the ballet you loved. I learned the habits and meaning of drink in your life and the life of Lena from Yuli Zilber, Igor Sereni, and Alcoholics Anonymous. I never knew how ignorant I was about this issue.

I learned about hospitals in Russia and maternity hospitals from Dr. Dina Orkin, Director of Anesthesia in the Operating Rooms at Sheba Medical Center, who also did shifts in the delivery room in Moscow; as well as Tanya Fishman, nurse in charge of operating rooms at Sheba, who also documented for me details of clothing and footwear, and the long queues in stores during the eighties'. Dr. Alice Khalila, a gynecologist who also worked in Russia, supplemented and corrected.

Concerning your communal apartment, I heard from at least four people and there seems to be a consensus because everyone gave almost identical descriptions. I conjured up your daily routine in my mind, but learned about adoption medicine from Dr. Eli Antman, Dr. Gary Diamond, and from Dr. Boris Bronstein. I learned about child rehabilitation during your time from books translated for me from Russian by dear Leah Belziuk, who donated the organs of her son after his death a few years ago. She also contributed the childhood songs her mother sang to her in Moscow.

You had two grandchildren, Ira, born seven years apart. In the year 1991 and in 1998. In order to learn about the characteristics of the period through the eyes of mothers, Olga Wolfson put a post in Russian for me on Facebook. Subsequently, Irena Shuminov, Yael, Ella Isotov, Yelena Pizetksy among others who emigrated from Russia to Israel, volunteered to tell me about what it was like to give birth at that time.

The Russian names I chose for the caregivers and the children at the orphanage as well as nicknames, I learned at the weight lifting practice of the ASA group in Tel Aviv.

Dear Ira, as the writing progressed, I loved you more and more. If you were real, I'd hug you now. Hard.

Sveta

Without Shai Golden, who insisted and insisted, your character wouldn't have appeared in the first days of your life and nor would you have opened the book. Thank you, Shai, for not giving up. I thought the request to write about the first days originated in your personal experiences. I went underground for a month to learn what one feels and, perhaps, thinks at a day old, or a week, or a month.

My sister, Yael, an early childhood expert, compiled a list of books for research, and Nurit Keidar, my cousin the librarian, took care to bring them to me. My friend, Noa Kimche, a social worker and family psychotherapist, made sure I had books and articles she'd written on the subject. It's important to say, my Sveta, that I borrowed from one of Noa's clients who wasn't happy about her pregnancy.

Dr. Tsachi Neter, a psychologist who worked at an orphanage in Israel for a decade, introduced me to a new way of thinking in the field that helped me build your character. Merav Bartela, a social worker at Ichylov Medical Center, added and instructed, even allowing me to observe premature babies who, during the Corona period, saw only expressionless nurses and parents in masks.

Ella

Your character is a distillation of many stories I heard from adopted girls who opened their hearts to me, and there are no words to express my gratitude for this. Not only adopted but also very brave: Rotem Keren, Shir Zrikel, Sharona Wagman, Lily, and others I knew from sessions and panels for adopted children, adoptive parents, and biological mothers, organized through "Mishpachta" – Israel's adoptive community, Sharona Duchna, founder of the adoption and fostering initiative and who, herself, adopted a child.

About your experiences at school I learned from your ballet class and about the names and movements I learned from Siki Kohl, an old friend and once a choreographer for the Bat Sheva Ballet Company, and a dance teacher.

About the self-harming you experienced, I learned from one of the adoptees and from Dr. Ronit Plotnik, an educational psychologist, who also expanded my knowledge of current research on abandonment and attachment. When I sat down to write, buoyed up by knowledge, I sensed you as deeply as the cuts on your arms, until tears wet the keyboard.

I learned about the characteristics of experiences of adopted children like yourself, and their parents, from Ruti Baruch, herself adopted. She is a social worker and, primarily, the major authority in the field of adoption in Israel, who has accompanied and supported hundreds of adopted children and their parents.

Tali

The details of your visits to Russia and the many challenges, I myself experienced – fifteen passport stamps in Russia – and I filled out more than a few original documents that I've kept. The chapter on your fertility treatments, "you must," said Ronit Vardi. There is nothing like following the instructions of a friend, and I continued to consult with her at many other stages.

Thanks to Avd. Ruth Ofek, whom I met in the context of the mourning that accompanies stillbirth, I was given the legitimization to conceptualize the bond and love a mother builds with a baby she hasn't yet raised and who doesn't recognize her. This, Tali, is the source of your strength to fight for Daniel in the Supreme Court in Moscow.

Your character was inspired by the many adoptive mothers I encountered both in life and during the research period, including the journey to open the adoption file. Riki Keren and Malki Zirkel don't know how much they contributed to shaping your character; I assume they will realize this once they have read it.

The realization regarding the similarity between adoption-related loss and losing a loved one occurred to me on the drive home from one of the hospitals, while processing conversations in my mind with Ruti Baruch.

When I finished writing, I wept again during your visit to the graveyard in Russia, after thanking the woman who had given birth to Ella and given her up for adoption, and when you discovered who Irena, the doctor, was for you.

ENCOURAGEMENT AND SUPPORT

To my family, friends, and colleagues who referred, sent, directed, connected, coordinated, supported, and expressed an opinion, consistently or only once: My sister, Yael, Rachela Ivanir, Tamar Nahir, Azi Kaneh, Yael Nitzan, Ruth Ofek, Ronit Vardi, Shira Yavetz, Lani, Bat Sheva Oren, Tami Pesahzon, Yael Bistritz, Asaf, Tami, and Michal.

To Dvorah Szerer for giving me a boost with the writing, for opening the door and encouraging me to send the manuscript to Yedioth Books.

MY FIRST PROSE WORK

When I first started the book, I shared it with a writing colleague, Miki Argaman, who donated his son's organs and who writes a lot himself. It was he who sent me the link to the writing courses of "*Notza and Kesset.*" Through directors, Shai Amit, Shai Golden, and Lital Mizrachi, I met well-known writers who dealt with various aspects of writing and each one taught me at least one thing that served me.

A MILLION THANKS

To Dov Eichenwald, CEO of Yedioth Books, who not only agreed to consider a debut novel, particularly during the Corona shutdown when all the stores were closed, but also appointed a wonderful process manager – Renana Sofer, who was a marvel at choosing editors and taking care of the small details.

Amichai Shalev, literary editor, who erased and shortened with a liberal hand until I suspected the book would end up as a notebook. It was only after the final version was complete that I grasped the extent of Amichai's sensitivity and intelligence. A great gift. And if I considered myself someone who wrote more or less good Hebrew, then the abundance of red lines from language editor, Rotem Kislev with correction software, disabused me. While she was working on the part about the rockets fired on Sderot in 2002, she experienced them live during Operation Guardian of the Walls in 2021, and we could compare feelings and fears. If I were asked to prepare a triangle for Rotem, I would write professionalism at the top, thoroughness on the second, and meticulousness on the third.

A large team welcomed me, even if I haven't mentioned them all by name. Thanks to all of you, as well as Adv. Gili Michaeli-Schiller, whose graciousness and willingness brought us to this point.

Printed in Great Britain
by Amazon